I

Billy's eighteenth birthday was yesterday. Transitioning to a new part of life he foresaw being ready to graduate high school would be the end to an uncomfortable era. Throughout all the years of schooling, he just did not fit in to anywhere, or was even allowed to. At first he blamed it on his adoption and somewhat unique looks; then to the some unforeseeable force was the cause. His unanswered questions moved him towards believing this 'outside force' was steering his life to something totally different than all the other kids. Without a belief in any religion, he did believe his fate was much larger than just a castaway. In the weeks ahead Billy discovered how all of these unexplained events came about, and all of the reasons for his life.

"Billy, I am NOT taking you to school today so you better call one of your friends to take you" said his sister Jewel, his half-sister that was three years older. Jewel was five-foot-seven with wavy thick strawberry colored hair and light blue eyes. Her relationship with Billy was motherly and somewhat jealous of Billy's abilities in sports, school, and humor. She did not express much ambition, but was happy with her simple life. She got a license for selling real estate shortly after graduation, worked at a local office and still lived at home.

"And I am not going that way either, so get on the horn young man. You're not skipping school today even though it is one of your last my dear," Katherine, his mother, was saying from her room. Being a mother of two, she was a very hard working person. Her hair was faded auburn with a touch of gray, and her appearance was a little on the skinny side. She had never married. Jewel's father left for what was only to be six months to do a construction job in the Middle East, but never returned. Katherine pursued all of the information she could as to his whereabouts, but never found any conformation of a kidnapping or murder. She finally quit with the hope that he would return, but never told Jewel her fears.

With the help of her mother and sister, she became a

LPN. Then she adopted Billy through her work at St. Joseph's Memorial Hospital. The hospital helped her continue her education, and she became a registered nurse. With the stability of her job, she was able to raise her two children mostly alone. She kept them all happy and healthy and she managed to do well financially. Her strength and tenacity showed the two children what it took to survive and that anything was possible; she always reminded them of that.

"Oh, whatever, you know that we are just going to sit here and talk about the past four years and wonder about the future, but I know I must go to that damn place if it kills me just trying to get there!" Billy said with the most sarcastic tone and sigh that might persuade his mother to let him skip.

"I'll try someone, maybe Francis is going today. He drives right by the corner store, and I could just meet him down there," he said mostly to himself, but loud enough for the others to hear.

"Don't be pullin' that shit again," his sister came to his door and said. "The last time you tried that one we found out that Francis was not even in the state, and you ended up drunk and high with all of your friends at Francis' house because you were supposed to be watering the plants and feeding his dog. So you better think of someone else to pick you up this time buck-oh," she said with a smile.

"Yeah right, BIG sister, go ahead and remind everyone of that time. Let me get my book out on the things you tried and failed, so I won't make the same blundering mistakes, Buck-Oh!" he sneered back at her while laughing.

"That will be enough out of the both of you. Bill, get on the phone. You haven't much time, and Jewel, mind your own business," stated Mom directly.

Katherine was fair with the two of them. Being the head of household, she liked that she did not have to discuss any parenting issues with anyone, but missed that she did not have a man to pass some of the other responsibilities to. Katherine had boyfriends and a couple relationships were long enough that should have become permanent, but when they got to that point, the guy would seem to go away and never be heard from again. One time Katherine went out looking for her boyfriend, Lewis and found him. When she came back, she was in tears. This happened six years ago:

"What happened Mom?" Jewel asked.

"It was awful. It was like he was a completely different person. He immediately told me to leave and to stay as far away from him as possible. It was like the last two years just completely vanished." She said this sobbing into a pillow.

"But Mom, didn't you ask for an explanation, or anything?" Jewel asked.

"I did but all he said was... 'I want no part of that'!" She exclaimed.

"A part of what?" Jewel asked looking perplexed.

"I don't know. He was so upset over something, but he would not explain. At least I know he is not dead or something." she concluded.

"I wish he was." Jewel said.

"Don't ever wish anybody was dead. That is terrible karma. Things like that come back to you if you keep that thinking up young lady." She said this with a stern look at her daughter.

"Hey what's going on?" Billy said as he walked into the room.

"Mom found out that Lewis is alive, but he refuses to talk to Mom or explain to her why he left her." Jewel replied.

"Well at least he is not dead; we thought Tom and Bill were dead after they left Mom the same way. I suppose they are not dead either, but I wonder why they all left right when we were all getting along so well."

Tom and Bill happened when Billy was five and ten respectively. Billy was twelve when the incident with Lewis happened. It was a turning point for Billy, it dawned on him that experiences were not as normal as he thought before. He really started to watch and remember the strange things involving him and his mother. As Billy got older, more of these memories accumulated.

He would all of a sudden not he welcomed over at his friend's house to play video games. His friends would say that it was their parents, but then also they would never hang out with him anymore. As he became interested in girls the same would happen, the parents would intervene. These things never happened to Jewel. Most of her problems were self created.

At the end of his fourteenth year he went into puberty. It seemed a little late to Katherine. Billy grew enormously fast. He repeatedly remarked that he felt like he grew in his sleep. He outgrew shoes and pants in less than two months. He said he felt like he was on some sort of drug and could think faster and retain more at school.

About this time he was allowed to go to the store for his mother and ride his bike around the neighborhood. Billy noticed that there seemed to be someone following him. He would see a man that would be walking the same time Billy was riding, or going down to the store. One time there was a car following him on his bike, Billy doubled back on the street to look at the driver, it was the same man. Billy once waited at a corner and walked up to the man and asked him who he was. The man smiled and said something in a different language and walked off. Billy even tried to be sneaky and follow him, ride faster on his bike, but the man would somehow always be there, then disappear, or change his outfit and try to appear disguised, Billy would see through it. Every time he left the house, no matter where he went, he would eventually catch a glimpse of the same man near him while he was out.

As Billy matured, his looks became very distinguished. His brow looked as if to have been chiseled from marble, square and noble. His hair had a perfect wave that never faltered. He had sharp eyes that were almond colored, naturally strong physique, light brown skin; at just under six foot tall. He was handsome. At school it seemed that he was born with an ability to carry himself with dignity and behave with poise and polish.

Billy got into sports in high school. He started with football, but he would see what he thought to be the same man at practices. He saw this man talking to the coach after the first game Billy started. From then on, Billy was put on third string and all the coach would say was, "That's the way it is Bill, it's out of my hands."

"What do ya' mean Coach? I give my all, I should be first string. What gives?" he would desperately ask. "That's all I know Bill my boy, that's all I know," was what Coach would say. He would tell his mother, and all she would be sympathetic to him.

Soon after, Billy quit football and took up baseball; everything was fine until he got hit in the chest by a pitch, and then he was taken off first string and put on the bench. That coach gave the same response: "It's out of my hands." So he gave up on sports.

Without sports in his high school life, Billy started hanging around the rest of the kids who did not play sports. They were the partying crowd who smoked marijuana and drank excessive amounts of cheap beer. This lasted quite a while. It did not affect his grades, and Billy maintained a straight 4.0 grade point average throughout the rest of school. However, he never really had any good friends. He would just become close to them, and then they would stop coming by or calling. Billy thought that was just the way it was with him and friends, he had them for a while and then they leave. This would always leave Billy wondering, until once when he went to his mother and asked:

"Mom am I weird or something?" he asked his mom.
"Why no, dear you're as normal as they come," she replied.
"Well none of my friends ever come around or call, and it seems like our family is cursed. Men leave you when things are alright, and the same thing happens to me when my friends start becoming close. I think sometimes that we are cursed or something. Is it because you adopted me? Do those people know something and are afraid that something bad is going to happen to them because they are my friend?" he asked almost in tears.
"I mean I know you said that my real parents had passed

away and you really do not know anything else about them, but where did I really come from? And why is it our family has so many troubles with others that try to be a part of our family?" he would question.

"Oh honey, don't ever think that. There is nothing wrong with you or our family" she said very sympathetically.

"That is just the way it is. Some people are different and neither you or I can explain the way they act or end up treating others. They just do what they do. Please don't ever think that it is because I adopted you or anything remotely related to that. I love you very much and so does Jewel and we are a family and will always be there for each other, don't you ever forget that. You will make friends, real friends. I didn't make any real friends until after high school. Maybe that is just part of the Ruoff family. O.K.?" she said with a smile and a kiss on his forehead.

"I believe you, Mom, but I can't help but wonder why our family, or mostly you and I, get ditched by the ones we want to be around. Jewel has never had that problem. Is it because she was not adopted?" Does that make a difference to other people?" he asked again.

"Being adopted has nothing to do with those things. Not very many people know you're adopted. They probably think of the fact that I can't keep a man. I do not think that even the teachers at school know that, so it is just like I said, some things are just unexplainable" she concluded.

That was not good enough for Billy. He knew in his heart that people just don't ditch others when things are going well. It never happened to his friends, and it also never happened to his sister. Billy knew that it was just his mother and he. There was some kind of connection to the reasons that he and his mother could not keep friends. This was right around the time Billy was finishing up his high school years, he wanted to make sure this type of thing did not follow him into the next part of his life or his mothers.

After Billy's graduation ceremonies from high school, a man came up to him after the ceremonies and offered him a place in the Army. He told Billy all of the things that would happen to him and all of the places that he would travel to see, exotic lands and whatnot. This man, however, was not dressed in any uniform and when Billy's mother came over to listen to what the man was saying to Billy, the man quickly gave Billy a card with an address, but no phone number and told him to come over and see the rest. He gave his mother a smile and walked away and out the door of the auditorium not talking to anyone else.

"That was a little strange" Billy's mother said while looking towards the door. "Yeah, it seemed like he did not want to talk or discuss any of the things he had to say in front of you Mom" Billy said. "Must be all of that testosterone, probably too afraid that I might take offense to what he was telling you" she replied. "I don't know, all he was saying was to come and see what the U.S. Army has to offer me" Billy said with suspicion thoughts coming to him. "What's the card say?" his mother asked. "It has an address but no phone number. That man looks familiar. Did that man look familiar to you Mom? Did he seem like he could be from another country? I'll bet he isn't even a recruiter. I'll bet he is a fake or someone that works with those people who are always following me." Billy was rattling off like a detective. "Oh really Billy you sound like some T.V. show detective, and wipe that look off your face, you look as if that man was suspicious or something. Now listen to me, I am not starting to play along with these silly thoughts you're thinking. Stop this right now!" she said as she grabbed his arm to move him along , Billy was still in thought.
"Now we have to go and see your Grandmother and Aunt Nellie so I want you to stop whatever you are thinking and do it later, I don't want them asking questions about this, so wipe off that look off you face!" she concluded with a jerk on Billy's arm. Billy was not even listening.
He was off on his own little tangent as to why or who or what. "Are you listening? Here they come, now straighten up, Damn it!" she said with another jerk.

All the rest of the afternoon Bill was trying not to think about it. He did want to enjoy graduation day with his family. After the pictures and commencements he was even invited to a party later that night and that really made his day because he had no real friends. He was glad to finally be with a group, even if it was the last day.

They traveled to Bakersville to Grandma's house and enjoyed the dinner she prepared. Things went smoothly before he left for the party. His Grandmother gave him $500 for making it through his hard times and it was also for his Mom who had also suffered for dealing with a teenager. Aunt Nellie was humbled when all she had was a handmade quilt for Billy that she had made herself. Billy was more surprised with the quilt; however, he thought it was a jacket. He kept thanking the both of them, he never expected anything. His mother was very proud of her son. She had thoughts of him dropping out because all of his troubles that kept on happening. Even Jewel was proud; she gave him her car since the company she worked for bought her one for her real estate job. She could not believe that she was going to give it to him, but she did anyway.

The family had a marvelous dinner; it was just the five of them. Grandmother and Aunt Nellie lived together in Bakersville, about forty miles away and that was all there was to the Ruoff family. Katherine had only her Mom and Great Aunt. They just had a small family, and it always seemed different to Billy that their family was so small.

He was thinking that thought when he started on the weird things in his life and he found himself right back to the man at graduation and everything he was trying to tie back into those thoughts.
"Billy, hello. Too much for ya?" Jewel said as she was coming over to Billy's side of the table.
"Are you in there?" she asked again.
"Yeah, just a lot on my mind, big day and all. You remember don't you? You're not that old." Billy said.

As Billy got ready to go, he became nervous, mad and happy all at once as he thought to himself. "I do not know what to expect or even who to talk to. I have some of my 'back drive' friends and then there are the ones who deserted me. Should I talk to them or ignore the people who abandoned me for no reason?" he said to himself, but it must have been out loud, because his mother came in to tell him some motherly advice.

"Just be the Billy you are, don't be someone they want. The ones who left you might come over to you and explain now that school is over, who knows. You have made it this far so don't blow it. School is done and you have the summer to put together new friends and experiences. I love you and I am very proud, so just have a good time and don't worry. I know you won't be home until late and since we will not be there I expect that you will have the sense to not drive drunk or anything like that, Will you?" She said this while giving him a kiss on the forehead. "No Mom. I already heard it from Jewel so don't worry, O.K. Mom. I'll just go there and be myself, whoever that is," he agreed.

This is great, Billy thought to himself, he had his new car and was out of school and ready for those kids and whatever they were going to be. He had time to think during his drive back and his confidence was high and when he reached the party, which was in full swing. No parents, just kids and at Pete MacDugal's house, which was very large and well stocked with liquor and food. When he walked in the door it was mostly the graduating class. Some older kids from the year before, but everyone was nice, and greeted him like he had always been there.

"This is strange, "he mumbled somewhat out loud. "What's so strange Billy my boy? You should know just about everyone, they know you," a voice said from behind. It was Francis, his one time friend from the list of dumpers. "I am surprised that anyone is talking to me. It's like in school everyone ignored me or did not want to be my friend, but now the curse is lifted and it's O.K." he said with a smile.

"Well I know of no curse but if you must know, most of us were told not to become too close to you, I mean literally. A lot of us were told that you had some unknown disease and some of us heard that you were dying and could infect us if we were over exposed to you, like in your home or something, I don't know. It seemed pretty weird to me but I wasn't sure and I was too afraid to ask, thought it might hurt you feelings," he concluded with a gulp of beer. "Well then why are they talking to me now? This is bullshit. I ain't got no disease or anything, what the fuck is going on?!" he screamed.

"I don't know bud but grab a beer, its freeee, and I guess that everyone is so wasted that they don't give a shit," Francis said with a laugh. Billy was not laughing, he was fuming. All this time he could have cleared things up, been a part of the school. This seemed a little far fetched. Most of his high school he was alone, all because some schmuck started a rumor. He is lying to me. He just wanted to say he was sorry or something. There is no way something this serious could have been going on that long, he thought to himself.

It was true. Throughout the night people said pretty near the same thing. He was either dying or diseased and was better to stay away from. It seemed as if everyone in the school knew he was ill but him. Teachers were told to not bring it up for it might trigger an effect or something one of the kids told him, and they would let him enter the sports just to appease his self-esteem, but only to be let down easily by being benched. The 'back drive' kids didn't care what he thought because they were the only ones to hang with him, but he found out that they didn't know about the disease or were too messed up to remember. Some stoners thought that he smoked it for his condition.

While standing there with Jenny a few of the 'back drive' crew came around and were whispering to each other until one of them came up to Billy and Jenny and said, "Hey Billy I heard about the false alarm on your condition, I just never had the guts to come and ask you about it. I wish I had,'cause you had a good arm for football and baseball. Remember when we used to throw the Frisbee and stuff on the drive while skippin'? I thought that there might be nothing wrong with you, but now we know and we can still hang out, right?" asked Greg, the only hippie in the school. "Yeah man we can still hang out. It was not anyone's fault, except the guy who started the whole damn thing. I sure would like to get my hands on him and find out what the hell and why!" Billy said.

Things immediately got better for Billy, at least socially. All of the kids in the class more or less came up to him when they found out the rumor about his condition was just that and soon after it seemed that it was a good thing. Girls were more attracted to him and people who he never thought would talk to him did. He was a social magnet. He surmised that it was now his time to develop further. Take back what was lost and move on, but now that he figured his life was now making sense, he wondered if his mother's would follow.

II

For the past three weeks Billy had been seeing Issa, a very pretty girl that was a year younger and very athletic and social, which was what Billy needed. Since it was summertime, they would mostly drive out to the river in Billy's car and swim or play tennis. He and Issa fell in love almost instantly. Billy's mother was happy to see her little boy shine like never before. Billy went to the mall and got a job and was working at Divine Burger when one day it seemed like all that happened since he met Issa was a dream.

The man posing as an army recruiter at Billy's graduation was sitting in the food court across from the Divine Burger and was intently staring at him until he realized who he was. About that time, the man came over to the stand where Billy was working and asked Billy if he remembered him. Billy said he did and the man went on to ask him why he had not come to see him. "Well I thought about it Sir and I did not think that the Army was for me and plus, your card did not have a phone number on it so I couldn't call."
"I think for your own best interest you better stop by and see what I, I mean we, in the Army have for a person like

you, out of high school and all. A hamburger stand is not place for the caliber of man that you are. There are a great deal of people who enjoy what we have and do for the country," he said with a weird smile.

"Like I said Mr. ....I am sorry, I don't remember your name?" Billy asked. "It's John Doe, I know that it is a common name but that's it," he replied.

"Well Mr. Doe I am very happy now. I have a job that gets me what I want and a girl that likes me very much and I don't think it is me, so ..." he was cut off by Mr. Doe.

"A girl, well why don't you bring her too, there are women in the Army now so maybe we could set you both up together. Here is my card again. I will see you soon, won't I?" he asked quite seriously with a mean stare. "Don't hold your breath Mr. Doe, I don't really buy it." Billy replied in the same grim tone.

Mr. Doe gave Billy a mean look and hit the counter hard with his fist and walked away. He was mumbling something under his breath and it was not in English. Billy was shaken. It was the first time he ever raised his voice to another adult. He thought he was right. Who does that guy think he is, telling me what to do? This is America and I can do whatever I want, he was thinking to himself. Then he thought of Issa and the whole thing seemed to go away until the man came back with two other men with him. Billy saw them coming from across the Mall and his gut told him to hide.

"Hey Ed can you cover for me I need to go to the bathroom, I'll be right back." Billy asked.

"Sure, go ahead and take your break it's past the rush, be back around 3:00 O.K.?" Ed asked.

"Great, I'll do that instead," Billy said and was off.

A few moments later, Ed was confronted with 'Mr. Doe' and his associates.

"Where is the young Mr. Ruoff?" Mr. Doe asked.

"Oh he went on his lunch break, he'll be back in an hour or so," Ed said.

"Well then we shall wait," Mr. Doe said.

The hour had passed and Billy was not back.

Being very persistent, Mr. Doe came up to Ed and asked why Bill had not come back. Not knowing that you did not have to be on time in the food court at the mall, especially after the lunch rush made Mr. Doe very uneasy. Mr. Doe walked away mumbling something. After another half hour, Billy peeked his head through the back door and got Ed's attention and immediately asked if there was anyone waiting for him outside. Ed proceeded to tell him about Mr. Doe and his friends that were waiting for him to come back. Ed seemed suspicious of the men and their mannerisms. He too thought that they were strange and possibly from another country, and they could not speak English perfectly. Ed thought that it might be better if Billy went home for the day.

"Are you in any trouble that I should know about? I mean these guys look serious." Ed asked.

"Hell no, I met Mr. Doe at graduation and he wanted me to come and check out the Army and stuff but I told him it was not for me. I don't know what they want now." Billy responded.

"Well just go on and I will tell them that something happened and you had to take care of some stuff and will not be back today," Ed muttered.

"Thanks man this is a little weird. I might have to do some snooping around on these guys. I am not going to let this happen every day until they get whatever they want from me, I thought that this stuff was over after I graduated" Billy said.

"Really, well be careful man these guys look like trouble," Ed said concerned.

Billy went through the back door and got in his car and started to think. He could not figure out why this guy was so interested in him joining the Army. Why did he need other men to accompany him to recruit some little guy like me? He pulled out the card that Mr. Doe gave him and looked at the address. "2711 Broadmore, I think that I'll go to the lion's den and see if it is real," and off he went.

Billy headed directly to the address and found it in an unpleasant part of Broadmore. When he got to the exact address there was no recruitment sign outside. It was just an office with a desk, a phone, and some chairs inside. He looked twice at the phone, wondering why there was one there but no number on the card. At that point the phone rang, which scared Bill and he jumped and got into his car and drove off. He circled around the block and when he came back around the two men and Mr. Doe were getting out of their car. Billy was not sure what to do so he slowly pulled away and tried not to draw any attention to himself.

Bill went straight home, got on his mom's computer and went online to find the local recruiter for the Army and see what their address was. It was not the same as he thought so he logged on to leave an e-mail for the recruiter, saying that there were three men posing as Army recruiters at this address and gave a little description of their tactics. He described the Divine Burger stand and wrote that they might be there tomorrow to do the same. Billy left another name and e-mail address just because he was nervous about leaving his own identity. He started to think that he was being set up or tested by the Army to see if he was good enough. It was how his imagination went, with all of the things that happened to him in the last few years of his life. He had hoped that he was right and these guys were some real bad guys that would get caught by him blowing the whistle on them and whatever they were up to. Maybe they're trying to get some young kids out of high school and then take them, like kidnap them and kill them or something. His mind was really racing now. He forgot all about the fact that this might be normal and was already making himself into some hero. Sensing this, he almost did not send the message, but his gut told him to and that if it was really a part of his recruitment, he would just plead insanity or something.

Later that evening Issa called him and told him of the events that occurred right after he left. At that point he settled down, because all of the time between him sending the message to the real recruiter and talking to Issa, he was going over it and over it in his mind. Issa assured him he was not crazy and asked him what they could do that evening. He mentioned some new movie by Sofia Coppola, *The Last Great Sun*, and noted that it was said to be her last and they should go see it. Issa agreed, they both liked most of same movies, and so they made plans to meet there. The theater was almost the same distance from either of their houses, so they got there the same time, but Billy was late and Issa was starting to get worried just when Billy pulled up, got out of the car and grabbed Issa by the wrist and ran into the theater.

"Why are we running? Ouch that hurts! This better be..." she was cut off by Billy.

"I am sorry, just come on!" he said as he was forcing her to crouch down.

"I know they were following me, I saw them in a car that was behind me. I know they were following me!" he was shaking. Nonetheless, no car came in front of the theater across the street into the parking lot. Billy finally was enjoying the movie until on the screen a man in the movie looked familiar, Issa started looking over at Billy and Billy was getting a strange look on his face while the picture was on the screen. The man they were looking at was flashed on the screen and off the screen. The man was on a news segment that was part of the movie. The scene happened so fast Billy was not sure why he felt weird about seeing the man on the t.v. and neither was Issa. They both passed up talking about it at the time. The movie concluded and they left the theater as if nothing happen. They were totally relaxed, got into just holding each others hands and walking. "Hey why don't we just walk around the park for a while?" Billy asked.

"Are you O.K. with that, I mean you're not worried, are you?" Issa questioned.

"Yeah I feel pretty good about the area and if they are out there, so what, here I am. I think they will find me no matter what. So let's just enjoy the night, o.k.?" Billy replied with a smile.

"Sounds good to me, I just love the fresh air and a late night walk," Issa smiled back.

As they walked, the night air surrounded them with soft breezes and warm whorls of summertime heat. Billy was forgetting all of the days' craziness, and even what might be next, until he suddenly remembered the man in the movie's face. Without even saying anything, Issa saw the look change on Billy's face and she thought of it too.

"Who does that man remind you of Issa? I saw you look at me when he came on the screen? Who was he?" Billy asked Issa worriedly. "The more I think about his face, I get scared Billy. I am afraid because he looks like... like... YOU, I mean an older version of yourself. I know it sounds crazy, but it is the only feeling I get when I think about it." Issa shuddered while she spoke. "It's alright to feel that way," Billy responded, "I feel it myself".

III

Everyday after the movie, Billy felt like some of that rumor in high school was true. He did not think that his life was his and that part of him was dying everyday. Issa was also changed by the way Billy was acting.

He went back to work at the Divine Burger, and it was a couple of days before he got any word from the Army recruiter. It seemed as though the message that the recruiter got was different from the one that Billy sent. The real Army recruiter, Fred Tarkington, acted like Billy wanted information about a local recruiter and wasn't trying to tell the Army of the imposter. Billy was really confused about what to do next, with the thoughts of him being someone else and some weird guys acting like Army people trying to get him and Issa being the only person who knew the whole situation, Billy just wanted to go somewhere and start over. Start over, start over that was the only thought that made sense.

He went to his mother and told her what had happened to him and she was of course a little leery of the story line, but it did have some solid stuff that went with the life that they had had together since she adopted Billy. She could remember seeing strange men that were always around when they would move from an apartment to their house, from the city and to the suburbs. She had shrugged it off back then, thinking they were moving to, or just at the same place and time. 'Just coincidental' she thought. As Billy was retelling the incident at the Mall and describing the same men, she came to the realization that he was not crazy and just going on his gut instincts. Something she had always done also. "Billy, I have always wanted to be normal," she spoke, "and most of our family life *was* normal, but since I adopted you, something was just a little... there was a little tingle or, some kind of energy around you. At first I thought it was because I adopted you, then I thought it was because you were a boy, but I tell you this now because you have also seen it. I have seen the man you saw in the movie too, and I just blew it off because I have seen those 'separated at birth' photo's of famous people and I thought that you were one of those types. Now, however, I think differently. Since you have graduated, things are happening more frequently with fewer answers, or at least, less obvious answers. So I can't believe that I am saying this, but I want you to run. Go somewhere with the money I am about to give you." she started to cry. "Mom I know I have to go, but how will we talk, I will need you up here", pointing to his head. "I am not smart enough to figure what or where my life is going. Issa...," he was cut off. "Issa can not know where you are. The men might try to get you, through her and she would probably tell them or be forced to talk. I really think you have to go this alone, or take her with you." She concluded with a look that he could be with her,(for she did not want Billy being alone at any time). Issa was a smart girl and two heads are better than one. These thoughts and more were going through her head while she looked into her son's eyes.

"Wow! I don't know if she would want to leave and maybe never come back, who knows what I am up against mom? These people are definitely not good people and they want something from me. They might put her life on the line, right in font of me, to get it." Billy looked off at the pictures of himself and his sister. "You'd better go to your room and think of how and *if* you can ask this of her. I know you want to but how can you get her to make the decision and stick to it, for if she does not, it might ruin you." She gave him a stiff kiss on the forehead and a long stare into his eyes. She left the room and closed the door.

Billy was left with his thoughts. What is going on here? That was the most frequent question asked. Where do I go? I must be crazy to think that a group of people want me or something from me. Just then, the picture of the man in the movie and all of the times his mother might have seen this man over the years went through his mind. Scrambled thoughts of how he was like him, who he might be in life, and why he felt that this man had such a grip on his life. "Am I going to run for the rest of my life, from something that I know nothing about? All I know is that my life is being taken charge of, by someone else, because I am scared and have no backbone to stand up and say something to these people who are trying to get something from me. And am I to ask Issa, a girl I feel I so much love and trust towards to go and risk her life for mine? I must ask her if she will go with me. I need a place to hide, someplace to collectively find out who they are and why have they screwed up my life and my family's.

IV

"Billy what are ya gonna do? You are way out of your league here and what are your resources? Where are these people coming from? Is this madness? Am I mad about this whole idea? Are my mother and I just in our own little world?" Billy was looking in the mirror thinking out loud. "Who are you talking to?" asked Jewel. "I was not talking to anybody." long pause............. Are you aware of what is going on in this family? Mom and I are at a threshold of fear from feelings of no control that is coming from all of this weird stuff that is happening in my life, and what has been happening throughout Mom's life." Jewel gave no response. Billy looked at her, waved his hand in front of her. "Hello!!" he said while still waving. "Guy's hassling you at the Burger, isn't that stuff normal for your age group?" she asked. "No ding dong, it is much more than that" he responded and proceeded to tell the entire story from graduation on.

She was fairly stumped when he told her about Mom's side of the story and the feelings she had since adopting Billy.

"I had no idea, Mom never mentioned it to me, and I thought we were close," she responded.
"Oh honey", Mom came into the room, she was eavesdropping." I am as close to you and Billy as I can get, Jewel, I love you but even in your life there will be things that you won't tell me or anyone, there are just some things that you just keep to yourself. I am glad you brought your sister up to pace on what is happening around us and it seems to be happening more and more every day," Mom said. With a look of confidence Jewel asked, "Are both of you guys thinking that we are, or Billy is part of something, out there?" she asked while pointing out the window. Just then there was a knock at the front door, they all jumped and gasped. "Jewel go and answer the door," Mom said. "Why me? " she answered with a no way look.
"Because you are innocent and they want nothing from you, and it might be for you anyway. Just go and answer the door please? She said with a look, brushing off the fright then seeming slightly desperate.
"You're right I should go and answer the door, 'cause I wouldn't want any of my friends to see either of you at this time," she said and ran off to answer the door.

"This is all too much, I never thought that after high school your life would be so involved in mine, at this time everybody else's kids lessen the weight of life and its cycles, but this is a new, heavy, and different and I know I have the strength to carry some new weight, you know what I mean Billy. It is kind of like a weight is now lifted to you and a new weight has been handed to me through the insight and communication our thoughts and beliefs. What we have seen is real and something is happening to us," Mom said with a big concerning look on her face.

"Billy. I think you should come down here," Jewel called from downstairs.

They both looked at each other with disbelief in their eyes.

"It's o.k." Jewel yelled immediately afterwards, "This person you'll want to talk to" she said.

They proceeded to go downstairs, slowly.

They were introduced to an Army Sergeant Mike O'Malley, from the local recruiting office. "I received your email Mr. Ruoff and traced it back to this house, I thought I should come over as soon as I could and talk this matter over with you and your mom. Fred Tarkington, the man you first spoke with did not wish to help, but I knew that you needed someone to explain this situation." he said firmly with a slight Irish accent. "Is it serious? Has Billy done something wrong? Katherine said with concern. "Oh no Miss, it seems that Billy here has been picked by one of the local ah... ah ... F.A.R., they are Foreign Army Recruiters. They come in from all over and try to pose as the real McCoy, us ya see, and reel in the ones that are dumb, take them off to fight 'deir wars and do da killin' for them. They either look for ones that are really into violence, or smart and don't fit in, kinda like your son here, Miss. Billy here he was smart and not fooled by their lack of tact and persuasion, were ya Billy? I thought not laddy." Mike finished that off with a smile.

"But anyway I have ya know that we went and checked out that address ya sent and the place was empty, we figured that they knew you might be someone who would call the real McCoy so they moved on. So ya might watch around for any more of those kinda people. I don't want to alarm you folks but these kinda people are out there and it is really hard for us to keep a hold of them and to police this type of thing would be outta hand ya see. Keep your wits about ya if you stumble upon them again and call me if anything else serious happens, that's about all I can let ya know about these kinda things, you know military and all, ya see?" he finished again with a grin.

"Well at least I know I am not crazy or anything, I was starting to wonder about those people and why they seemed so persistent, and easily agitated when I said no to them." Billy said this with a look of relief.

"They are like that from every country we have caught in *this* country, trying to recruit our kids. We only get the ones that overexpose themselves. This group will probably not bother you again since they have left their office and all, they usually move on after that. So on that note, I will not bother you nice folks any longer, here is my card if anything else should arise, feel free to call. Good Day." The Sergeant was out the door without anyone saying a word but feeling slightly relieved.

"That just ends that part of that, they will be back. I know someone will," Billy said, while looking at the ceiling. "Oh what do you guy's think is going on with this, these ... feelings, and that someone is really after you?" Jewel asked with crazy, raised eyebrows, and hands in the air.

"Well young lady you better drop any belief that this family is normal, and that we do not have a problem surrounding this family. I, for one, have dropped the feeling that this is not real and that this is just our imaginations running away. This is serious and I am afraid that we are going to be looking over our shoulders from now on and that there's some trouble coming to our family 'til we figure this out. I..." she was cut off by Jewel

"I do believe you Mom, you have never really acted this way or with so much... conviction, and I did see things that I dismissed as just something weird or just society being this way due to too many people living together in one area. I am starting to believe, but of course do not want to, I will find the... the strength to look over my shoulder and look out for the, whatever I am looking for. What am I looking for Mom?" she finished with a non-committal look.

"Well that is a good question Jewel and I am not sure any of us know what to look for. I am getting a thought though, I know that you two are going to love this but I need to go somewhere else and talk about all we know and to figure out what we can do to rid us of this. I think we should leave for the weekend, go to Seneca Springs and soak in the hot springs and think of a couple ways to guard ourselves and be cautious with these people. I know that could do it better away from this place." Mom finished with one of those smiles that only come from a mom.

"Great idea Mom, I can go ask for the weekend off, Ed won't care and I will tell him that if any of those weird guys show up to tell them I quit. But I am not really quitting, am I Mom?" He finished with a mischievous smile.

"Well I don't know that one yet, but as of right now you are just going away for the weekend. O.K. young man, can you two swing it? I mean we have to realize; this is serious!" Mom said looking between the two.

"I know I can after making a few phone calls to cover myself at the realty office and one to Danny and I will be set." Jewel replied.
"What about Issa, Billy are you gonna call her?" Mom asked. "I will call her and just tell her that we are going to the Springs and I call when I get back. I don't think that she should come, this is family business. I fill her in once we have talked." he finished again with his usual grin. "Good, I have a few personal day at the hospital so

V

Mom had a cooler full of food and drinks and Jewel had some good music to listen to, but Bill was mostly in a daze, just going through the motions of packing. Suddenly, Billy broke the silence and said, "What are we really going up there for Ma? Do you think that when we come back that they are going to be gone? We are not the type of people to try and outsmart the men who do this 'spying stuff' for a living. I am just not sure what we are doing here, o.k.?" Billy was saying this with some anxiety. "Billy I understand the tension you are feeling, we are all feeling it., I need you to be strong, this is a little much for me too, not to mention the little maneuver you just pulled, thankfully, but when are you not going to slip past them, then what? Now come on, we will do as much as we can, until we get some good evidence that we can give to some of the authorities and not sound like we are crazy. So until then young man, you have to believe, we are all we got, and someday this will be all over." She stopped with him in her arms, giving him a big motherly hug.

Jewel came back in to the house and asked, if everything was ready she was going to call her boyfriend and then she would be ready. Mother nodded and so did Billy, and as that happened, Billy saw over his mother's shoulder the black car go by their house very slowly. Katherine saw Billy's face go from look of disgust, to anger, but then to clarity. He felt a change in his heart and knew he could not lie down and die, he had to fight. "What is wrong Billy?" she said excitedly, what is wrong with your face? Why are you smiling? Is this supposed to be funny? "No Mother I just figured out a little bit of it and I am glad." He did not tell her about the car, not wanting her to be alarmed; he knew that it was his fight. Since the day he graduated this has just gotten more intense and Billy felt a spark in himself get hotter and it made him feel a part of something bigger. He realized that he must remove himself from them, as easily and quickly as possible.

"So are you ready to go?" Jewel asked coming back into the kitchen. "Yeah sis lets go out through the garage and go. I will check the doors and come out to meet you." Billy said.

Mom and Jewel went to the car and Billy went around to the back door and was walking through the dining room which led into the kitchen. He looked again out the front window and saw the same black car go by; luckily Mom and Jewel were already in the car and not outside of it. Billy could see this as he walked through the kitchen. Billy was wondering what to do now and not cause any real panic, as he got into the car his mother noticed the flushed look on his face. "Is there something wrong with your face again Billy? I mean this is starting to annoy me? You can't keep changing like that, it will totally give you away," she asked with careful anxiety. "Well Mother, I am going to suggest that we go out the long way because I just saw that black car go by again and I think we should actually go the longest way, but definitely leave now. This is beginning to ruin my weekend," he finished and they all sort of chuckled. So Katherine pulled out and went the longest way possible and they were never followed. They headed down highway 21 and off to Seneca Springs, which was two and a half hours away.

They arrived at Seneca Springs Lodge around three o'clock and Mother went in to get the key to their room, Jewel and Billy sat quietly and looked out at the nice lay out of the springs. Seneca Springs is a tucked away hot spring that is privately owned with a single lodge and a naturally heated swimming pool. The guests that rent cabins get access to little natural caves that have small pools at constant 102 degree water and to a club house that has a pool with the 102 degree water and with ten miles of trail for walk or bike, saunas and massages. The Springs were known for the sensations you get after swimming in the waters. She had been bringing the children up here for a long time.

Katherine came back out and drove around the long way to their cabin. She said "It's good to know that not all good things were gone." as she drove around the other cabins.

It was a very nice log cabin with real solid logs that were large. "This is real cozy, I could get used to this," Billy said with a lot of enthusiasm. "Well it is good to see you excited about being here, too bad it is only for the weekend, Buck-oh," Jewel smirked back. "O.K. you two, let's not start, I wanted us to come together on this one and really, really, uh pull our thoughts to the facts, hell I don't know we need some drinks, I think... so let's not get into the swatting sibling routine," Katherine concluded. "I thought we were going to stop by the library and see about books on people following people or something like that," Jewel asked. "Well with that black car and all, I did not want to take any more chances in town so we will have to see what we can find out here. I know of a book store around here and they might have something there that we are looking for, but first let us relax and enjoy the evening and then start with our heads fresh tomorrow." she concluded.

"Sounds good to me, but I am hungry, I think I will walk over to the lodge and buy a few snacks for us until dinner. Mom can I have some money?" Billy asked "Sure this weekend is on me, buy some ice." she said with another big smile.

As Billy was walking over to the lodge he thought of the trees and all of the calmness that was around him and he thought that this would be a good place to come again if it got any rougher for him with his family. He knew that Issa would love it too. He was thinking a lot about her and how much she was already involved. He was sad that his whole life up until now was so boring and lonely and now he was going to be on the run and detached from the friends he finally got to have. Oh well, he thought, life is so strange, but now I must face the world and all that she is going to give me.

As he concluded his thoughts he came upon the lodge and a man outside smoking a cigar. As Billy approached him, the man formed the most peculiar look on his face, and then turned into a look of disbelief. Billy tried not to stare at the man but his look was so profound that he could not look away.

"Is there something wrong sir?" Billy asked trying to be as polite as possible. "It is just that you, young man, look extremely familiar. It is as if I just fell through a time warp of some sort. Please pardon me for staring but you look just like.... well I went to school with a chap in Oxford some forty years ago and I will be dammed if you are not the spitting image of him. I say what is your name boy? He asked with a heavy English accent. "My name is Billy Ruoff, and I have never been to England. Who exactly do I look like, sir?" Billy replied giving a most inquisitive look.

He looked at Billy as if he did not want to answer but the man thought to himself. He mumbled, "I opened up this jar of jelly so ... Well ...his name was....(heavy English overtones) Rafkar Suddain in school, but I heard that he died in a terrorist attack in his own country. I had quite a few classes with him and we played soccer together quite often at Oxford, yes it was a shame that he died in his own country, like that." The man faded off into his own past, and frowned while taking a drag off his cigar. "Rafkar what?" Billy asked. "Rafkar Suddain I am very sure. Where are you from young man?" he replied. "I am from around here. Say what is your name, sir?" Billy asked this, trying to change the subject, for now he was becoming suspicious.

"I am Thomas Mallory, from Sussex, England and I am just visiting these marvelous springs. Oh how refreshing they are. I find it remarkable how you resemble him. It makes me feel like stepping back in time." he finished again with a heavy English accent.

"Well it was nice to meet you Mr. Mallory, are you staying for the weekend?" he inquired. "Why yes ...yes I am staying 'til Monday morning. And you?" he finished. "Yes, but I am leaving on Sunday evening."

"Good, well then maybe I'll see you around. Good day young man." After extinguishing his cigar Mr. Mallory was off.

Billy turned right around and went back to the cabin. He did not even get some snacks. All he could think about was the name Rafkar Suddain. Billy was sure that it had something to do with his life, but *what* he did not know. Billy was starting to get a burn in his stomach that seemed to be telling him this. It was stronger than ever and he knew that this man could tell him a lot more than just his name. Rafkar Suddain was not just a person that Billy looked like, he must have been more. Billy was walking fast while he was thinking and before he knew it, he was standing in the foyer of the cabin and his mother and sister were staring at him from the kitchen table.

"What's up with you? Did you even make it to the lodge?" Jewel asked.

"Mom.... I just ran into this guy, this English man...who ....who thought that I look remarkably like, this....person," and he said softly as in disbelief, 'Rafkar Suddain'. He said that I looked just like this person Rafkar Suddain. And that he went to Oxford with this guy about forty years ago and that would have been right around the age I am right now." Billy finished while looking out the window toward the sun, just being shadowed by a large dark cloud.

"What are you talking about Billy? You mean to say that you just met this English man in his late sixties and he just stopped you and told you this?" she said waving her hands in the air.

"Pretty much, pretty much, he was standing outside smoking a cigar and was starring at me so intently that I stopped. I asked him if something was wrong and immediately said because of the resemblance I had to someone he knew. I was not too stunned, needless to say, so I figured that I should go ahead and listen to this guy. So I did and he went on to say he felt like he was in a time warp or something. All I could think about was the guy's name Rafkar Suddain." Billy kept on saying the name over and over.

"Jewel, that's not so crazy. I saw this movie, *The Last Great Sun*, by Sofia Coppala and it had this..." As she was joined in unison with Billy to say that 'this man that they saw in the movie looked just...,' they were cut off by their mother. "Billy we know about the man who looks a lot like you so this just might be another example of people that look alike in this world, what do you think that these are the same people?" she stood there pointing her two fingers together. "No, he said that he died in a terrorist attack in his home country, well he heard that he died. But I feel that this guy, Rafkar has something to do with our situation here. The way things have been going mom, I think that every time something like this happens it is just more to the story and,..." he was again cut off by mom. "Now look here, Young Man, you better slow down so as not to jump the gun," she was serious looking. This English fella' had nothing more than to say than you looked like some Chap that he went to school with some forty years ago. And that he is dead, remember, so I am not sure what you're really getting at but you better slow down O.K. Buck-oh?" She was worried even more. She sat slowly in the chair and sipped her drink.

"Well I would like to finish my story that was

partially joined by my little bro. After I saw that movie I saw him again on a magazine, a foreign one, I can't remember the name, but his name was Shah-something, or, I don't remember exactly, but it was definitely the same guy because he...He really looks like you or like you could look as you get older or when you get older, I mean." She was laughing at the idea of him getting older.

"I know about that man too," mother said. "His name is Shahpur, I heard that he was given this sacred name by the people whom he represents. He mostly came to power of this territory through land ownership and money. He is very well liked and keeps the peace, which is also where he grew up. It was in the country of Iran, but now the area is a territory owned by he, and his family. The power he has gained since becoming dictator has been great." She paused to take a drink. "I noticed him a long time ago by the match of their eyes. They are so unique. When I saw the Shapur for the first time, I noticed it, but thought that there is someone with the same eyes, no big deal. As time went on, I never thought that the resemblance would get closer. The adoption agency said your mother was that of Indian descent not Middle Eastern." She acted very sure of herself. "But Mom you did not see the look in this man's eyes. He seemed so... amused by the reality that I was he." Billy interjected. "I understand that it might not have been all that, but the English people are very, very presumptuous and dramatic about their stories so they're a bit hard to believe sometimes. This one lady at work was from England and she would just go on and on about things and be so, so dramatic. I asked her if all English people were like this at some point, and she said mostly yes. So I am not so sure that the man you met wasn't really just, 'pissing in your pocket', that was something they used to say to each other when trying to impress someone." She laughed and then Billy was acting like he was pissing in Jewel's pocket and they all laughed really hard together.

They came out of their laughter only to find that they could still not believe that any of this was real. Katherine went into the kitchen and fixed herself another drink. A screwdriver was her favorite so she made it a double and came back into the room. Billy was there all by himself. With his head in his hands he was thinking of what his mother had just said about the English and all. He really thought that Mr. Mallory was telling the truth. He seemed older and established, as if he would not have to act that way to get attention, he was so enthusiastic about the resemblance of Billy to his friend.

He looked up to his mother and wondered how he could get away and take whoever it was that was harassing his family away. He knew it would hurt his mother, but it was the best thing to do. The next thing to happen could bring his mother over the edge.

"Where are you Billy, my sweet? Are you all right? I did not mean to burst your bubble but we just can't go crazy every time that we encounter a... coincidence, like that one or any one. We must assess and then maybe write these things down and see if they have enough weight to be real. This is why we are here, to address these...these circumstances and write them down, to show someone who can help us." She took another drink and shook her head only to finish by saying: "We must not go this alone Billy, we must get help, but we need some evidence, some proof to show somebody." She took another drink.

"What are you drinking?" Billy asked.

"Vodka and orange juice, why?" she replied.

"Can I have one?" he said.

"Well, I guess so, I think that you're old enough." she said and smiled.

They went into the kitchen and Katherine made Billy a fairly stiff drink, in a tall glass. She handed it to him and clinked her glass to his and just then Jewel walked in and demanded one to join the celebration.

Afterwards they decided to go to the lodge and get some dinner for it was around six o'clock. They changed into some casual clothing and started to walk their way over to the lodge. It seemed as if the two drinks that Billy and Katherine had had was getting to their walking abilities by the way Jewel was giggling at the way they were holding onto each other. She was smiling at the sight in spite of all that was said earlier.

Billy and Katherine went into the dining area of the lodge and were seated toward the back. While walking there, Billy saw Mr. Mallory across the room and pointed him out to Katherine and told her also that he was staying the weekend and maybe he could get some more information from him. She told him to stop the nonsense and that this was dinner time and they were not going to discuss the matter in public or at dinner and that was final. Billy did not like the idea of letting it lay. The subject was never going to rest in him until he understood who, and or what, was behind all of this.

As the waiter left the table up walked Mr. Mallory and he proceeded to tell Katherine the same story that he had told Billy earlier. Katherine let Mr. Mallory tell the story to see if the enthusiasm was as Billy described or if he was just another amusing English man. She was rather confused by the look in Mr. Mallory's eye when he was telling the story and looking at Billy. Even Jewel was watching him and later noted the same feeling. Katherine and Jewel nodded and smiled, but did not say anything except 'Nice to meet you and Thank you' they were silent after Mr. Mallory told them to have a great evening and he'd see them around the springs. They finished their desserts and were walking out the front of the lodge went Billy finally spoke.

"Is dinner over yet? I mean we can talk about anything yet? He was asking as politely as possible.

"I am just a little tired of taking so much in at once. I just want to go to sleep and start in the morning, o.k.?" Katherine finished with a sigh and slowly sat down in the passenger seat of the car.

"I am tired too. That Mr. Mallory was too much after dinner. I just want to take a shower and hit the hay." Jewel said while pulling out of the parking lot of the lodge. "How about you little Buck-oh?" she interjected. "Yeah, me too I guess ... I guess I knew all along." he mumbled to himself.

"What was that last part?" Katherine asked.

"Nothing that can't wait till morning Mother," he finished with a heavy sigh also.

By then Jewel was to the cabin and they all got out and went inside. While getting ready for bed no one said anything. They were like zombies moving in slow motion. Later that evening, Billy woke up and went to the kitchen for some water and all he could think about was the name Rafkar Suddain. And that he might still be alive and he was his illegitimate kid or something.

Billy was constantly thinking how Mr. Mallory acted when he first saw Billy today at the lodge. He needed to talk to Mr. Mallory more about Rafkar, was he from a rich family, exactly what part of the world was he from, and if he was for sure killed in a terrorist attack. Billy chugged some more water and then turned his world to Issa for a moment. He really wanted her to be in his world, safe and tucked away from this constant follow-me game and trap. Why after graduation? Is it really an army from another country that really needs me to help them conquer whomever? It can't be. This is something huge. He could just feel a part of him that somebody else wanted. He hoped it was not the whole thing.

After that final thought, Billy put his glass down and went back to the couch and as he fell asleep his thoughts went back to Issa, he imagined her in his arms, on the beach of some far away island.

VII

Billy awoke to the sound of bacon and eggs frying and the voices of angels; he thought for a moment and then chuckled to himself wholeheartedly. The sky was clear and the air was just around seventy-five degrees. He felt like this was definitely going to be a good day. After breakfast, Billy was waiting for someone to start in on the whole discussion. He came out of the bathroom; saw his mother reading a book and Jewel lying in the sun outside. After thinking that he should let the chat wait, he said out loud that he wanted to go soak in the hot springs then go swimming in the big pools and asked if anyone else wanted to go. Katherine waived and said 'No', he did not even ask Jewel. So, Billy went off to the springs.

He sat alone for a bit and then heard someone come into the sauna area. He had his eyes shut for he did not wish to look at them. Through the steam came a....

"I say is that you, young William boy?" It was Thomas.

"Why yes it is, but it is Billy, not William. Is that you Mr. Mallory?" Billy replied.

"Why yes it is, and you can call me Thomas, Bill," he stated.

"How delightful, I say you have been on my mind since we met. Not trying to be tempestuous, but you have stirred at lot of interest in me and my colleagues, but please let me digress... The water here is too refreshing to talk of this now let us enjoy." He stopped while getting in the water.

Good, I am not quite ready for all of your information, yet. The water here is marvelous Thomas, I mean it makes me feel really alive. My Mother always brings me and my sister here when she can. It kind of makes me feel.... alive," he looked over through the steam at Thomas. "I say Bill you even talk like that bloody Rafkar the way you were just talking. He was always talking about feeling alive and how he wanted to stay alive forever and nonsense. He was a very imaginative person, Rafkar was. I wish... I. Never mind, let us enjoy." he faded off.

They sat for a spell; Billy was watching a clock that he could see through the steam. His mind was full of questions.

"Is he really dead Thomas?" Billy asked. "That is what I don't know. I wish I did," Thomas paused. "Do you know about the Shahpur in what was Iran, and who those people are?" he looked at Billy seriously. "My Mother just told me his name the other day, but I saw his face before that and it gave me and my girlfriend a weird feeling, kind of at the same time.

"What sort of weird feeling? Did you know this person? Is that why you felt so weird?" Thomas asked.

"Well, Issa thought that he looked like me, or like what I will look like when I am his age. I just felt a sort of jolt of energy off of her, but then the more I looked the more it did kinda' look like me, then that part was over. But what has that got to do with the Shahpur of wherever?" he asked.

"The Shahpur and the man you saw in the movie are one in the same, my good boy. What I don't understand is the way I feel since our first meeting. We, I mean some of my friends and I, were discussing the Shahpur and his intentions in the new Middle East. He is someone that is not very stable." He stopped to wipe his face.

"His rise in power was just and well fought for, but recently, he started abusing his power and many former allies of his are, let us say not 'endorsing' his actions. Just recently there was the leak of a raid on a small town outside of the borders of the new territory that is now what the Shahpur calls his, that had supplies and arms. But the raid was lead by Shahpur's men, which is conflicting information. Is someone helping or hurting him? You see I have friends who love to talk when they know something. This is quite disturbing now that I put it all together. I mean you and this Shahpur news, the resemblance the... the... fact that you and Rafkar look so much alike at this point in your youth." he was dwindling, Billy cut in.

"Where did this guy come from anyway, with this rise to power, was he elected or appointed?

"Being a general in the army, he was victorious in an important battle for the territory that he now rules. The people felt a great honor to him for taking charge and leading them in some direction, for they had none back then. And not to diminish the fact that his family owned a lot of the important areas of that territory. He chose the name Shahpur, and so the people loved it. After that and his real name was never used and up until now no one had ever pursued it,......and come to think of it neither have I." Thomas drifted for a moment.

"Through some further campaigns of war that started when Saddam Hussein fell, his power became big and was voice for the people, in an area that needed it. Shahpur then brought together some very rich people and got their backing to try and establish an area of their own. Through the gathering of people and the words of Shahpur, the people came together for the most part and now they stand as a... a united people." Thomas stood and grabbed another towel after speaking.

"Wow... he was like Hitler or something, just rose to power by using words, now he is trying to war with those who are his neighbors." Billy said and shook his head.

"Not quite, but a close affinity to the likes of old Adolph. These people in these areas live very hard and often, violent lives. We in the West have no idea what it is like in those places. I for one cannot, nor do I wish to see." He leaned back as he finished.

"So you know he is up to something, but what has that got to do with me? Why do you Thomas act as if I have something to do with this?" Billy was starting to come out of the little boy of tell me a story, to the reality, remembering at to why he was up at the Springs.
"I am not sure, my good boy, But you caught my eye the other day and it, along with the conversation I have had with my colleagues, has made a connection inside of me,I know it. You see these things happen to me quite often throughout my days. Although I have not had one in years, I kind of thought I was losing my touch, so to speak," he finished off more proud of himself than the answer to Billy's question. "But why..... Thomas?" Billy asked assuredly. "I say old boy ... this world is nothing but day by day. I have seen things and know things that are not good to talk about. As I believe that fate and chance are one in the same. We don't need to try and answer one of the oldest questions, but just be thankful that we met. Now when it sounds like you need someone like me on your side, Right? I am thinking that you are as intrigued as I, but we need to be very careful." Thomas suggested with a slight tilt of the head and warm smile.

"I am very intrigued, Thomas, and as far as my life

goes...." Billy was thinking whether to tell Thomas or not, so he made a leap of faith." There have been some rather strange things happening to me, since I graduated from high school and actually I am lost on how this, I mean us, have come together at this place and time in my dilemma." Billy had the most absurd, wrinkled look on his face. It almost seemed as he was coming apart.

"Good god boy are you thinking that I have a part in your life as much as you are a part of my story? ...Ah, damn it I would really like to know how 'strange' things have been getting in your life since graduation." he finished by grabbing his chin and rubbing it.

Billy started with graduation day and the so-called Army recruiter and then back tracked over his mother's boyfriends suddenly not wanting to talk to her anymore. Billy talked about as much as he could remember and tried to conclude at the present. At this point Billy got up and while grabbing for his towel, stretched his arm and just then Thomas looked over to watch and....

"Good god boy ... Is that a rather large mole, near your arm pit?" he gasped

"Well, yeah, it is kind of huge." Billy said embarrassed

"Rafkar had the same ...sort of mole in the same place. I remember him cutting it open once on the soccer field. It was the only time I saw it, but I remember that's what it looked like." his eyes were coming out of his head as he got up and slightly spitting as he talked.   "Well I don't particularly like the mole, but all people get moles on them; I mean, why are you so excited Thomas?" Billy was utterly confused as to all the excitement.

"Don't you see boy," Thomas pause and then mumbled. "It is almost time." he said questioning himself as well.

"See what? Time for what?" Billy was still in the dark.

"How old did you say you were boy?" he asked.

"What?? Ah, eighteen, just turned." he said proudly.

"What are you doing Thomas, I don't like the ah ... ah. Way your ah...ah questions are... ah." Billy was starting to get up again and grab his towel. Just then Thomas said in almost a whisper.

"William what I am getting at .... You could be his clone." he finished off with his fingers to his lips. As if he did not believe the words himself. "Billy please do not think I am against you I am just speculating." Thomas was trying to direct his sincerity to Billy as Billy grabbed his towel and started to the door when he stopped, put his towel around his neck and sighed. "You know," he said, still staring to the door, "That is the last thing I would ever believe Thomas. Me, a clone of some mad man that rules a country that I don't even know about. You're telling me that I, Billy Ruoff am a clone? I don't understand you folks sense of humor sometimes but this is redic...." he stopped after turning around and seeing Thomas getting his towel and walking toward Billy.

"You are right Billy. I should not have speculated with your personal life like that. I sincerely apologize for I did not realize the magnitude of saying that you are a clone. Please accept my deepest apology." He humbly stuck out his hand, to shake. Billy stood there for a minute, looking at Thomas and then to the sky before saying. "I do accept your apology Thomas, for I know that you really, did not know... at what you were implying exactly,..... so ... I don't hold anything against you, alright, all is cool I guess. So, I'll see you around, o.k. Thomas?" he said while shaking his hand. " Right, Old Boy, see you around." he said with a firm hand shake and heavily emphasized 'old' to make Billy feel respected and trying to undo any damage that might have been done.

Billy walked away from the pools trying not to think that he could be a clone of this Shapur. Some mad ruler on this planet of..., were to clone children for his own, pleasure? Or to carry on some plan, live forever? He stopped and looked upward, shook his head. He did not want to believe this, but why else would someone have been watching his every move since he was able to go out on his own from the house. He stopped again and said aloud 'NO, this was not going to be the case. I will not believe that ludicrous idea for another minute.'

Billy thought to himself, but as he approached the

door of their cabin, he was thinking of how his face looked, he thought about Issa and that changed his face but not his thoughts. He was wondering whether to tell Mom and Jewel about the morning talk with Thomas. He walked on in, still not sure when Jewel popped up from the kitchen.

"How was the bath Buck-oh, a little too hot for ya? I thought you would be there all day," she said while sipping her tea.

"Ah... they are...fine... I just... had enough of that talk ... or time, I mean tubs. I need something to drink, what is that?" he said while trying to look away.

"It is tea, Are you o.k.? I think that you were in them a little too long. Mom is outback, you should go out and lay with her for a while, cool off, ya know?" she said with a little hug then starred at him. She was thinking that he has had enough.

Jewel walked on by with a smile, but Billy just stood there with wide eyes and head hung down. He went on into the kitchen and got some tea. Katherine came into the kitchen and looked at Billy while getting her own tea. Stopped and looked at the wide eye and plastic grin on his face. She knew that he was trying hard to hide something, she could always tell.

"What is it little Buck? I know this is a lot for any teenager to deal with, hell it is enough for anyone, but I feel that you are extremely down about something now, or am I just loosing my touch?" she said while rubbing his arm. "Mom, do you know who my parents are?" he said shyly.

"Well, no not exactly who they are, but I think that they were just people who could not take care of you, so they gave you to me. Did something happen at the pools or something? I mean you left so happy, but now." she finished with the worried mother look.

"Not exactly bad, but just disturbing. So you really do not know exactly who my parents are, do you?" he asked. "No I do not, but what has that got to do with your this mood swing?" she asked.

Billy was still not sure whether to tell her about Thomas' accusations. This is your mother, he thought, and she is one of the only people to trust. "Mom I saw Thomas again at the pools, and I told him of the reasons we are here, and he told me of the Shahpur and that he and the man I saw in the movie are one in the same and that also... also ....." he was hesitating.

"Also what honey?" she interjected.

"That I might be a Clone of him" he almost burst into tears. "Could that even be possible? They can't do that with people can they? I thought just animals," he was whimpering with tears on his cheek.

"Oh... honey, no...there is no way that you could be anything like that. They don't do that. It has never been made public that they do that. Stem cell production was as far as the world governments would let that go. Thomas was wrong and I am going to have a word with that man the next time I see him. How dare he impose such a thing as that on someone. Especially my boy!" she went from total compassion to almost rage.

"Now wait Mom, I already said something back to Thomas and he saw the impact of the idea and immediately apologized, so there is no need to go confront him on the subject, o.k.?" he said while wiping the tears from his cheeks.

"I don't care about his apology, I want an explanation as to how he could come up with such an idea.... cloning, how absurd. I...." She was cut off by Billy.

"Mom I really don't care about his ideas anymore, I could tell he was sincerely sorry for the accusation and that is all I want to hear about this crazy idea of cloning, o.k.?" He was acting very stern while trying to finish this Thomas business.

"O.K. I guess, but what kind of a person would even think that you could be a clone?" she rebutted.

"Well he saw that mole under my arm and he went on to say that his friend Rafkar had the exact same mole, in the exact same place. So I guess the idea of cloning popped into his head. The thing is though is that Rafkar is dead, or that is what Thomas said about his friend, although Thomas was not positive about that." Billy said with a perplexed look. " Anyone can have a mole that is near another persons or even look like one, so he must either know more than he is saying or is just plain strange himself." she said shaking her head.

"Yeah.... maybe he knows more, but just had to say something about cloning for his own sake. Because when he said it, he kinda whispered it, it was very strange." Billy noted.

"This mister Thomas knows a lot about things. Do you know what he does or is?" she asked.

"No I don't, but he mentioned that he and his colleagues do talk a lot about things and just recently they have been talking on the subject of this Shahpur and his doings in the Middle East as he called it.

"Interesting, what else did he say?" she inquired.

Billy just started from the beginning of his time spent with Thomas earlier that morning up to the cloning accusation. His mother listened intently while stirring her tea. When he was done talking she just stood there and looked deeply at Billy. Starting to wonder herself how big this whole thing could be.

"Mom.... Hello.... did you hear anything I said? It looks as if you are staring right through me." Billy exclaimed.

"Yes....Yes I did hear you and it is rather interesting that all of that information came to you from a man that you happened to meet yesterday. Not to mention the fact that...." she was cut off.

"What that it could be TRUE!!" Billy interjected.

"No... that is not what I was going to say. I was going to say that Thomas was so in awe of the fact that you look like his friend and that you and he had the same mole and all." she finished.

"So you are saying that it could be true Mother!" he was almost back to tears.

"Honey... settle down. I am not saying that it is true. I am just trying to put all of this together. It is quite a bit of information to take all at once, and for us to solve or figure this out we must look at everything. I mean we came up here to try and figure a way to get some answers and here comes Mr. Mallory and BAM! We got all kinda facts.

Maybe you're the lost son of Rafkar and some of his relatives want you back for themselves or something. It seems that you are part of all of these facts and it is up to us to figure out how they fit. That's all I am saying Honey, I have raised you your whole life and if you think that for one moment that I am going to let anyone, I mean anyone tell me that you are a clone or whatever. I will have to see solid proof and then I would even still doubt it. O.K. I love you so much, you must believe that if you believe anything that I just said." she was weeping too.

"I do Ma,..It is just that I don't want to be a clone. I want to be me." he was just about to cry.

"William Ruoff, that is who you are, and don't you forget that. Even if someone does tell you, you are a clone of some mad man. You are not mad, you are you and that is the most important thing you must never forget!!" she was holding him by the shoulders and looking directly into his tear filled eyes.

"I won't Mother. I just want my old life back. Not this running and looking over my shoulder bit." he again wiped his cheeks.

"That's my Billy, this is not the first time that you might hear something this disturbing or..or extreme. We will get to the bottom of this ordeal and return your life back to normal, even if it kills me, I promise," she was holding Billy very tight.

"No death, Nobody is going anywhere without me, you got that Mother?" he was staring into her eyes this time.

"O.K. my little Buck-oh." she said with a big motherly smile.

"Hey what's all of this about. I thought that you guys were coming back outside? Why are you guys crying?" Jewel was perplexed.

"It's alright honey, Billy and I just needed to talk, that's all. Let's go back outside, it is so NICE." she grabbed her tea and was moving out toward the back door.

The afternoon went on and Jewel inquired if they were going to talk anymore about the reason they came there in the first place. She was answered with "We already have" almost simultaneously from Katherine and Billy. She was satisfied, asked no more and just went on enjoying the sun. That however, just stirred up Billy's emotions on the subject so he went inside to be alone.

"Now don't you go moping too much young man. I want you to enjoy the rest of this day," she exclaimed. "I won't, I just need out of the sun," he said going inside.

She knew that he was going inside to think. She saw how much it crushed him, to entertain the idea that his body was cloned from someone else. It was not his life that was cloned, she realized, but his individuality as a human. He really had no unique mother or father. Her heart poured out for her son. She then thought about the fact line that Thomas was going down, could he be right? Could the mole be the proof that her Billy was a clone from this Rafkar? She wanted to find out the rest of what old Thomas knew, and to what extent he could get information.

As he went quietly out the front door, he figured he'd just walk around until he found Thomas. It was a pretty nice day with little clouds, a good time for a walk.

Billy walked for about an hour and no sign of Thomas. He was starting to get hungry and thought he'd walk over to the lodge. As he was entering, he overheard someone talking, and it sounded almost English, but then the other voice became familiar. Just then he rounded the corner to the lobby and sitting there, on the couch, were Thomas and his Mother?

"What are you two doing? he asked. "I have been looking around the springs for you Thomas, but I see that my Mother has found you first," he said staring at the both of them.

"Well William, I can talk to anyone I want, especially if it is on your behalf. It seems that Thomas here does have a little more information about the Shahpur and Rafkar. Is that what you were looking for him for, young man?" she asked earnestly.

"I am sorry to come off like that Mom. It's just that I.... I wanted to find these things out.... first I guess. I mean you understand? Don't you?" he said with his head down.

" Now look here old Boy, anyone who just had something of this magnitude laid upon them would act the same or even worse, why I know some people who would have gone mad actually. I think you are handling it quite well "he said with a reassured smile.

"So it IS true." he said rather loudly. "You were keeping something to yourself, that you could have told me at the pools this morning, weren't you?" he asked somewhat distraught.

"No, No, good boy, we still are just speculating, calm yourself and sit down, good Lord we'll have everyone looking in no time." Thomas said pulling Billy into a chair.

"Honey, all Thomas had told me was the background of Rafkar's family and how he could be tied into this. It was something you did not mention, so I thought it might be relevant." she said reassuringly.

"Is that all you know Thomas?" Billy asked.

"Not exactly, that is where I was when you came around the corner. Rafkar's family was fairly wealthy, to say the least, and they were have thought to save their son's life for he was in a coma. It said in the papers that he died. I never really followed up on it until, well actually until I saw you." Thomas noted to himself.

"But I thought that you and your friends were talking about..." he was cut off.

"We were talking about the Shahpur... not Rafkar." he finished with a quick nod.

"Your mother tells me about the men you have seen that you thought were following you your whole life, or you keep seeing them, the same men, but now they want you to join an army of some sort?" he asked.

"Well that is what the real Army, I mean the American Army says that their some kind of foreign....army...people.... or something. Why? What's their role in this?" Billy asked.

"Boy this is exciting!" Thomas said with a smile." It is

amazing this whole story and..." he stopped... looked at the two of them and finished with a modest: "Right".

The three of them sat and mostly went over all of the things together. Towards the end of it Billy was starting to get a little more uncomfortable with the situation becoming more real and not just a bad dream, but sick human reality. Billy started thinking of his first sick reality after everyone at school really came around after the fact , but it never left him that no one during all of those four years came up to him and asked. So his larger than life new reality was unfolding before him. At this point he stood up and excused himself.

"Oh honey, are you all right? I am sorry; Thomas and I were just going off. I should have realized how we sound." she asked concerned.

"Oh Mother I am just going to the bathroom, I am o.k., besides we are just talking, right?" He fake smiled and walked away.

"I hope he is going to be alright. This is starting to get worse. Ever since graduation things have just got worse. I thought this weekend we could pull together and really find some... things... out," she slowed. "And boy we sure did. Not what I expected, but we have made a start." she said rolling her eyes and sighing. She took a quick drink.

"I am not sure Mrs. Ruoff, oh...Katherine, sorry, but I am not sure that he is a clone, but I say, what was he like in High school? Was he athletic at all? he asked.

Katherine went on to tell Thomas all about Billy's abilities, and being placed on the bench with no explanation. Which led her slightly, due to the vodka, towards her 'men' problems, and how all of sudden the men acted scared of her. As she went on, Billy came back and Thomas gave a small nod to acknowledge Billy's arrival.

She stopped that part of her conversation, with a slight slur. Billy sat down and said to his mother:

"Are you catchin' a buzz ma?" he chuckled.

"No, Yes, So what... I think it was all... this

....Sun...that I am getting today. I think that I am going back to the cabin, Billy would you escort me back there, please?" she smiled.

"I would love to. Thomas, we will see you later, I hope?" Billy asked as he stood.

"Yes, indeed old Boy, later." he said with a quirky grin. Billy smiled back at the expression.

They walked slowly back to the cabin. At first Katherine asked if they could just walk first before talking. She wanted to enjoy the outside while she had a slight buzz, plus she was afraid of what she might say in that state of mind. So they walked and Billy felt the wind pick up and he started to feel clear again and he puffed his chest out and stood up he was trying to feel this... person... that he could possibly be made from. At this point, Billy realized that he had been walking a while with his eyes closed and his mother was leading the way and they had arrived at the cabin. He opened his eyes just in time to go over the step, but he still staggered.

"Hey, I am the one with the buzz on. You are supposed to hold me. ..Old Boy!" she said with her best English accent. They both bursted into laughter.

"Where was everyone? I woke up and everyone was gone. Where were you two?" Jewel came around the corner, slightly pissed.

"Well young lady " Katherine slurred," I decided to have a drink, and then Billy came and rescued me from this boring English man," she sort of nodded towards Billy.

"Oh was it that man from the other night. I thought he was weird; I would stay away from him. I just..." she was cut off.

"Now don't worry Jewel, it is all... good. Billy rescued me. Now I am going to lie down, Billy will you bring me in some water?" she asked with a wink.

"Sure Mom, be right there." he said

"Is she buzzed?" Jewel asked.

"No, why do you say that?" he sad smartly.

"You better watch it, Mister," she snapped back.

Billy took the water into his mother's room

and when he sat the water down she held his arm and pulled him to her. While they hugged, she told him how much she loved and cared for him. Saying that she would do everything she could to put a stop to this. She wanted him to just keep it to the two of them for now; Jewel did not need to know all that they had learned from Thomas. At least not now, then she went on to say that:

"Your life is very important, and you must never give up. These people want something and if, and I am just saying if. What Thomas has said is remotely true, YOU MUST NOT GIVE UP!" she was holding him very tightly with tears starting to gather in her eyes.

"Mother, I....have" he paused and pulled away. "I am going to be o.k. So are you and Jewel," he smiled, to himself and then to her, remembering his inner voice.

She smiled back with a proud, but nervous look as she sat down on the bed. Billy said he would be outside and for her to get some rest. He left the room and closed the door. He felt o.k., but nervous, like the hug that he had just received. He had known that he was up against something big and thought it was very overwhelming. With this new speculation, Billy felt the last piece of his old reality slip away.

VI

They all got ready for one more dinner time over at the lodge. Katherine insisted that they eat out, saying sarcastically that she wanted to treat her children to one last meal. So they put on nice clothes that Katherine had asked them to bring, and Billy insisted that they drive over, no walking.

The three of them walked in, Billy had each of them on an arm, and he felt special. Two fine women on my arms and I fell like a king of the world, he thought. "Well that's a thought" he said out loud.

"What is Buck-oh?" Jewel asked.
"Oh nothing sis', just thinking out loud."

"Yeah,... well keep it to yourself. and...." she was cut

off by Mom.

"Enough... let us sit and eat just like last night. Please?" she begged.

They asked to sit in the back hoping to not see Thomas. No one said much during dinner. Billy and Jewel each figured that they should not talk about much.

"I know we are leaving tomorrow, Mom but we have not really done anything about Billy and .... his problem," stated Jewel.

"Well, honey I think that we actually have done a lot, even it does not look so dear. Don't you think so Billy?" Mother said confidently.

"Yes.... I think so." he said.

"Well I don't believe either one of you, but I don't have the strength to argue. Tomorrow I will so I will want a little more information. I think all that food is making... mee... tired.... Ahhh." She yawned and did not say another word.

They arrived at the cabin, roamed around for a bit then Jewel and Katherine went to bed. Billy was not that tired since his nap. After sitting out back in the warm air, he again thought of Issa and if all of this would drive her away, but his immediate feeling was no, she is going to stay. He joked to himself that he hoped he heard the right voice. He caught himself falling asleep in the chair then made his way into his bed.

Morning came and check out was before 11:30 a.m. Jewel started making coffee. Katherine was packing her belongings and Billy was just sitting out on the back porch, overlooking a beautiful field. While the breeze picked up, Billy felt a feeling of strength and desire. He was to fulfill an empty spot that had been open since he found out he was adopted and what that meant. Just then there was a knock at the door, and it was Thomas.

"Thomas what brings you here......old Boy?" he asked with a chuckle.

"Well I remembered you said that your stay was until Sunday, so I came to bid farewell and also...." he reached into his pocket, pulled out a piece of paper, slid it into Billy's hand and whispered, " Call me if you find out or even if it gets to be too much. This could be my last one." He pulled away giving a jolly smile.

Thomas kissed the hand of Katherine just when Jewel entered. Jewel gasped slightly and then turned in disgust. The three of them laughed behind their muffled hands. Katherine went on to let Thomas know that Jewel was a little 'in the dark' about the possible news. Katherine hugged him, Thomas laughed childishly and he bid them farewell again and was gone. Jewel came back in after hearing the door slam.

"What was he kissing your hand for?" she demanded.

"He was saying goodbye," Katherine replied.

"Well at least it was goodbye. I didn't like that guy; I don't know what you two saw in him." She crinkled her nose. "I think it's what he might have seen in us Sis." Billy smiled at the fact that he had found an ally and a true friend.

"I think he saw something in mom Bro... I didn't see him give anything to you?" she smarted back.

"Oh... but he did ... he did," he smiled even bigger.

It was approaching check-out time and the car was packed. During the ride back Billy was sitting in the back staring out the window thinking about what tomorrow would bring. As he looked out the window he saw horses gracefully running free. That thought filled his head until they were almost home. Once they got close to home, Billy had Katherine drive past his car.

After checking his car he had the unnerving feeling that their house was not safe and probably being watched. Billy must stay somewhere else, but not be followed. He wanted to try Issa first, but didn't want to involve her just yet. He thought she could decide that on her own, so he called her and told her to meet him tomorrow morning, at the park, which was walking distance from Billy's house at eight-thirty sharp. Billy went to be thinking only of Issa.

The alarm went off and soon after he was walking to the park. Billy knew a way through backyards and woods, he could go virtually unseen. When he came out of the woods, he saw her sitting on the hood of her car and he ran to her and they hugged. She pulled away.

"I am glad to see you," she kissed him. "What's up, you seem so serious, Mr. Ruoff?" she asked with a smile.

He grabbed her hand and went over to the bench, sat her down and then proceeded to tell her about the entire weekend. Thomas and all that he knew and the synergy they had with the knowledge they shared. Issa was holding her head in her hands; she had been since he told her about the possible cloning. When he said that was all, she did not look at him, only threw her head on his shoulders and went on to say she did not care if he was a clone or not. Issa pulled away and stared directly into his eyes and said that while he was gone she had some very intense feelings, about him, and all of the things happening around him. She told him she loved him and if his was the body of another, he alone owned his mind. Billy was speechless. Not in all of his thoughts did he think that she would be and say all of the things she did. He embraced her for a long while before speaking.

"I am not sure what will happen next. I wanted you to know that I love you too, but I would not have blamed you for leaving. I know that it is going to get way worse before it gets better. This crazy world and the crazy peop....." he was cut off by her finger touching his lips, followed by her lips.

"Let's just take it day by day. We do have some facts and we'll find the rest. You must sneak back home and go to work, and so do I. So call me later, I am not coming to see you at the Burg. I love you." She kissed him again, got into her car and left. He knew that maybe that vision of them on the beach was a little closer to reality. He ran all of the way passed his home and to his car. There was no black car in sight, so he got in and left. He thought that even if it was there he would still leave, he felt invincible.

VII

Billy's life becomes very content. He and Issa

became entirely comfortable with each other's needs and wants. To the point of talking about eloping and being on their own.

A few nights later, Katherine called Issa's to talk with Billy.

"Billy are you watching television?" she asked.

"Yes and why do you ask?" he replied.

"Well I am on channel twenty-one and they're doing this thing on the Shahpur, and ...?" she was cut off.

"The Shahpur?" he asked. "Oh, what channel? Twenty-one?" he asked again.

"Yes and they say he is very ill, " she said with concern.

They watched and found out that his pancreas is failing and in need of a transplant, he however has the rare A negative blood type and time is running out. They also saw his face a few more times throughout the broadcast giving both Issa and Billy chills. When they showed pictures of him when he was younger, he looked exactly like Billy! Katherine called right after the broadcast was over and asked what he thought. He and Issa discussed his and the Shahpur's likeness and how it would be if he was of some royal blood and stretched that into a fairy tale with a happy ending. By the end of her story Billy was quite amused and said that she would be his Princess and they laughed a little, which faded.

The next day seemed to start out as a nightmare. Billy was leaving for work and found that one of his tires was flat. He begged Issa to get up and take him in and that he could hitch a way home later. Issa agreed and they proceeded to drive to the Mall when soon after pulling onto Speedway, Billy noticed the black car a few cars back and told Issa to slow down and let the car catch up.

"Are you crazy?" she insisted. I am not provoking anything; let's just see if they follow. I'll go a longer way."

"O.K. whatever, but don't be obvious," Billy said as he slid down the seat to get a better view of the car.

The black car did follow but right as they were turning into the Mall, it sped up and passed them very closely. Billy knew it was the same car and felt the uneasiness rise in him again. Issa was not entertained by the thought that now they are back, they know about her. Billy got out and said to be careful and he would see her after 5 p.m. or so, and watch were she parks, so she does not get a flat too.

He thought of Thomas, and found the piece of paper with the number on it and went to call.

"Is Thomas Mallory there?" Billy asked.

"Yes, and whom may I say is calling?" they asked.

"It is Billy, William Ruoff, I say," he said with a little arrogance.

"Is that you old Boy?" Thomas said.

"Why yes, old Boy, it is,...Uh huh." Billy and Thomas laughed together, and Billy felt that he was still his friend.

"I am so glad you called. Did you hear about the Shahpur and that he is dying?" Thomas asked.

"Yes, I did. My mother and I saw it during a news segment on him. I could not believe the resemblance I have to him. They showed some pictures when he was...." he was cut off.

"You see. That is why I was so astounded by your likeness to him, yes?" he said.

"Well ... I did, so what is up? What have you heard since that news, anything?" Billy asked.

"Yes. You know he needs a pancreas, and he has his rare blood, so the news is leaking that it is some kind of bluff on the Shahpurs part to see if the country is behind him; to raise his popularity. He does need a pancreas, and he does have rare blood, but he has one with his blood type. He is waiting for more attention it seems, as if he is playing with his life, skating on the edge,.... somewhat mad my colleges and I tend to think, but they do have a pancreas. Don't worry old Boy, your not needed, or whatever you might have thought of from this news. Well enough with me. Is there anything new in your world that has any correlation to this news?" he finished while blowing his nose, near the phone.

"Well.... it seems that someone is still playing with me. Billy went on to tell about the black car following them and how this occurrence is happening more and more. At his conclusion, he insisted that he have a number to call.

Billy gave Thomas the number at Issa's, so he would not be likely to talk to Katherine.

It was only Tuesday, and Billy and Issa were waiting for the weekend, their weekend to get married. Billy had four days off and Issa had a week, so they were just going through the motions waiting patiently. Katherine was somewhat suspicious of Billy's 'happier than thou' attitude, and how friendly Issa was toward her on the phone. Jewel came right out and asked Billy on the phone if he and Issa were getting married or something. He denied it and said he was just happy.

Now it was Friday and Billy went to work that morning with the thought that nothing could step on his buzz. He was about to marry the girl of his dreams.

Billy went to work and then came home from an uneventful day. They got the rest of their stuff ready and were on the road quickly. Issa was telling jokes, Billy was responding to it and finally said to hell with it and stated that from now on it was just her and him. He did not need any more friends. He had her and he knew she was true. That made Issa very relieved and happy to know that she was first and foremost was fine by her.

Wakimlee Beach was where they were to tie the knot. They heard from a friend of Issa's that you could get marriage licenses there cheap, plus they loved the beach. Wakimlee Beach was very nice and low key with just one pier and about ten miles of shoreline. One could sleep on the beach if desired, and the locals did not bother you. Billy and Issa decided to get married tomorrow but sleep on the beach tonight. Just as they were pulling into town, Billy noticed head lights in his rear view, and started to think that he had been followed. The lights soon turned off the road and he dismissed it as having butterflies in his stomach. Issa laughed.

They woke to the sun drenching them at 5:30 a.m. They

just laid there and talked about the future.

"Should we leave the area, sometime Billy? I sure would like to see the rest of the country," she said.

"I don't know. It might be best to pull these people away from Mom and Jewel. I just don't want them using Mom and Jewel against me. You have already agreed to be with me, even though I have some problem with someone I do not know." he finished by putting her arm around his shoulders.

"I know that sweetie, but I think now or soon that we should venture off. Save some money first then leave. How about that?" she asked kindly.

"That is good. I want to see this country too. Hell that could lead them to following us around the country, we could surely lose them out there," he emphasized.

"Well don't get your hopes up. It will at least raise their expenses for watching you." They both laughed and fell together.

They kissed for a while and then got up and walked out to the pier. They marveled at the sun and how the waters danced with the wind. An older woman who was passing by them noted out loud that they were a picture of love. They had the beautiful sky and the two of them radiating love off of one another. The lady smiled and waked on. They walked exactly that way all the way to the Court House, where they had made all the arrangements earlier that week. Billy pulled out a wreath of small flowers and put them on her head, and they walked in and got married. Billy also had a ring. It was dark, almost brown, with a design of leaves and ivy on it. Issa was delighted at the ring, seeing that it was so different from all other rings she thought he would get. She felt very proud and excited as he slipped it on her finger. The Justice pronounced them man and wife. They kissed and then went screaming, yelling and just whooping it up and out of the Court House.

After a long walk up and down the beach, they became hungry and went into the restaurant next to the hotel they were to check into. They did want to spend at least one night in luxury. They spent the rest of the day relaxing on the beach and going back to the room to enjoy their new status of being Mr. and Mrs. Ruoff.

Billy awoke to the sound of a loud car sometime later that evening. He swore that it was right outside their door. Being awakened by such a sound, Billy ran to the door to see the car. By the time he was outside, it was gone. He attributed the sound to the likes of the black car and that maybe they followed him to the beach. He did not go back to sleep at all. Issa slept through the whole thing. She woke once and asked why he was out of bed. Since he could not sleep he decided to turn on the television. Issa did not care; again she slept right through it. He was flipping channels when he came across the news. It was about the only good thing on at that time anyway. They were flashing through the day's top stories when up came the Shahpur. Apparently his organ donation did not come through and he was suffering badly. They thought he could go into a coma at any time. The time was 4:22 a.m. and Billy thought of Thomas instantly, he was an hour ahead of Billy so he could call him in two hours and probably not wake him. He watched the news again to see the top story segment. He wanted to see if he had missed any other details of the story. He did not. All he knew was that the Shapur was in severe trouble.

Billy started to drift back to sleep as daylight was peeping into the window. He thought of the day before; lying on the beach with his wife. The thought delighted Billy. His world seemed a little bit stronger and normal. Issa was very much in love with him, as he was with her. He was not too worried about the Shahpur stuff, he remembered: one day at a time. Issa woke up and started fooling around with Billy.

"Hey Mr. I am allowed to do anything to you I want, that is what being a wife is, right?" she smirked.

"That means the same for ME!" He jumped on top of her and tickled her to the point of screaming. Issa made a promise to do whatever he says, and said she would trust him forever. He seconded the notion and sealed it with a kiss. Just then he remembered to call Thomas, as he glanced at his watch. Issa was confused as to why he was calling Thomas. She thought that Billy was nuts.

Thomas answered the phone.

"Thomas I thought you said that he had a donor?" Billy inquired.

"Yes but he apparently died before getting to the hospital. They think that one of the Shahpur's enemies killed the donor on the way. He died with an exploding gunshot right to the pancreas area. They could not even use his blood because of contamination from the exploding bullet. I don't know what he is going to do next, Are you in a safe place William?" he asked.

"We are not near anyone we know in case of emergency. You are the only person that knows we are here. Do you think that we should head back toward home?" he replied.

"It could be wise. I tried to call your house when I heard the news. I was not sure what to do. I thought of calling your mother but then remembered what you asked me, about not telling her. So I am sure glad to talk....." he was cut off by a beep.

"Billy, are you still there? Could you wait a minute I have another call on the line?" he said.

"Yes, I will hold" he responded.

As Billy waited, Issa broke in and said she was sorry for saying he was crazy. Billy finished by saying that he forgot to tell her about what he saw on the news.

"Old Boy!" he said quickly, "Are you there? I say, are you there?!" he was frantic.

"Yeah, yeah Thomas, I am still here. What are you so excited for?" he asked smartly.

"I hate to do this to you, especially on your honeymoon old boy, are you sitting down?" he said calmly.

"What are you saying Thomas, yes I am sitting down?" he asked with extreme caution in his voice.

"Well I was just informed that the alleged donor was ....." he paused.

"Was what Thomas?" Billy yelled.

"He was a clone," Thomas said straight out. "The picture of him was released to some people in England that have kept me informed since I met you. I knew something bad was to come about this, I just knew it." he finished in silence.

Billy was almost crying with rage right behind the news. On his wedding day he finds out whom his parents are and that his body and his life for the moment was someone else's. Issa almost knew by the look of terror and pain on Billy's face. She held him as tight and long as she could. After a minute or two she could hear Thomas' voice asking if he was still there. Billy did not move. Issa took the phone and told Thomas that they would call back, the only thing he said was to call back soon. He would have some ideas as to what to do next and that time was not a luxury anymore, he also said he was sorry and that they were not alone. Issa hung up the phone, Billy was still in the same pose. He laid back with his arm over his head and a blank stare on his face.

He did not do anything for about an hour. He answered a few of Issa's questions: Are you in there? Is there anything I can do? Billy was filling up with his own feelings. He was establishing a self, one he could always come back to. He realized he had been quiet for a while. Billy played through his mind the possibilities at hand. The first thing that he knew was that he was the next guinea pig, and that the black car might know where he is, and would be sure to follow him closely. Billy was going over these thoughts to the point of saying them out loud. Issa started to hear him, she reminded him to call back Thomas, to find out what information he had. Billy got on the phone. "Thomas it's me, old Boy, I am o.k. to talk, what else do you know?" he asked slowly.

"I say, I am glad you are taking charge, my boy." He was trying to keep him in good spirits." The most important thing I learned is that there are possibly more than two clones; in fact my resources tell me that they are sure of it. Which leads to you not being in immediate danger and you're not alone either." I think you should get out of wherever you are, during the night, and tell your mother only, and go far away from where you are. Travel at night only and maybe even sleep in your car on back roads, in the middle of nowhere. William, you need to disappear, Now!" he was very emphatic.

"We don't have very much money, but I do feel the same way about leaving." Issa was tugging on his arm asking: "What are we doing? I can get some money from my parents, and tell them, I will...." she was cut off by Billy "I am sorry Thomas, what?" he asked.

"I need to go now; there is not much else to tell. Billy keep your head on straight and don't talk to strangers. If you have to work, let Issa, you must stay low, I mean think about ten years from now. It will be the only way you can stay alive. Call me in a week, good luck old chap, Goodbye." he concluded.

"Thank so much Thomas, you are really looking out for me and I appreciate it. I'll call soon, Goodbye."

Issa was frantic because she could not tell what they were talking about. She was done romping around the room when Billy came out of another stupor. He proceeded to tell her that they needed to sleep in the car and basically run away. Tell his mom and get as much money together and go. Issa was mostly clued in on that part, she wanted to know what else was said about being a guinea pig, she did not know how to put it. Billy laughed a little to himself, and then told her there could be others, and that he was not alone. Issa gasped. She started to think of seeing not two or three, but seven to ten people looking just like the man she just married. Issa started to cry, not knowing why. Billy asked, but she just shook her head and said she did not know.

After they settled down, she told him of her vision and that was what started her crying. She fell into his arms crying again, only saying that she loved this Billy and this one only, he was tearing up with all the emotions washing over his face one after another. He just buried his head into hers and they wound up lying there before falling back to sleep again.

When they woke, it was 5:30, check out was at 1:00. Billy started to get dressed and go over to the office to see if they still had to pay for another night. Issa packed anyway and got their stuff in the car. She was just ready to pull the car around, for the chance of a quick getaway when Billy turned the corner.

"Do we have to pay?" she asked.

"No those people were so nice, they knew that we got married and said we can leave later on if we like. If we stay the night they will only charge us half, a small wedding present." Billy was smiling, their first wedding present.

"Splendid, old Boy, she said with an English accent. Let's go back in and watch some television, before we leave." She was pulling her shirt off as she walked through the door. Billy was right behind her.

"It really gets dark around 8:30, and I think that if we leave around 9:30 and get home around 11:30, it will be safe." he said as they lay in each others arms.

After a few hours of honeymooning', Billy went out to the car to check the oil, and pull it around to leave. As he closed the hood he heard the sound of a car that sounded like the one outside his door last night. He waited for it to go by, and as it did, it pulled into the Hotel's parking lot and then parked at the office. Billy watched the person getting out of the car very closely. It was a younger kid, probably Billy's age. When the kid came out of the office, Billy walked over to the guy and asked him if he was revving the engine of that car the other night, and the guy said he was. Billy at first was relieved that it was not the black car or something, but then he had to say that it did wake him from his sleep, and that he should be a little more considerate toward other people. The guy was a little bit smaller than Billy, so he said sorry and walked off, only to rev his engine again and light up the tires as he drove away.

Issa came out and asked what that was all about. Billy said it was nothing. Issa hugged him and got in the car. As they pulled out, they honked to the office lady who was looking out the window at the time, and drove toward Bakersville.

Most of the way they did not talk much. Billy was trying not to check the rear view mirror too much, and Issa was trying not to notice. Finally Billy said aloud that he could not stop looking at it. Issa grabbed his hand and said that it was only natural to look out for oneself. He squeezed her hand back and said "thanks". Issa fell asleep with her head in his lap. They went through Bakersville, right past Grandmother and Aunt Nell's house and headed home. Soon they were home, but Billy did not want to stay at their place or his mother's. Issa woke and mentioned that they should get used to sleeping in the car so why not tonight? He agreed and they went through town. Billy knew of a road on the other side of the hill behind his mother's house and proceeded there. Issa however, wanted to get some things from her car since it was dark and insisted on going there now. Billy responded by turning down a back street and heading back to her place. As he got closer to the house, his gut told him to stop and walk around the building, not drive. He found an alley and parked next to a dumpster.

"What are we parking here for, it *is* night?" she requested. "I still want to play it safe,.... I am a commodity, to someone ... but not for long!" he smirked off as he got out. Issa got out and followed. The alley was dark and they could just jump over the back fence and be there.

"Come on you can make it babe," he said from the top.

"I'm a coming, honey," she whispered back.

   While Billy was standing up there he looked over to what he thought was the black car, but it was a police car. He jumped down and told Issa to wait. A moment later the police car was coming down the alley. Issa ducked beside a car and waited for it to pass. She came out not being sure that she should go over the fence, so she said she would go in the back entrance alone and let him in. He said to keep her head low and blew her a kiss, adding "good luck,"

   They just made it over the back wall when another car went by the alley way. Billy thought it more likely to be the enemy than the cops. He came out of the alley with his headlights off. They made it three blocks and then turned into another alley.

"This will take us all the way out of town, we'll just go slow

and quiet," he smiled to her.
"Can you see without lights?" she queried.
"Mostly ... I know the road is straight. and there are few street lights." he said.

They made it to the end of the alley and turned onto Speedway. No other cars were out, and they saw none the rest of the way. He pulled the car off the dirt road to a level spot and just then he saw dawn arriving. Issa had already crawled into the back and was asleep, so he just nuzzled up to her and tried to sleep.

A truck drove by the car and Billy woke and quickly looked to see it. He rubbed his head and Issa awoke too. He thought she should drop him off down a ways, near his house, then drive the car up a ways and wait for him there, she wanted to stay with him. He thought it would be better for her not to be there for the 'whoever' might be there. She argued, but then responded, by giving him a long kiss and starting the car. Billy knew these woods well, so it took him no time to get to the house. As he came through the back door, Katherine almost jumped at the sight of him.

"You scared the shit out of me Billy, Where have you guys been? I have been calling, Jewel went by the house, and I am just beside myself over this Shahpur news ... Well..?" she asked throwing her hands into the air.
"Mom,... let's go into the kitchen and sit down, there is a lot to tell you with very little time. It is very important that you listen." he was stroking her arm as they walked into the kitchen.

Billy started that he and Issa just drove to Wakimlee Beach for the weekend, he was not sure when he was going to tell her that they got married... yet. He told her of both his conversations with Thomas, in order. She almost cried, her eyes were full of pain for Billy. He keep on saying that it would be alright, 'maybe in ten years', Katherine would rebuttal through her tears.

After she calmed down, he went on telling her he would have to leave, and if she had any extra money to lend. She asked about Issa and if she was trust worthy. She was becoming scared and asked if Issa should leave because it would be so much? Billy finally told her that they were married. She cried again, only they were happy tears. Now she knew that her son would not be alone. Billy told his mother that Issa knew what they were up against, and they would run to the remote corners of America first and then out of the country if need be. Katherine was smiling somewhat, after hearing Billy's plans. She knew he was smart enough, but she could not help wondering, being so young, how tough they could be. She went and got four-hundred dollars, it was her emergency money.

"Mom, I love you and no matter whose body I am, I am your son!" he grabbed her and kissed her on the cheek then placed his head on her shoulder only to stare off while hugging.

"I will only write, which I'll try for twice a week, hopefully more. Issa is really with me on this, she knows that this is not a game, or something to be taken lightly. Were gonna' head up to Colorado,.. that's all we know right now. I love you, tell Jewel I love her too. O.K. I have to go, Issa is over the hill on Paddycorn road, thanks for the money,.....Bye." He let go of her and started to run, looked back once and was gone.

"Bye?" she whispered through her tears.

She stumbled back into the house and called Jewel to come home, she was at a boyfriend's house. When she arrived, Mom told Jewel the entire story and the new news. They both wept in each others arms. After a while, Jewel offered to make some coffee. Mom accepted and they went on upstairs to turn on the television for something to look at. They were both confused as to how could this be and who was behind it. Not just the Shahpur, everyone. Katherine wished she had gotten Thomas' number, she wanted to be able to call someone to talk about all this.

Billy came upon the car, at first he did not see Issa, as she was lying in the back.

"How'd it go?" she asked.

"Smoother than expected. She did not cry as much which I was glad for, but you could tell that the truth about the cloning just crushed her. The way she was looking at me afterward was..... I just knew." Billy was getting into the car.

"Did you tell her about us?" she asked.

"I had to, she was questioning your... your ability to stay with me and not leave me when it got rough, and all. So I had to tell her, O.K.?" he said.

"I am glad she knows. I love your mom, she is so great, and I am proud to be her daughter-in-law." she ended by grabbing him around the neck and pulling him closer.

"Now how am I gonna drive to Colorado with you around my neck?" he asked.

"I don't know. You figure it out, Mr. Ruoff." she said smartly.

Billy started the car and drove to another pull off that was shaded by trees and far enough of the road not to be seen. He thought they could stay there until dark, get some food at a store and then make their way north. Issa started rubbing his thigh as he shut off the car.

"You know what I need, Mr. Ruoff?" she asked coyly.

"What?" he replied.

"You with me until dark we part." she squirmed.

"So be it!" he said.

VII

A gust of wind blew the blanket that was blocking light through the windshield. Issa was aroused, said out loud that it was getting dark, which arose Billy with a smile.

"Let's get out of this place!" He jumped up front and started the car.

"Issa, I am so glad we are leaving, I hope that......" Issa put her hand over his mouth.

"Don't say another word about anybody...or nothing. William, don't you jinx us,... not now." She finished by replacing her fingers with her lips.

"Well I would gladly stop talking' all day if you kiss me like that, good thing this is a back road, we would have wrecked for sure. O.K. now you start looking out for...... nobody, Right!" he was caught by a fast stare from Issa.

They got out of town without noticing any black car, and

made it all the way to the state line before stopping. She asked if he was scared, and he said no, but they both knew he was. He kept thinking that something would happen to his Mom and Jewel.

They found a side road off the highway; it was already close to dawn. Billy threw one blanket on the windshield and one over himself and Issa. They felt safe. Billy had said he felt safe at Seneca Springs, and he felt the same safeness here. So they slept 'til dusk again. As Issa got up and started the car, Billy asked where she was going?

"North, I want to see some Mountains," was her reply.

"Well just head West and we'll be there in no time.." he jumped over the seat and put on his seatbelt.

They were coming into the mountains just after dawn. Ended up near Alamosa, Colorado when they felt they were in the heart of the Rocky Mountains. Neither one of them had seen mountains that big before. Mostly "Wow" was the common word spoken between them. They were extremely blessed with an almost full moon setting behind the mountain. Billy pulled the car over and go out.

"We sure picked a good place to come,.... or what? We'll be able to hide in these mountains for a while, hell I might even get used to winter!" Billy was tickled with his surroundings.

"Don't get too attached, Buck-oh," she said impersonating Jewel.

"Very funny, I would prefer it if she was the only one to use that term,.. Sweetie , o.k.?" he asked.

"Oh, alright. Sorry, but you know we won't be able to stay for long. We'll have to move on and go farther west or north, I would love to stay here, but eventually we will go. " She said with sad but concerned eyes.

Billy shrugged off her comment and walked off up to a small crest. He sat down and started to cry. Issa came up slowly and sat down, she was whimpering also. What freedom and joy they felt as a result of their surroundings, was suddenly lost to the reality of being fugitives.

"We'll have to find a good spot, or we might draw attention to ourselves. I will drive for a little while, keep looking for a dirt side road without a "No Trespassing' sign." Billy sounded game for the idea.

Issa saw a road with no markings, Billy turned and after a few hundred yards, they did see a sign, but they could tell that it was old and not very visible so they went on. The road got narrow and the car started to scrape the tree limbs, it looked as if a clearing was up ahead and Billy turned the car off. Issa jumped out of the car first and jumped and yelled. Her voice was drowned out by the wind, but she was still jumping and laughing. Billy looked around and saw a place to park the car, in the shade, he pulled it in and got in the back to lay down. Issa came over slowly and asked him to move over.

The light got lower in the car, but still daytime. Billy stirred and pulled out the money in his pocket. He knew at the rate they were going they only had two weeks till they were out of money. Issa mentioned that a job would be o.k. for two weeks here somewhere and then they could move on. She did not want to work more than two weeks somewhere anyway. Billy agreed so they had a bagel and cream cheese, some rice milk and straightened up the car so it did not look like they lived in it and headed back out on the road.

Eventually Billy drove slowly through the little town of Alamosa, Colorado. They said the names of the hotels out loud to remember their names. They figured that they could say that they were staying at this hotel until they got a place and then switch names if anything got suspicious before they left. Issa saw a local newspaper receptacle, so Billy stopped. When she looked she saw a cashier's job at a restaurant on the main street. They drove a little further and saw it. Billy turned in and shut off the car.

They went into the Southern Wrangler restaurant. It was a typical steak house set with Western scenery. Issa turned up her nose to Billy as they were looking around. After a few moments a hostess came and asked if they were going to eat. They all exchanged names after Issa acknowledged that she wished to apply for the cashier job. The hostess, named Jodie, told them to wait and she would get her an application. Issa filled it out and after a short meeting with the manager she had the job and was to start the day after tomorrow. They felt a little strange when Jodie was staring at Billy. At one point, Issa gave a real long and hard stare towards Jodie. Jodie caught her staring and quickly left the office area. Billy said something to Issa about it, but Issa noted that she was just interested in him and not who he was. Billy smiled and left it at that.

They did get some fries to go and Jodie did not charge them for it. She said something about her being hired and that she would see her on Thursday. Issa was somewhat excited and Billy was too. They now had money coming in, not just going out.

While cruising back through town, Issa spotted a hotel with a special deal: two nights for the price of one. Just what they needed, for staying another night in the car did not sound good. Billy agreed, so they got a room for two nights at the Red Hill Inn, thirty dollars for two nights.

Their new life in Colorado was beginning to look alright for the moment. Billy was anticipating talking to Thomas, since he had been out of touch with the rest of the world since they left home. Issa was talking about a shower and how nice it was going to be to take a long hot one. Billy interrupted with his thoughts on a bath for the two of them. It seemed as if they were at a slight ease on life..... for the moment.

VIII

Eight days later, a letter arrived from Colorado. It was not from Alamosa, it was from Trinidad. Upon reading the letter it seems that it got a little uncomfortable for them in Alamosa, people were asking questions everyday. Well mostly to Issa because she was out in the public. The real turning point was when a dark skinned man came into town and stayed for about four days. They said he ate at Issa's restaurant and always asked to sit in her section. One evening though, Billy was picking Issa up from work and he was waiting in his car for her. The dark skinned man came out first, and as he drove right by their car, he smiled real big and sort of laughed.

From that day on someone was following Billy around the area. It was not a big area, so sometimes the person was on a bike or walking. He knew it was not paranoia, because they were the same guys. Billy ended the letter by saying that they left there in the night again but were heading back in their direction thinking that it might throw them off for a while. He promised to write a lot sooner than last. He said not to worry and that he might see them soon.

Katherine and Jewel spirits were lifted. They made a promise to not get their hopes up, however th next evening around 10:00 p.m. Katherine heard something in the back yard. At first she thought it was a cat, but she saw its shadow and it was moving slowly like it was coming across the lawn. Then she realized it was a person, two of them. She ran to the stairs and called for Jewel and told her to turn off the lights and get under her bed and that she would be right up. Jewel started to ask why but Katherine walked away and turned off the lights downstairs and was coming back up the stairs while Jewel still stood there. They got under the bed and at that time she told Jewel why they were doing this. Right then they heard the door rattle, Katherine was sure she locked the door, but just then they heard it open.

They were both holding each other as they heard the foot steps walk around the downstairs. The foot steps went into the study where the computer was, and stopped. They could hear the floor creaking as the person sat in the chair in front of it. She knew they were looking right at it. With the screen saver on, anyone would know that it was turned on.

After fifteen minutes they started to come upstairs. Then someone else came into the house, there were two of them. Both Katherine and Jewel were trembling holding each others hands. Katherine noticed that no lights had been turned on since the people had come into the house, and now that they were coming up the stairs, she saw no flash lights. She instantly thought of hit men with infrared night goggles. She started to whine, as she suddenly realized they were going to die. Jewel grabbed her mother by the head and pulled her into her chest to quiet the sound. Jewel was looking out the door to the hallway, just waiting for them to come to the room and look for them. It seemed like an eternity.

It was two hours later that Jewel woke with her mother in her arms still. They had both fallen to sleep. Jewel started to speak into her mother's ear and wake her. She wanted to come out from under the bed and see if the people had left. Katherine wanted her to stay, but knew that they could not stay there all night. As Jewel got up and walked around the bed Jewel heard noise from Billy's room and as she came into the hall it sounded as if the people were sleeping! She could hear two sets of breathing coming from his room. Jewel thought that she and her mother should make a run for it, she went back into her room and got Katherine up and whispered to her what they were doing. Katherine thought that was a good idea. As they were walking down the hall the floor creaked right in front of Billy's door, they both looked at each other and then into the room. It was barely lit from the street light outside. Katherine was scanning the room when she noticed that there were a pair of tennis shoes and socks near the door and as she looked closer she noticed another smaller pair. When she noticed the second pair, she grabbed Jewel's arm and told her to wait. Katherine then started to walk into his room as Jewel was pulling her back, after she saw what Katherine was doing. Right then, the floor creaked again. A slight moan came from Billy's bed, Katherine gasped, followed by Jewel chirping 'Mom' and then another moan from the bed. "Whaaattt's.... going.... on ?" the person said in a drowsy low moan.
"William!! What the....." Katherine said, her voice rising from a whisper to a slight yell.
"What mom, I .... we ..... what time is it? "Billy was still drowsy.

"Billy is that you.... I am gonna really kill you this time." Jewel came storming in.

"I told you to wake them." Issa said from the other side.

"I am sorry Mother, I should have woke you, but can't this wait till morning?" he asked as he rolled over.

"Hell no, Buck-oh, we have been under a bed since you came into this house, thinking you were someone coming to kill us both and when I am through, you'll wish they had." Jewel was mad as ever.

"What are you talking about?" he exclaimed back at her while rising from the bed.

"She's right," Katherine said. "We heard you come in and then you used no lights and were extremely quiet, so being as paranoid as we are at the moment, we thought that someone was coming to kill us. " She finished by sitting on the bed.

"Wow, I never thought that you guy's imagination was that powerful. Well now that this is clear, can we finish this in the morning? Issa and I have been driving all day and are very tired, as are the both of you, so can we finish this tomorrow, Jewel, please?" He ended drearily.

"I guess so, it's at least good to see you both, safe and not someone who I thought was going to kill me. Goodnight." She walked away.

"Goodnight you two, it is good to have you home, for now. We'll talk in the mornin' young man." She said this sternly but with compassion.

"Sorry mom, it won't happen again," he said as he rolled into Issa.

Katherine thought to herself that she hoped that it would happen every night. Then she would at least know that he was safe that night.

Morning came and Jewel and Katherine were at the start of their routine until they hear the unmistakable sound of a man peeing into a toilet. They both looked at each other and laughed. Billy came into the kitchen to see them still giggling at the thought.

"What gives? Are you two laughing at me?" he said as he went for the refrigerator.

"A little,... We are not used to having... men around." Jewel replied with a smile.

"So... YOU'RE not still angry with me, are ya sis?" he asked with a big grin.

"Oh yeah, but you're on safe ground... for now," she muttered.

"Enough you two, now William.." Katherine demanded, "What in the hell ARE you two doing here. You come into the house late and I hope you did not park near, we think that you are killers, I mean, ... next time ya come back , could you include us in the plan? This whole damn thing is enough without you pullin' something like,.... this." She was nearly crying, pacing the kitchen.

"I am sorry, Mom. I thought it would throw off the people looking,...... I wanted to come home." He went over to her, leaning up against the counter. He grabbed her and held her tightly.

"I am glad your are safe," Jewel started to whine, "Little Buck-oh, but sh... you really scared us, don't do that to us." She went over and joined them.

"I was starting to feel slightly normal, but then someone discovered us and all of the feelings came right back," Billy said.

"Who found you?" Jewel asked.

"Well one of those dark-skinned men came into the restaurant that I was working at, after that we saw him everywhere we went. So, when I got my last paycheck, which was for only twenty two dollars, we left." Issa finished.

"So that was when you decided to come home or.... what?" Katherine asked.

"Well at first we wanted to head farther northwest and we did, but on the way out of town we saw one of them again, so we decided to take him on a little tour of the area. Since Issa was at work I would sometimes go on little drives to check out the area, so I sort of knew my way around the back roads of the county. Well we had this guy all over the road, it was.... " Billy was cut off.

"Hilarious," Issa jumped in. "You would have been so

proud of your son Katherine, he had that jerk drivin' like he was chasing gold.

Katherine looked to Billy, she could tell that reliving the moment was a lot for them.

"Mom, we wanted to see you, I have never been away, and well, I am scared." His lip was quivering" I am sure that I can handle this but only in small doses for now, and I need to come back to you for strength and security. I am not quite as strong as you yet. "He tried to shrug off the feeling of crying, and it took a few minutes.

"William, I am so glad you are here and I know that you are still a young man with the world on your shoulders, and I, *we* are here for you at any cost. Your life is very important. You must be the one to stop this Shapur son-of-a-b... He is not in charge here, you are. Jewel, Issa and I are here to help you and we will find a way to get you a normal life, if you wish, or to find a way to stop this cloning madness." She had him in her arms and he was in a full cry.

Mom you are so strong, where did this come from? This does not seem like you?" Billy asked.

"Well, while you were alone in school, I was alone in the world. Every man I got to know would suddenly run away as if I were a witch. Well I have put two and two together and they spelled 'Shapur'. You see my life has been controlled by that ... a hole since the day I adopted you, and that has set me into the mode of strength, not scared. I know you will be the same," she smiled.

XII

The next week came and went with no one being followed or watched. No strange cars parked up the street or across from Jewel's work. Billy was getting bored and was reading every book and magazine in the house. At night, Billy would ask if he could do anything to help with the bills or something, but Jewel and Katherine just made him cook and clean the house while they worked. Billy really did not mind this, but he would sometimes forget that he was not a normal person in society and just want a return to normalcy.

One day the phone rang and it was Thomas.

"Hello old boy how are and your lovely family doing on this fine day?" he said in his cheerful English way.

"Just fine Thomas. What do we have the pleasure of hearing from you, on this fine day?" Billy replied with a slight accent himself.

"Well, the pleasure won't be too much. I am afraid that the news I have *is* somewhat.... how do you say unnerving?" he replied softly.

"What is it Thomas, I think I can handle anything these days." Billy said.

"Well in that case it should not be too awful, you see my friends have told me that the Shapur is planning a visit to America in the coming month and I hear that he is looking for a good doctor. Now I don't know what kind of doctor he is looking for, I just know that he is coming and what his business is. .... Are you there William?" he was asking curiously.

"Oh yes, quite so. I was just pondering the idea to go see the man myself and.... get a good look at him, you know." Billy said sarcastically.

"You mean to go and directly meet the man in person, as yourself?" Thomas said with much concern.

"Well not exactly as me, you see I have been experimenting in disguises and I think that I have found one that would not give me away so easily. I have been dressing up as an old woman and my sister's friend showed me how to do has some incredible make-up so and I look pretty good as an old woman, or something of the sort. I have been using it to get close to those goons that have been following me for the last month or so." Billy said.

"How rather interesting, have you spoken to these 'goons' as you say?" he asked.

"Oh yes, they think that I am an old woman named Gloria who has seen them parked and comes over and acts nosy and is pestering, like some women do. It works quite well, except that the shoes and the boobs get to be a little much after an hour or so." Billy explained.

"Good show my boy, that is a marvelous idea. You keep practicing your Gloria act and I will find out more details on his trip to the states. By the way, why would you want to risk it, I mean going to see him and for what reason, if I may ask?" he questioned.

"I am not sure, but I know that I should go and get a good look at the man I am going to expose to the world as a fake and exploiter of humans. I don't really know ...... I just want to look him straight in the eye and then expose him." He said this very slowly. Billy knew something had to happen.

"I know that you feel uncertain of yourself William, but do as you heart tells you, and be careful. I will be in touch soon with more information. You are a very strong man William, keep your head up. Cheers." Thomas finished and hung up the phone.

Billy was full of anxiety and wanted to go directly to the Shapur and tell him everything he knew and then straight to the news stations with his story. He did not want his mother to know his plans, at least not directly. He came out of his bedroom and ran into Issa.

"Who was that?" she asked.

"It was Thomas," he said.

"Really! Does he have some news on the Shapur?" she asked excitedly.

"Yes, but I am not sure how to handle it." he said.

Billy went on to tell Issa the conversation they had and his intentions. Issa said it was risky but new that Billy had to do something to end it.

Issa's feelings made Billy very happy and relieved. He had thought that his idea was mad and he was just going crazy over the whole thing again. Issa reassured him that it was perfectly normal to feel crazy, even though being a clone was not normal. Billy heard her but made no response.

She promised him she would not tell the family until all was known about the Shapur's trip and his plan.

Billy would have to be on his toes since the Shapur was coming to America looking for a doctor. This could only mean that another clone would have to be used for whatever surgery was going to take place. That's what really weighed on Billy's mind.

XIV

"Well something is bound to happen soon, I can feel it. Things have been a little too quiet lately. Have you heard from Thomas at all?" Katherine asked as she took off her coat.

"As a matter a fact, he called today." He said as he looked at Issa, giving him a wide eyed look.

"How funny, what did he have to say?" she asked.

"Nothing..... really, he was..... just uh.... calling to see how I was." Billy tried to think and was not doing a good job of covering up.

"That tone in your voice does not match what you are telling me William. Did he have some news about the Grand Goonie?" she said in her motherly tone.

"Well kinda, he was not to sure on his information and he said that he would be in touch soon..... with more info." Billy was not looking at her as he spoke.

"Now Billy if we are going to be in this together, you must tell me or else I will not be..... be.... alright. It is enough that my son is a clone of some mad man who probably wants you only for body parts. I live with that thought every day. So you must tell me what Thomas said." She was trying not to break down.

"I am sorry...... I am just nervous. And sometimes I just don't want to involve you and Jewel all of the time and I just want to do this on my own and I get scared to tell you....... Do you understand? Sort of?" He came over and sat down beside her.

"I do understand but that is not how it should be. We are a family and we must know. So we know what to expect and when, O.K. What did Thomas say?" she asked while stroking his head.

"He said that the Shapur is coming to America and

he is looking for some sort of doctor. He didn't know what kind or when. He said he would get back to me when he had more detail." He was looking into her eyes and saw them filling with tears.

"I just know he is coming for you. Whatever kind of surgery he needs, he is going to need something from you, and I just know it." She was holding her head and shaking. Jewel came over and sat beside her.

"Now Mother you don't know this. Thomas is going to find out more and then we can start to ...... see what is going to happen. Don't become so worried so fast. We will do something, this is not going to happen the way you think it is." Jewel was trying to stop her from crying.

"Jewel's right Katherine, you need not worry so quickly. Billy is not going to just let something like that happen, are you Billy?" Issa was glaring at Billy, willing him to say something to ease her thoughts.

Billy stood up and walked away from the couch and then turned, as if to say something. He instead asked his mom if she wanted anything to drink. He went into the kitchen, Issa following.

"Are you going to tell her? I mean look at her, she is realizing the truth. What are you going to do Billy?" Issa was getting in his face.
"What ?...... You want me to tell her now that I am going to go see him as Gloria and look into this madman's eyes before I expose him to the world? She would be even more scared. I ...I... I don't know what to do. What do you think? I think that now is not the time to tell her, we should wait until we learn more from Thomas. .....and that is what I am going to do." He turned, filled a glass with water and walked out to the living room, Issa followed.

They finished supper and ended the evening in the living room with laughter, telling stories of the family's past. Issa learned a little more of Billy's past and that of the life they lived, without knowing why the things happened the way they did. Now they knew someone was protecting Billy from harm or from a potential father figure, the reason for

Katherine's sorrows and Billy's inability to make friends and participate.

After three days of holding their breaths every time the phone rang, Thomas finally called with his information. It appeared that with the success of the previous pancreas transplant, something that had yet to be accomplished did not happen. The doctors that performed the transplant were skeptical, although they did not know it came from a Shapur clone. It seemed that the boy had developed diabetes before the removal of his pancreas and since the Shapur's body was not yet diabetic, it was rejected. Also, with the amount of time that the pancreas was in the body, he had overworked his kidneys to the point of shut down. So the Shapur was now looking for a new pancreas as well as new kidneys. So he is coming to America for a doctor and also for ...... Billy.

At that point,, Billy dropped the phone and put his head in his hands. Issa immediately grabbed the phone. Thomas was very concerned and sorry he couldn't relate this disturbing information more easily. Thomas summarized what he has just told Billy to Issa and then added that there were only three clones in the beginning. One had died very young and the other was killed for the first pancreas. That left Billy as the only remaining clone. He also said that the Shapur was desperate.

Issa was listening and somewhat shocked by the news. They were not expecting these extreme measures from the Shapur. They thought that there were more clones in the world and were not prepared them for these hard facts. Issa had a blank look on her face as Billy pulled his head out of hands. He slowly pulled the phone from her ear, and heard Thomas still talking.

"Thomas it's me, I....I ... I am not sure what to do now. I was thinking of going to see him face to face, but risking that would be suicide. What do you suggest?" his voice was cracking.

"Well one other bit of information you need to know is.... Well old boy, I am afraid they have you tagged, meaning that you have been bugged." he said.

"You mean my house?' Billy said.

"No, ... I mean *you* have. It seems that at birth, all of the clones were implanted with a very small device giving them the ability to locate you. The only advantage to you is that they must have a receiver within a thirty mile radius, but it will give the direction you are going away from the signal. It is all that I know of the device. I am working on the exact location of the bug. Unfortunately, my source that had gave me this knowledge was unable to probe any further into their origin without risking detection. When I do find the location, we will have to find a doctor willing to remove it. For there will be a risk during the procedure, and they'll also wonder what the purpose of the device is.. Are you still with me William?" Thomas was trying to be sympathetic.

"Yes I am. I am just a little lost in my ever changing world. It seems now that it was never mine to begin with. I am, however, ready to claim it as mime and take whatever chances there are to do so." He said this emphatically.

"That is an astounding statement my Boy. I am always amazed at your resiliency; we shall get your life back. Now I suggest that you be on the lookout for the ..... goonies as I believe you now call them, and have your Gloria get up ready at all times. The Shapur will arrive soon, but he has to find the right doctor for this procedure, if you get my meaning. Not just any doctor will do. The doctors in America are not so easily persuaded, now that the new operating laws are in effect. That is another factor helping you also, after we find the location of your apparatus you will need to find a willing doctor to do some, ...how do you say, back door surgery? Do you follow me my Boy?" Thomas asked.

"Absolutely, I need to get organized now, I don't need anymore information. Thomas, I want you to know that If ..... well if I ever thought as anyone as a father...." he was cut off.

"There, there my Boy, I understand you very much. I will contact you as soon as anything and I mean anything, comes my way. You and your family should act as normal as possible not alerting the goonies that you are aware of anything. I will be in touch, and William ..... I am honored to be a part of your getting a new life." Billy could hear that Thomas was smiling.

"I am equally honored, Sir. Thank you." As Billy hung up the phone, he felt a small relief, knowing that Thomas was looking out for him. With the contacts that he had, his life was once again going to be his. The word destiny was prominent in his mind and he felt his actions from here on out were already written, he just had to play them out.

While waiting to hear back from Thomas, he wanted to test the ability of the location device he now knew was inside him. Alec probably knew that he was in the area but not standing right next to him. He wanted to be sure though, so he thought of a way to test it. He recognized that they did not know that it was he standing there as Gloria or were they just playing dumb as well as he was playing Gloria? He wanted to see how far he had to go to ensure a chase.

He told Issa all of the rest of the conversation that he had with Thomas. And that he wanted to go back to the beach to see if they would follow them. They needed to get out of the house. Katherine and Jewel were also filled in on the details of Billy's plan, however, they were not told of the Shapur's plans for Billy. They were told of the implant and what they were going to do to test its strength. Katherine thought it risky, but after Billy explained that it would be just like him going anywhere, and that since it had been there all along, there would be nothing different, just that Alec was being lead somewhere. Katherine agreed, gave them some extra money to ensure some-what of a good time.

The next day they set out for Wakimlee Beach. They were excited to be out of the house and the neighborhood, since it had been two months since their last adventure.

Billy had come up with a plan to see how much time it took Alec to find him after he would loose the signal. He was going to dress as Gloria and drive Issa's grandmother's car to lure the signal. Then once out of town and on the road to the beach, Billy would set a dummy next to him that looked like him from a short distance. Once the Alec realized that the grandmother's car was where the signal was traced to they would leave the car with the dummy, and then travel on to Wakimlee. The figured it would give them a little more time alone and hopefully Thomas would find out where the bug was so they could lose them for good.

They set out with Issa following a mile or so behind. After an hour on the road, a car came up on Billy rather swiftly and then passed him, he had just put up the dummy. Further up the road Billy saw the car pulled over. A short while later it happened again but when he passed the car the driver was out of the car and very intently looked at the dummy as he passed. Billy saw through the rearview mirror the man scratch his head and look at his cell phone again, he also saw Issa's car in coming up the road. He thought that it was time to ditch his car.

Issa looked at the man as she passed him. He was looking at what appeared to be a cell phone and the man did not even look up to see Issa's car pass. As she crested the knoll she saw Billy's car starting to turn onto a dirt road, she followed. Billy saw her follow then sped up and pulled off the road and got out of the car.

"Well he is now contemplating what the hell is going on with his tracking devcice. I hope that he thinks that this dummy is me and then stays with this car. It just might work." Billy said while scratching his wig

"He was looking a cell phone or something as I passed him. I say we go back out to the main road and give it a shot. There should be a little town up ahead that we can leave the car. You go in and then go out the back somehow and sneak into my car. I will try to scope out the area so we can play with his tracking device. It should buy us some time." Issa was feeling sure of the plan.

They kissed and got back in their cars and Issa went out first and Billy followed far behind. Not long after Billy pulled out, Alec passed him going the other way. He quickly turned around and followed.

Issa came upon a small roadside shop and gas

station. There was a long straight part of the road coming into the area. Issa could see Billy behind her so she put on a left blinker and pulled around to an area in back of the shop. Billy did the same but parked under a large cottonwood tree that was beside the shop. Got out and walked like an old lady into the store. As he closed the door he peered over his shoulder to see Alec just parking across the street.

He took his time in the shop and then asked if there was a restroom. The clerk was an old man that seemed unhappy. He rolled his eyes and said; "It is for paying customers, but it is through the back."

Billy smiled and said; "When I am finished I will come out and buy that hat." Said with grumpy tone.

He went through the door and notice the back door that appeared to be unlocked and without an alarm. He went on to use the bathroom and afterwards just as he was about to go out the back he heard a man out front talking with an accent he knew all to well. He really wanted a good look at him, he could not help it. Billy walked up and slowly opened the door just enough to see, he had a clear shot at the goonies back, he could hear him talking.

"There was older lady come to store. Is she still hear?" he asked the clerk while looking around the store. He was taller than he looked as he passed him on the road. The clerk hesitated and shook his head. "What old woman?" he replied.

"I saw her come to store, I need talk to her. You are sure there was no lady?" He asked and pointed around the store.

Ah maybe, there is some gal in the back using the john but she don't look old. He responded.

At that point Billy had the thought that he should be a younger lady, but as he looked up from his thoughts, he saw the clerk walking towards the door he was peeping through. His only thought was to go back in the bathroom and shut the door.

As he closed the door he heard the clerk ask if any one was still in there. Billy did not answer him. The clerk asked again while he wiggled the door handle to the bathroom. Billy still did not want to answer. The clerk cursed and mumbled, 'Dummy locked the door and left, hope I can find that key.'

Billy heard him walk away and after he heard the front door of the store close he opened the door quietly and walked briskly to the back door of the store. He came out on the side that his car was on and could see the dummy. He thought that he should put the dummy down. He started to hesitate, then ran to the car. Stuffed the dummy down on the floor board, closed the door gently and ran around the back of the store to see Issa just across the lot. By that time his wig almost fell off which reminded him that he was suppose to still be an old woman. After all of that he realized he forgot.

He came to the car somewhat together and got in and then got down on the floor. She leaned to start the car just as their pursuer came around the end of the store looked at her car briefly and then crossed the street. She waited, started her car too but was unsure of which direction to take.

"Billy, do you think we should drive right past him or away from him?" she was looking around to decide.

"Can we circle around the area. It looked like their homes on both sides of the street, go around the block a few times, real slow. See what that does." He winked with his answer.

"All right old lady, we'll see." She snickered back and pulled onto the street then right onto another street.

The houses were laid out in a big square and after two times around in a twenty minute period, their man started to drive towards Walkimlee. Billy said to just stay were they were and to keep circling like they were. About ten minutes later as they rounded a corner they saw the tail end of his car going the opposite direction so Billy instructed Issa to go on and head to Wakimlee and once they got there, hopefully Thomas would know where the bug was and end this pursuit once and for all.

They pulled into the town of Walkimlee and went to

the same hotel as before. They even got the same room and after a little honeymoon reminiscence, they decided to go for a walk. Billy dressed as Gloria but just put his hair around his face with some big glasses. As they walked out the front door, Billy saw Alec's car across the street from them, however, it was empty. Billy decided to walk by the car and try looking inside of it, for any kind of locating device. Just as he walked up to the car, a man came out from the shop it was parked in front of and pulled out some keys. Billy thought that this was the man, so he and Issa kept on walking. He did not want to stare at the man, but was compelled to. The man just smiled back as he passed, then proceeded to get in the car, but not start it. Billy's head was reeling with thoughts of what to do next. Issa sensed it and suggested they go on down to the pier, walk to the end and see if he followed. The pier was about a mile walk down the beach and that was what their plan in the first place.

They walked mostly in silence towards the pier, and as they got closer Billy mentioned children after his thoughts drifted to their activity back in the hotel room. Issa burst out laughing and commented on how Billy sometimes brought up the most off-the-wall things in the middle of chaos. He could tell that the reality of his life and all that they were trying to do to save it, was coming to the point of reckoning. He hoped she could keep it together. The little bit of scariness in her laugh just then, was his tell tale sign that she was trying and the thoughts of children did not even phase her. They got to the pier without another word. As they started down the pier, Issa placed her hand in his and held on rather firmly. Billy remembered the day that they walked down that same pier as newlyweds. He was about to cry for at that moment, he felt as helpless as ever. Not even twenty years old and about to try bringing down a world leader? He could not control himself any longer. Just as they passed the only other people on the pier he started to cry out loud.

"Oh honey......... what..... is it?" Issa grabbed him as he was just about to lose it.

"I.......just........Oh what isn't it? I don't know. Here I am, not even twenty and I have to face this." he paused.

"I am so unbelievably grateful that I have you. You are still here even though your life might be in danger and we know that mine is. Yet I don't know what to do next." he was speaking through a rough cry.

"I have this bug in me that has told someone else were I have been, even when I did not know where I was. The person I am made from needs enough of me so that I can't live any more. And to top it off, I almost feel like killing myself right in front of the guy, just for the pleasure of knowing for sure that he has no chance of getting me or a better life." He was yelling it to the ocean, as if no one else was there. He looked over at Issa and collapsed.

The two just sat there while Billy wound down. Issa stroked his hair and held his head in her arms. She was crying as well. She lifted her head and saw that the sun was setting to the west horizon and a beautiful full moon was rising up from the sea. That sight at that moment brought a small smile to her and she told Billy that everything was going to be alright. Billy sniffled and gave a little 'Yeah' and went back to embracing her. A few moments later Issa started humming the Bob Marley song 'Three Little Birds'. She kept singing the same verse: Every little thing is gonna be alright'.

"I am a strong .....man. I will ....deliver. I must deliver. You are ...... my greatest strength. And I am not going to die and I am going to show the world what this man is trying to do to lives he thinks he owns." He dried his face and turned to her, pulling her close.

"I love you Issa Ruoff. You will not be alone. I can't tell you in words what it means when you speak to me from your heart, because I know that this is where your words come from. As I .... feed off of your strength, your words, I become more ....confident, more assured, more everything as you spill out your feelings to me. I need to let out all that was pent up inside of me. I was not sure, but it did feel ......good in a way, and you just held me, bringing me through. I guess that I am or was so messed up, that I thought that you would be different or something,..... I'm just not sure of a lot of things at the moment." He was holding her head against his chest. She pulled back and just smiled as big and as happy as she could, and then she started to sing the Bob Marley tune again. He joined in and as they sang, three little birds skated along the water's surface. They laughed and kept on singing as they swayed slightly.

Issa and Billy talked about their future as they headed back to the hotel. They wanted to be positive and strong, as Billy put it. Issa wanted to go to some sort of specialty school to learn more about the earth and ecology. The few hours before were not forgotten, but merely put aside to enjoy the walk back. The memory was brought back when they walked in the door of the hotel and saw the message light on the phone blinking.

Billy just smiled at Issa and sang, 'This is my message to you ouu ouu' another line from their song of the night. He called the front desk and found that his mother had called and to call back immediately. That worried Billy instantly.

His mother picked up after six rings, by that time Billy was pacing the room with the phone. Issa just looked out the window trying not to show Billy the look on her face. Katherine was in the bathroom and did not hear the phone directly, as she answered the phone Billy sounded glad to hear her voice.

"What took you so long to answer, are you o.k.?" he asked very worried.

"I am fine, where have you two been? I have called twice. I just got off the phone with Thomas, and boy what am I to make of his message?" she sounded confused.

"Well we were down at the pier watching the sunset and well, I was just trying to sort things out in my head. So what did Thomas have to say?" he asked nonchalantly.

"Well I am not sure what it means, but I was to tell you that it is in between your big toe and your second toe. Now what in the hell are we talkin' about here William?" By the tone of her voice she was a little perturbed.

"Well it is kinda hard to say Ma, I .... am not sure how this is gonna sound." He was looking at Issa for some help.

"Since the beginning of all of this Billy till now, I think nothing will surprise me at this point, so just say it. I don't want to be left in the dark." She had the motherly tone now.

"Well was there anything else that Thomas said?" he said stalling.

"No, now damn it tell me or else I am....." she was cut off.

"O.K. O.K., are you sitting down because it hit me kinda hard, o.k.? Well, I guess before they gave me to the adoption agency or whatever, they.....umm.....ummm...bugged me." he stopped.

"They what!!" she exclaimed.

"They put a small bug in my body so they would know where I was at all times. .... Mom are ya still there?" he asked.

"Yes......I .... can believe it, but I don't want to. Now the real question is: Is it between your two toes?" she asked half heartedly.

"I guess so, but which one. Did Thomas say?" he suddenly realized.

"Oh yeah, he did say the left big toe, but what are you going to do now, remove it?" she wondered.

"Well yeah, I am going to. That would be my first move to freedom, eh Mom?" he sounded very assured.

"You've got a good point, but how? You're no surgeon. What are you going to do, hack it out and tear up you foot?" she now acted like it was no big deal.

"Not exactly Mother. I just found out where it is. And actually it is in a rather easy place to get out. It might be rather painful to walk afterwards, but it must be done." he exclaimed

"Oh Billy, so much makes more sense to me now. I just wish you would tell me these things when they come up instead of like this, over the phone. I feel the need to hold you and I can't help it." she was crying slightly.

"I am sorry again Mother, I am so unsure how to treat things. I was sure you would be opposed to my plan to see how strong this thing is and how well it works in a crowd." After he finished he wished that he had not said what he said.

"What do you mean by a crowd.' She paused, Surely you don't wish to get close to this madman?" she said sternly.

"Well, just dressed as Gloria. I really want to look into his eyes and see him. Now that I can get the bug out I can go and they won't even know that I am in the room. Ya see, now there is no need to test anything. I am surprised how fast Thomas got the location, he must have some important friends somewhere." he said joyfully.

"I think you're skating on thin ice, Buck -oh, but it is your 'game' as you say, so think it through and don't take any unnecessary risks. Do you understand me William?" She said this sternly.

"Believe me Mother I know they are all risks until this man is either dead or exposed. I have the best team to work with and we are going to win." he was smiling at Issa.

"Well, when are you coming home?" she asked.

"We have the room for another two days and then we hope to be debugged and on our way home, I will call you when we leave, I love you Mom and thanks for understanding." he said sincerely.

"I love you too, and I do understand. Keep up the teamwork and give Issa my love. Good bye." she said as she hung up the phone.

They decided to lay low as the next day passed.

Billy wanted to see the sunset and then go directly home. They finished packing and then drove through town looking for Alec on the way to the pier. When they got there the sun was getting close to the horizon. They had a little time so they walked slowly so they could enjoy the entire setting. They were about half way when they heard a car come quite quickly into the parking area of the pier. Billy said that it was not the car, they walked a few more steps, as a car door slammed, and Billy had the feeling that he new that car. He stopped walking, Issa looked to him and just the he heard a faint call, it was his mother's.

Katherine was almost running down the pier as they both turned. She was calling Billy's name in a loud but not shouting manner.

"Billy, Issa wait, Stop. " she was breathing heavy," I knew you would be here, I just called the hotel from my cell and they said you had just left. I thought you would come here and watch the sunset." She was trying to be calm.

"Mom what in the hell are you doing here? What is up? We were coming home tonight?" Billy asked this oblivious to her nervousness.

"I came, because uhh......," she was looking around, and trying not to cry.

"Mom, take a breath and then tell us what, I can tell that it is something serious. Did Thomas call?" He was holding her by the arm.

"Yesss......" she was starting to cry.

"And what did he say, ...come on Mom hold it together, breath. What did Thomas say?" He was trying to hold her steady.

"He said that they are com...." she was cut off by the sound off a car pulling into the parking area very fast.

They all looked and as the car stopped, four men, large men, got out of the car one looked like Alec, and started walking down the pier.

"They are here for you, I wanted to call but you weren't answering. I drove as fast,...." Billy stopped her.

"Why Mom? What did Thomas say. "The men had stopped at the end, one of them on a phone.

"He said that the Shapur was in Washington D.C. and that he had found a doctor, now all they needed was you." I wanted to find you before.......It was too late.....now it......" she was crying.

Billy was thinking fast. He knew that there was only one way off of the pier, and going through those men was not it. They must go to the end, jump off and hope that they would not be followed.

"Mom, Issa, start walking to the end acting like we don't

know what they are up to." he said in a whisper.

"What are you thinking Billy, are we just gonna wait at the end? Besides I did also call the police and tell them that I just got a death threat, man with a gun, and that I was at this pier. They said they were coming. she said crazily.

"Sort of .... We'll wait to see if they come or we'll have to jump, it is the only way. I am not just gonna walk into their hands. They could kill you two and drag me off before the cops come." he said as they walked.

"I love you Billy, I...... just wanted.... to .....see.... you." Katherine was still crying.

"I love you too Mom, and this is not the last time you are going to see me. The sun is nearly down and it will be too dark to see after we jump. The only danger is that the tide is coming in so we will have to stay clear of the pier poles after we jump. Mom you have to clear your mind, and be ready to jump. It is about twenty feet. I know you can do it, I know you can." Billy said as he looked over his shoulder, the men were walking toward them.

"I ...... will make ...it, I am with you and I feel ... better... how are you Issa?" she was trying to be motherly.

"I am fine, I will hold your hand .... Mom and we'll swim together, o.k.?" Issa said.

"Great!" she replied between breaths.

They were at the end and Billy said not to turn around, but he did. The men were about halfway to them. He told them to slip off their shoes and sit up on the rail. He would tell them when to jump. He would count seven and then they would jump, him following. Katherine noted that she thought it was higher than twenty feet. Billy said for her to imagine it was not. He was not sure of the height, but imagine it so. One of the men spoke.

"Are you William Ruoff?" one asked.

"Why, who are you?" he replied, rather scared.

"We are with the government and we wish to ask you some questions. Would you come with us please?" he said as they approached.

"You're not with our government are you?" He started counting in a low voice to Issa and Katherine.

"We are, who do you think we are with?" he answered.
"No one in our government has such shitty accents and
dark skin that's how I know, " he was up to five." So you
can tell your Leader!, that he can't have any part of me and
he is going to have to die just like the rest of us. As a matter
of fact, you're probably gonna die after he finds out you let
me slip right through your fingers, SEVEN!" and the girls
jumped.

Billy quickly stood on the rail and saw them running
towards him. He quickly flashed them his butt, and
jumped. As he descended, he saw Issa and his Mom hit the
water, holding hands. Issa yelped as she hit.

One of the four men yelled Noooo! very loudly, as they
ran to the railing. They definitely were surprised by his
actions. Two of them went to each side of the railing and
looked over. The sun had just gone down and because of
the cloud cover daylight was fading fast and the waves were
rolling in. They were yelling at each other for someone to
jump in.

Billy knew he had to draw their attention. He took off his
shirt and dove down in the water and towards the pier. He
let go of the shirt thinking that they would focus on it for a
while. He came up looked around. He swam closer to the
poles and watched as best he could for the waves rolling in.
He saw a splash near one of the poles where there was no
wave, and swam to it. He could still hear the men on the
pier arguing.

As he got closer to the splash he saw that it was Issa,
trying to get up the remains of an old ladder. Out of the
corner of his eye he saw a wave breaking towards him and
Issa, who was almost out of the water. He dove down and
towards the wave, to avoid being slammed. When he came
up he could not see Issa, but then he hear a 'Psssssst' from
above, he looked and saw an arm waving. He swam to the
ladder and began to climb up, before the next wave could
hit.

"Where is my Mom?" he whispered, with great fear in his
voice.

"We lost hands when we had to swim. I think she went to

the right, after we came up. There was not time to think, I just swam and the waves pulled me back to the pier, lucky I saw the old ladder, I thought I was a gonner. Then I saw you, I thought at first you were her......" she was stopped by the sight of someone jumping off the end of the pier. He said something, maybe a prayer, in his language as he was falling.

"Oh sh..., I did not think that one of those bastards would follow. I thought that they would just run down to the beach. We'll need to go up under further, this ladder must be for a roost under the walk." he was looking around as he spoke.

"There, towards the end is a platform, quick!" Issa whispered .

They moved along one set of cross braces to the middle then up and sat right under the walk. They heard the rest of the men above them, they were barely breathing. As they looked down in the water the light was changing so fast that with the waves getting bigger it was hard to see things in the water. One of the men yelled something in their language and Issa and Billy saw the splash of a swimmer going towards another splash, it was Katherine.

Once Katherine saw the man coming, she dove under the water, from that point under water, she lost her direction and swam toward the pier. When she came up she was close to a pole, the next wave hit her from behind and into the pole. Billy and Issa hear the low thud of something hitting a pole, then they heard a low moan.

Katherine was slightly conscious, but the barnacles on the pier had cut her hands and arms. The sting of the salt water was starting to burn, she moaned louder as she went under the water. She came up and trying to swim away, she swam right into the arms of her pursuer.

Upon realizing that he had caught a woman, and not the Billy, he immediately tried to drown her, she fought as best she could. As they struggled, the man was having trouble swimming with his pants and shoes on, but they both were coming back toward the pier at an alarming rate, Billy and Issa could only watch, for the rest of the men were just watching, Then the man yelled something up and the others quickly ran off.

As they heard their footsteps get farther away, Billy and Issa could hear police sirens off in the distant, they could only hope that they were coming to the pier. They then looked down and saw neither of the two below. Billy started to go back down the ladder to get closer to the water. He still saw nothing, as he quietly called his for Katherine.

Issa came from behind and yelled too, nothing. Being lower to the water he could see the lights from the police car coming from the parking lot of the pier. He told Issa to stay on the ladder, waited for break in the waves and jumped in. He swam between the poles looking for his mother, at each coming wave he dove into the water, but he too lost his way under water and came up next to a pole only to push off of it at the last second. Billy got out from under the pier on the other side. By now it was dark and from the silhouette of the police lights he could see just three men being questioned by men with police caps, he could only hope his mother had made it to the beech.

Billy swam all the way back around the pier to get Issa. The police lights were off, but they were still there. As Billy came up the ladder he was crying, he feared the worst. "I..... could not find.....her." he was breathing heavy" The cops are talking.... to those..... men I think that my...mother is .....gone.." he head lolled onto Issa's chest.

"No.... No.... she is hiding under the pier , I know it , she....she. she would not have looked for you. She saw the cops too and is waiting for them to leave, just like us, I know it." she was stroking his head.

"There were only three of them. The other is missing too, now do you think that he is still in the water? He could barely swim, he would be on the beach." He was speculating.

"We'll have to wait 'til they're gone, so no more bad thoughts about your mother, Got It?!" she was holding his chin and looking into his eyes.

They waited for what seemed like hours. Billy and Issa heard cars pull out and they waited for a break in the waves, then swam back into the water. They came ashore and Issa was exhausted, but Billy went running toward the underside of the pier, still looking for his mother.

When Issa joined him, she saw him weeping uncontrollably. She went to him and held him, she was crying too. They saw no signs of Katherine. Billy wanted to cry as loud as he could but refrained. They knew that they could not stay there and that the men were close and they must act fast. They walked to the parking lot and Billy saw his mother's car and started crying again. Issa looked into the car and saw that Katherine had left the keys in it, she was in such a hurry to save her son, Issa thought. She got in Katherine's car and started it. Billy looked at her morbidly, she then explained the urgency of this act.

"This car is faster and better than mine, we can't just leave it." She said. He got in and crawled into the back, still crying.

Through the tears Issa was not sure she was ready to deal with Katherine being gone. Although she thought she could handle the fear of being the wife of a wanted man, she did not think that Katherine would be the one they would lose. She thought of Jewel and how they all bonded and then the strength of Katherine throughout the past days and years. She looked over at Billy, who had just been staring out the window as she started driving out of Wakimlee. He looked over to her as she looked at him.

"I gotta get this bug out of me!! If I don't, they will know that I am going home. Pull over." he said sternly.

"What do you have in mind?" she replied.

"Well, with what mind I have left, I am going to take this damn thing out and leave it in the ocean, or something. We'll need some ice and a towel. There is a gas station, pull in there, please." his voice was breaking.

Issa pulled into the station, went in and got a cup of ice. When she came back, he had his left shoe off and was prodding with a knife between his big toe and second toe. Issa immediately got in and pulled the car around to the side of the station.

As soon as she shut off the car, she heard a deep inner

moan held in from Billy. He had sliced into his foot, between the two toes, rather deeply and blood was running on to the towel below it, he made the comment that he felt the bug. Issa swallowed loudly as she watched the knife being turned inside of his foot. The concentration on Billy's face turned to tears as he felt pain from both the knife and the loss of his mother. He said he could not believe that he was doing this. She replied the same.

He pulled out what appeared to be a large sized piece of rice that was silver and hard. Billy held it up to the light, squinting then just said, "That's it". As the blood was pouring into the towel, he grabbed the ice, wrapped it in a shirt and then asked Issa to turn back to Wakimlee so he could leave all of his past there. Just then he gave a large laugh as he saw a dog run near the car.

"What is so funny now ?" Issa asked.

"I want some chocolate, will you run in and buy me a Snickers Bar please?" he said with a smile.

"What the..... well alright, but I now know you are crazy." she laughed crazily back.

By the time Issa came back to the car with the candy bar, Billy was talking to the dog that was now by the car. Issa handed the bar to him and he ripped a piece off and stuffed the bug in the piece of chocolate, then gave it to the dog. Issa burst out laughing as Billy turned to her with a large smile. The dog was waiting for more, Billy was however bleeding badly. He smirked at her and asked her to quickly go back to Wakimlee St. Matthews Hospital.

"What are you going to say to the doctor? It looks like you just gouged yourself with a knife. I wish you had thought of that before you cut into yourself." she said concerned.

"Well I did and I'll just say that as I was body surfing a wave, I came into the shore and my foot dragged the bottom and snagged on something. When I came up I was bleeding and in a lot of pain..... How's that, not bad, huh?" he grinned.

"I guess that will work, ... It was definitely a good snag! "She laughed.

They pulled into the Emergency entrance and Billy

hobbled into the waiting area while Issa went to the counter. The shirt wrapped around his foot was dripping blood and when a nurse passing by saw it, she immediately took Billy into a triage room, properly cleaned the wound and lightly dressed it. The nurse quickly went to the nurses' station to tell them that he needed an i.v. drip for he had lost a lot of blood.

Billy thought of his mother while he was there and while talking to Issa she thought of his mother's insurance card that carried Billy and Jewel on it. She went back out to the car and found it in her purse. When she returned he could tell that she had been crying, her eyes were puffy and swollen. It also took a while for her to return.

They were able to use the card and about three hours and twelve stitches later, they were back in the car and on there way home. All Billy could think about was his mother. Then later, how he was going to tell Jewel. At one point during the discussion, Issa had to pull over because she could not see through her tears. Billy tried to drive a little, but the medication he had been given for pain was making him drowsy.

When she pulled into the driveway of his house, Billy was asleep and Jewel's car was not home. Issa was thankful that she was not there, for she would have had to tell Jewel.

She was just getting Billy to wake up, when he lifted his foot up and across the dashboard to keep it elevated. He could not feel his foot for all of the blood he'd lost.

"I can't walk, Issa , would you pull the car into the garage so this is not so difficult or obvious, in case someone is watching." He grunted this towards her.

"No problem. Jewel is not here, so hopefully we can get situated before she comes home." she said.

Issa helped him out of the car, as his foot would not bear any pressure, and the drugs were wearing off. Billy moaned rather loudly as he hopped into the house and saw a picture of his mother on the wall. It was of her and Jewel at the beach, the same one they just left. As he collapsed on the couch, his eyes started to fill with tears. The room was mostly dark, for the shades had been drawn, but the garage light was shining on the picture.

As Issa came in and saw him, she closed the door, blocking the light on the picture. Billy asked if she would leave the light off and just come and sit beside him. They sat there in silence until they heard a car pull into the driveway. Thinking it was Jewel they just sat there waiting.

There was a knock on the door and unexpectedly it was a police officer, Issa answered the door.

"Is there a Ms. Ruoff at this residence?" he asked.

"Yes she does live here but, ..." she pulled her hand to her face.

"Well I am afraid I have some bad news, are you her daughter?" he asked again.

"No I am not, ...I am her daughter-in-law what is .....it." she said.

"Have you seen Ms. Ruoff today or yesterday?" he asked.

"No I have not, what is it wrong, officer?" she asked.

"Is seems that Ms. Ruoff had an unfortunate accident at Wakimlee Beech pier last night or early this morning. We found her body on the beach this morning and as far as we can tell she drowned. There were no signs of foul play indicating anything else. Is her son at home?" he asked.

"Uh.... no, he is not here at the moment, he.... is.... at work, he should be here later, ... I just ..... don't know how I will tell him. This is too much." she was starting to cry.

"I am sorry to bring you this news, we are relatively sure that it is her, although her car could not be found at the scene, that is why we are here to see if she was here or her car, ..." he paused.

"Uh ,....... well her car is not here. Are you sure it was her?" she said.

"She had on an I.D. badge from her work. I am truly sorry. Here is my card with a number, would you please call if you have any further information, and have her son call me as soon as he comes home, he or her daughter will have to come down to identify the body. Again, I am very sorry." he concluded.

"Could I...... could I come down and identify the body, for I feel that they will be unable to deal with the task, I will come down later if that is possible." she asked

"I would need one of them to call me and say that you were coming down to identify. I am sure that it would be fine, you just call when you can. But please, let it be no later than day after tomorrow. Thank you, and good day. "he tipped his hat and walked off.

Issa closed the door and started to cry. She sat down on the steps and heard Billy crying in the other room. She ran into the room and lay next to him.

XII

A few hours later, they were awoken by the sound of a car pulling into the driveway. Billy pulled his foot onto the coffee table and tried to awaken. He was not sure how he felt, losing his mother was and seeing her in the water was the only thing he could think of a the moment, just then the front door opened abruptly.

"That no good son-of-a-bitch, I can't believe that he could do this to me after all this time." Jewel was mostly talking to herself as she walked upstairs to her room.

Since the lights were off, she did not notice that there was anyone home. She yelled for Katherine. After receiving no answer, she came downstairs and asked who was there.

"Just us, uh.... what is up with you?" Billy asked with a broken voice.

"It's just that Derek happened to tell me that he had found someone new in his life and was basically ending our relationship after four months. Can you believe the nerve of that guy? I almost asked him if some stranger had approached him and told him to lay off of the Ruoff girl or something like that, I mean this just infuriates me. Why were you guys in the dark when I came home?" she asked as she finished.

"Well...... we were asleep, are you...uh o.k.? Maybe you should sit down for a moment. "Billy was easing up from his position.

"What happened to your foot? It is all bandaged up, and you look like you have been crying, ... Where is your car Issa?" Jewel was still feeling unsettled by her break up.

"Oh ...... It is .....a ...long story..... I think.... that you....should sit......down. "his voice was breaking and he was starting to tear up.

"What the hell is going on here? I mean where is Mom, she should be home by now? Did something happen at Wakimlee? Is that why your foot is bandaged up? Tell me now Buck-oh, before I..... " everything was becoming too much for her. Billy cut her off.

"Sit down. This is serious, I ...... am...trying to tell you, Issa will you come in here, please? "Billy was shaking and had a mean tone.

"What ... What.... What is so damn serious, Bill?" she was staring to get up. Billy grabbed her and pulled her to his side. He started to cry very hard, when Issa entered the room crying slightly.

"What is it with you two It's as if someone died, or something...." Jewel was looking at Issa when she said that. Issa slightly shook her head.

"Where is Mom! Damn It ! If she..... is ..... Oh NOOOO!!!!" As she said the words the grip on her arms from Billy became tighter and he pulled her to himself. She let out a quiet but convulsing cry. Issa came over and sat next to her and turned off the light reflecting off the picture of Katherine. They all sat in the dark and wept for her.

With the release of all of the emotions, Billy's foot began to pound with great pain. As he tried to pull away from Jewel for some relief, she would not let go of her brother. He just stroked her hair and dealt with the pain that he was feeling through his body and soul. He asked Issa to go and get the medicine for his foot. Just then Jewel pulled away and wiped her tears. Still sobbing she tried to ask what happened to his foot, for she did not yet want to hear what had happened to her mother.

He decided to talk about how Thomas found out that he was bugged and where it was. Jewel just nodded agreement and did not question the reasoning, for she was in a dreamlike state, and nothing at the moment was going to bring her back. Billy was starting to drift off also for the pain killers were taking affect and Issa was also drifting off from exhaustion. Jewel however, just stared at the shadow of her mother's picture in front of her. She didn't move until almost daylight. The three of them became part of the couch as their feelings, and the lack of, overcame their urge to move.

The sunlight was just coming into the room as the pain was coming back to Billy's foot. He awoke to see Jewel and Issa asleep. He reached over them, grabbed the bottle of pills and took two more. He washed them down and closed his eyes. A little while later it was Jewel who woke up and actually gave out a small laugh as she found herself on the couch, thinking that she had just fell asleep on it and not the real reason why. As she looked around the room, she noticed the picture of her mother and out of the corner of her eye she saw Billy's foot and it came back to her rather quickly why she was on the couch.

The morning was very cloudy and gray, somewhat unusual. It set a fitting mood over the room. A low cry awoke Issa next and she rubbed Jewel's back as Jewel slumped into her lap and cried. Issa just stared at the window and wondered how such a morning could occur at this time. She felt the need to get up and let Jewel lay there. She said that she would be right back. She did, however, slip up to Billy's room and call Thomas. After many rings, he picked up.

"Hello?" a voice said, somewhat groggy.

"Thomas? Is it you?" she asked.

"Yess,..... umm Yes, who pray tell is this?" he snapped, rather rudely.

"Well It's me Issa, Thomas, as in Billy Ruoff and Issa. Um, did I wake you?" she said shyly.

"Yes you did my dear, I was taking a noon nap you see,

nothing to worry about. Is everything alright there my dear?" he asked.

"No not at all, I .... don't know where to start, It all.... happened so fast, I ....just don't," she was sobbing.

"Now there there my dear. I take it you are relatively fine. Is Billy alright?" he said.

"Yes, well .... he is but he tore that bug out of his foot yesterday, but that is not the big thing, it's just that......that..." she paused.

"Just slow down and breathe my dear. Relax, and then you can tell me." he reassured her.

"Katherine is dead!" she said rather fast and then let out a cry.

"Good heavens! My dear, are you sure?" he pondered.

"Yes she is, we heard her hit the .... pier..... pole. And the .....police... came last night.....I am sure Thomas." she could hardly talk.

"Oh dear, oh my, Is Jewel..." he stopped.

"She was not there, she.... is fine." she said.

"I take it this happened last night, or yesterday, right?" he asked.

"Yes, we just told Jewel last night and they are downstairs sleeping. I just needed to talk to someone, someone who would understand. I just don't know what to do Thomas. They are not going to be coherent enough to think and I know that we are going to have to do something fast. In hours those goonies are going to figure out that the bug is no longer on Billy and the first place they are going to is here. We do not need to be here, I just don't know what to do, please help us, please." Her voice was whining and rising to a cry as she finished.

"Now of course my dear Issa, I will do all I can from here and you do need get them going. Somewhere, anywhere, but you must be as calm as you can. I must tell you that I am glad you are there. They are blinded by sorrow, and you had the notion to call me. They will come there first as soon as they find out. Now you must find another car to use, for they know of all the ones in your family. You need to go somewhere where they already know you are not. Now I know that this misfortune must have happened at Wakimlee and I am just suggesting that you go back that way or at least in that direction. They are not smart enough to go back there, especially if it was where Katherine died. I know that will be very difficult for them, and you. At least being there will give you more time to gather your thoughts on the next move. By the way, how did Billy remove the bug?" he asked.

Issa was crying, " He.... He.... just told me to pull over and while I was in a gas station he got out a knife and he cut up some strips of cloth and then just cut into the top of his foot where you said it was, until he found it. Then we went to a hospital and he acted like he cut himself while swimming in the ocean and they sowed him up, no questions asked. Then we came home. "She stopped crying and was sitting there wide eyed while talking.

"My,. .... It sounds rather desperate to inflict that upon himself like that. Is he alright now?" said Thomas.

"Yes, they gave him some drugs to relieve the pain. The doctor was rather worried about the deepness of the cut, so he prescribed some pain medicine. He and Jewel are downstairs asleep on the couch; I was awake and knew that something must be done immediately so that is why I called. You don't know how glad I am that you are home. I just needed to talk to someone about this whole ordeal." she stopped.

"I would say so my dear, it would be hard for anyone. I am rather exhausted just from listening. Now I want you to gather up some of Billy's clothes and definitely the Gloria outfit, for he must go into public wearing only that. You don't know who is who and especially after they find out that he is no longer bugged. By the way, what did you do with the bug after he pulled it out?" he asked.

"Well that is one of the lighter sides of this. After Billy pulled it out and looked at it, a dog ran by the car and around the gas station we were at. So being the joker that he is, he asked me to go and get a candy bar and then he put that bug into a piece of it and then fed it to the dog. He knew that they would eventually find the dog or the pile of dog poop that the bug was in. Billy knew that it would give us some time, quite funny, huh Thomas?" she was smiling while reliving that moment.

"What a piece of work your William is, I must say that he is quite his own person, regardless of his maker. If you remember to tell him I said so, it will give him some confidence to make it through the following days. So you have a little work to do and call me later. You should not stay there another night, at least stay at a hotel and get out of the area as soon as possible, Godspeed my child and keep your head up. I will talk with you soon, now run along and do what I said, o.k.?" he talked rather fatherly.

"Yes...yes.. Thomas, thank God for you and bless you for being there. Billy would be dead by now if it weren't for you, I'll do as you say and call you as soon as possible. Thank you, bye-bye." She hung up the phone and her lip started to quiver. As she looked up, she caught her reflection in the mirror, straightened up and went over to Billy's dresser and started getting their clothes together.

About and hour later, she heard movement downstairs. She was just finished packing and went on down. Jewel was coming out of the bathroom when they met.

"Are you doing o.k. sis?" Issa asked.

"Yeah... somewhat." Jewel said, wiping her face.

"I know that we need rest, but we also need to leave this house soon. The goonies are going to find out that Billy is no longer bugged and this will be the first place they come to look for him. From the way they acted at Wakimlee, they won't be in any mood to talk. I have just gathered up some of Billy's clothes, so we can leave as soon as he is awake. Can you go and get some of your things or would you like me to? I would be glad to do it for you." she was holding her hand.

"Well,..... I think I can, but would you help me? I just don't want to be alone right now." she was squeezing her hand.

"Of course, lets go to your room." Issa smiled back.

They got some of Jewel's clothes and through some tears and hugs, they got a small suitcase together and brought it down by the door. They heard Billy moaning and moving

around. Jewel went back upstairs to get Billy's suitcase
from his room   .

XIII

The next fifteen minutes seemed to take forever for Billy
and Jewel. They had to get as much stuff as they could,
that would sum up their existence and experience at their
house. Jewel found a stash of money in her mother's room
as she looked for things to remember her by. Issa kept
suggesting that there was no more room. After gathering all
they wanted, they had to go back through that pile to really
take all they could. Issa was loading the last of it, when she
saw the two of them go back into the house for the last
time. She just waited in the car and watched for anyone
coming.
    The two of them were unconsciously holding hands as
they stood at the threshold of the living room.
Jewel's lip was quivering and Billy tightened his hold on
her hand.
    "I am sorry to be putt-...." Jewel cut him off with a hug.
"This is not your fault, it is either this or I have no more
brother. Do you understand? I love you..... now let's go."
she pulled away.
    Billy looked at her in a very different way. He looked at
her with pure admiration and respect. Issa then called from
the garage that they should be going. The two of them
whispered that they loved this house, smiled and walked
out together. Issa started the car and pulled out of the
driveway.
    Five minutes after that, two large black cars ascended
on their house and its occupants proceeded to break in and
search the house. After a quick sweep, the six men got into
their cars and left, knowing that they had lost the Shapur's
clone.

    Billy's head hit the car door armrest and he woke. They
had been driving for seven hours and Issa had to pull over.
They were almost in Tennessee. They thought that they
should head to Washington D.C. and that some of Thomas'

connections could find a way to prove that Billy was a clone of the Shapur.

While driving, the endless quietness was getting to Issa, so she decided to sing. She started singing 'Three little birds' as Billy and Jewel realized what she was singing, they were all singing along and trying to figure out the lyrics to keep it going.

Billy's pain was fading and decided he could drive. Soon after they changed places, he noticed a car behind them. He had noticed that it had also stopped at the last rest stop they had and was traveling at approximately the same speed. Of course, his paranoia was high and he was frightened for all, so he opted not to say anything yet. He decided he'd just wait until the next exit which offered some kind of food, so he could get off the highway and see if the same car followed.

He kept a watch as the girls talked a little bit about the fact that neither one had been to Washington and all of the things there to see, but the air was mostly silent.

Billy was humming his own tune in the back. 'Three miles high, and I don't give a.....' He was saying. Apparently a few gas stops back, Jewel bought Billy a 40 oz beer, since the pain pills were gone, and was just finishing it. Jewel was snickering when she heard her brother wailing to himself in the back. The look of a comforting smile came across Jewel's face. As Issa said good morning, Jewel said "Yes it is."

"Billy, "Jewel yelled from the front.

"Get up front and tell me where I'm going!!!?

"O.K. I am. Now is it just me or is that a helicopter keeping up with us,. perfectly?" Billy was peering out the window and he could see the pilot's silhouette outlined with the black helicopter. Then he grabbed the map.

"Jesus, I didn't even notice that son-of-a.... I need to become more aware of my surroundings. This has got to stop." Jewel was ranting.

"Enough. Has anyone seen this road..uh, NC 1282?" Billy asked.

"Well here comes NC 1200. So I guess we are not there

yet .." Issa said.

"Take it. It will lead us to a fairly populated area. We need to find some cover." Billy said.

XIV

The road lead them into a small town with a few old and new buildings and in the middle of them was a three story parking garage, Issa noticed as they were driving into town. So they went there for cover. Seeing how small the town was, Billy figured that it would unfortunately be the place they would have to commit their first crime; stealing a car.

Billy instructed the girls to grab what they needed. As he was talking, he was getting into his Gloria disguise. He figured that he could scope out a potential car inside the parking garage, as Gloria. He asked Jewel to park on the second level and after parking, for the both of them to walk away from the car with their stuff and wait for him. Billy was almost ready, as Jewel pulled into the parking garage. He seemed to have sobered up since he saw the helicopter.

Billy got out just before the car ascended the ramp and walked, looking around for police or anyone rapidly coming his way. His ability to assess his surroundings had been immensely improving. Billy knew he had to act fast. He walked out and around the garage and saw no one coming. He took the elevator to the third level and started to evaluate the types of cars on that level. He found one that could possibly work, so he walked over to the edge and watched the entrance for a minute and then walked back to the possible car.

It was an old car that might not have an alarm, so Billy thought that it was their best bet. As he walked up to the car and went to touch the handle, he lost his step, a combination of the alcohol and not walking in heels for some time. This caused him to stumble to the ground, only to see a set keys behind the front wheel. Billy could not believe his eyes. He grabbed them, found the right key, got in the car and started it.

He shut it off and then gave a loud 'Hootie Hoo' twice out the window. He saw their car pull up onto the level. He waved his arm out the window and they pulled up next to him, unloaded their car into the new one. The girls got in with mouths open, but not talking. Billy whispered "Be cool", as a group of people walked by and as they got out on the road, Jewel was lighting up a cig and speaking through the smoke.

"How in the hell did you do this one William? I mean Gloria?" She said as she exhaled.

He proceeded to tell and as he was driving he saw a black car coming at them and he told one of them to get down. As it passed, he could tell it was a goonie and that he was clueless. They were safe again, for the time being.

XV

They pulled out with no commotion and back on to the highway. Jewel and Issa laid low for the next half hour until they were way away from the scene of the crime. Not much was said until Jewel broke the silence again about how cool the car was.

"This car is older than I am.. it makes me feel old." she said sighing.

" Well you're not that old and if it makes you feel any better, the car is a good one, even in its 'old' age." Billy returned.

They kept on going north and decided to drive until dark and get a motel along the way. Their next move would be dictated by what Thomas had to tell them upon their next talk with him. Billy was left thinking of possibilities, while the girls started to talk about girl's stuff.

It did not seem long until it was dark and everyone was very tired. Issa went into a roadside motel to get a room and Billy hid in the back, so to the desk clerk, it looked like just two women checking in. Once they parked the car in the back of the lot, they hustled into the room. They ordered some room service and Billy immediately took off the Gloria outfit. He was almost naked when Jewel demanded that he put something on. Jewel was switching the channels after her shower, watching the news when a story on the visiting Shapur was shown. It immediately caught everyone's attention.

It seemed as the Shapur came to the United States the rumor got out that he was here for an operation. What sort of operation was unknown, but he was not talking to the public when asked about his situation. The segment went on to say that he was staying indefinitely at a clinic in southern West Virginia, known for transplant surgery. Afterward Billy use Jewel's cell phone and called Thomas. "Is that you old boy?" Thomas asked.

"Yours truly." Billy claimed. "Thomas we are just about three hours out of Washington D.C. and we don't know what to do next and we are almost out of money. What do you suggest?" Billy concluded.

"Well the Shapur has just entered the country, but his health is slowly deteriorating and he is in dire need of a pancreas. My colleagues are not sure of his next move, but we know he has a doctor in Baltimore that he has used in the past. We believe that he is going to him next. As for you, find a place to receive a money order and get that information back to me, I will send you two hundred of your American dollars in order for all of you to get to Baltimore. In the mean time I will see if there is some way to retrieve some substantial information that will prove you are indeed the clone of this man. This doctor will have blood samples of the Shapur and with that compared to yours will be the proof that will foil this man's madness and rid you of this constant chase. You are going to have to sell something in order to get to Baltimore. I will be in a safe house and can help you more from there, but I can not help you right now. I want no trace to you until it is over. Now remember William that you must stay in the Gloria outfit at all times. It is the only thing that will hide you at this time. Stay on your toe's young William you all are going into a lions den. Thomas said sternly.

"Wow that is what I envisioned. I knew we were going to have to have some proof before we blew the whistle, but I never knew how. It sounds like we will have to get into these doctors quarters and find some hard evidence. I'll have to use the girls to do something. We'll put our heads together and think of something. The road has a tendency to promote a lot of thinking. We'll probably sell the car for we have no other valuables, but as far as seeing the doctor, that might be a little tricky." Billy concluded.

"Do the best you can William and call me. I must be going. Best of luck ol' chap." Thomas added.

"I will, we will. Thanks." Billy said and hung up.

He was as quite as he could be and slid into bed and after an hour of lying wide awake he decided to go outside and stare at the sky for answers to questions he did not even know. The sky did respond with a falling star which in Billy's mind was a signal to go back to bed and wait for the morning. He at least knew that it would be new and to take them one at a time.

Jewel awoke first and went out to find some coffee and breakfast material for all of them. When she came back it seemed that her timing was perfect, for the two were breathing heavy with smiles on their faces. After everyone ate, they showered and hit the road. Issa was driving and Jewel was navigating.

"Up here a ways you'll be getting on 81 north, then to 66 East on into D.C. I think that we are farther than 3 hours away, it seems more like 5." Jewel said.

"Well, whatever it is, it gives us more time to think of how to sell this car, get into the doctors office and get…" Billy was cut off by Jewel.

"What are you talking about? Sell what and go where?" Jewel asked.

"Oops I forgot that I had not talked to you all about the conversation with Thomas." Billy said with a smirk.

He went on to tell them what Thomas said and the next things that needed to happen. The girls agreed that the car had to go, but as far as the doctors office they both agreed that it was not going to be easy and that a good plan would have to be made as well as a back up plan. They were all learning that this 'game' they were in was very unpredictable and they needed to constantly cover their backs.

XVI

They were about two hours out of D. C. when the silence broke. They all were deep in thought when Issa finally spoke.   "I think I have and idea for both of our problems" Issa said with a smile.

Issa's plan was first for her and Jewel to dye their hair and change their looks. Which of course got Jewel excited, Billy was unaffected. Then they were to find a motel near the doctor. The next thing was to find a sleazy car lot that would buy the car without a title. They new or hoped that in that part of the country the likelihood of finding a sleazy car lot would be high. Then Issa said that here was where the plan got very dangerous. Before they sold the car they would be caught up in an accident with the doctor. One of them, while in the car with the doctor exchanging numbers and addresses, would pull a gun and force the doctor to drive to the motel where Billy was and tell him their story. Upon all of this happening the doctor would hopefully be on their side, however, since no one was to be trusted, Issa had not figured out what to do next. Especially if the doctor decided to double cross them and be on the Shapurs' side.

To all of them the plan sounded good but Jewel said it needed all of their input. From what Thomas had told them, they needed proof of Billy's cloned life by a blood sample. This would be a direct genetic proof from the Shapur. "Without that Billy's story would just make a good book." Jewel commented.

Jewel thought to get the map and direct them through the heart of the capital, for none of them had been there before. After seeing the Jefferson and Washington memorials and driving by the White House and Capital building, Billy felt good about what was going to happen in the upcoming days. He saw all of the places he had only read about in books and on television. It was more exciting than he expected. It felt right to him that this was the place where he was going to bring down the Shapur.

Not knowing where to start, they knew it would be best to go to a small suburb of the area and look for a cheap hotel.

After getting out of the city and what ended up being three hours the best they could find was a hotel that had weekly rates of $250 for five days. They hoped by then, they would have more money and a good start on their plan. On the way there Jewel spotted a used car lot with a marquee reading "No Hassle Trades". It was not far from the hotel they saw so Jewel went to the hotel and got the room for one night so she and Issa could change their looks. Soon after, they went to the car lot and started strutting around then out came a seedy salesman and then Issa started to work her charm.

They had defiantly found the right place, however they were only going to get $700 for the car. They asked if there were any cars that they could trade and get some cash for. After waiting for about an hour, the salesman came back with a very ugly car that barely ran. They took it and $250 cash and made their way back to the hotel. Billy was quite nervous upon their return, for to him it seemed that they had been gone a long time considering they had not been separated since leaving home. Billy was happy with the deal they got. The car only had to last them the week that they were in the hotel anyway. Jewel and Issa were also happy they got what they did and reenacted the scene with the salesman for Billy's enjoyment. Issa could tell that Billy was getting tense as the whole situation that was coming to fruition.

While the girls were gone, Billy called Thomas and informed him of their plan and asked how to proceed further. Thomas noted their plan was good but their b-plan quite thin. Thomas suggested that the use of a gun was persuasive but left them in trouble if the doctor called the law. After throwing ideas back and forth, he and Billy thought it was the only way, unless the doctor was sleazy enough for the girls to persuade back to the hotel for a more private way of dealing with the situation. At which point, they could use that as leverage in their favor against the doctor. Thomas then gave Billy the doctor's name and location. He was a resident of the St. Andrews Hospital in Springfield, Va., just north of the D.C. triangle. He was married and a prime candidate for the Shapur's 'private' dealings, for the doctor was said to have had many affairs and not high on ethics. Thomas told Billy to go over the plan and every detail as many times as possible with the girls, for this was a very intricate and bold plan. They had to make it look real and if not planned correctly, the doctor might see through their scheme and all would be lost. The ability for them to prove Billy's identity weighed on this meeting with the doctor. His name is Vincent Montgomery. Thomas wished them luck and also told Billy that if all went as planned, the next part of unveiling the Shapur was going to be grand. Thomas was working on a way for Billy, disguised as Gloria, to get into a dinner at the Kennedy Center that the Shapur will be attending. There, Billy would expose the Shapur in front of all the world's representatives and media. This was only ten days away and they had to move quickly with the doctor. Thomas left Billy with that and finished with "good luck ole boy". Just then the girls came back with the new car and their story. Billy was doing all he could to handle this enormous task. Then he spotted a gray hair on his chin, he really had no idea why he had a gray hair, but his gut was telling him that it was because he is a clone.

XVII

Billy brushed away thoughts of gray hair and after Jewel and Issa told their tale, he told them everything that he and Thomas talked about. The girls were excited and nervous about the new way of luring Dr. Montgomery back to the hotel, but Issa thought they should get a fake gun for backup. Billy told the girls to start working out the details while he took a much needed shower. When Billy came out a half-hour later, Issa asked if he was alright. Billy never took that long in the bathroom. He said it just felt good to stand under the hot water and then his mind drifted back the pier. He said it gave him some needed strength to endure what was about to happen. The girls sighed and stared off in different directions, pausing with their own thoughts. Billy broke the silence with the question, "Well, what have you come up with?"

They started to make a plan. Jewel was going to be the one doing most of the acting. She said she wanted to, for the loss of their mother compelled her to make sure this happened, for Billy and her mom. The big sister taking care of little brother thing, as she put it. Issa smiled at the words Jewel spoke and looking at Billy with a slight mist in her eyes. Billy decided to get ready for bed and while he did, the girls began making up a few scenarios and then also got ready for bed. It was 3:30 a.m. and tomorrow they would go and check out the scene at the hospital.

Billy awoke first and looked at his Gloria outfit. He thought that this could work. For some reason he did not go out as Gloria and went out to find some take-out breakfast. His mind started to wander as he strolled through these streets as a stranger. He was trying to feel as normal as the people around him and could not. Luckily he looked up and saw a coffee shop that looked like it could also serve breakfast. His mind came back to reality and he went in. When he came out, he felt uneasy again. The whole world was looking for him, a clone. Washington is a large city and the views that he could see, just from the street he was on, made him wonder about all the world's great moments, a lot occurring in this city. He thought that within a few days he hoped to be at the heart of another one. No one looked at him as he returned. He felt nothing coming at him. He made a note to self: this feels good.

Jewel and Issa were up when he returned. They were styling their new hair and trying to find a 'cool outfit', as Jewel put it.

Before Billy got dressed as Gloria, the girls had bought a new outfit and wig for Gloria and decided to make her a sexy younger Gloria. Billy said he had the same idea for Gloria and was amazed as how good he looked and more excited when he saw the shoes that they found to go with the outfit, they were flats. After practicing in the mirrors and walking he went out to check the car. He thought he better get used to being a woman in public again, since he was going to be one for the next week or so. Being a full-time woman might take some more practice. Looking at the car as a woman would do for starters. It was his first look at the car. The car appeared to be a late 1997 Japanese import with a lot of miles but it actually sounded good considering. The thirty day tag was only good for thirteen more days. Billy smiled, as he considered thirteen to be a good number. After acting as a woman in plane view, knowing this was to be his role. He assessed his performance only to have Issa come out and lay a big kiss on him, 'that is definitely encouraging', he thought. Jewel climbed into the back seat as Issa took the front. Billy, now as Gloria, pulled out with Issa navigating their way up to Springfield.

They drove around the hospital and found the staff parking lot lay out was very good, one way around. They were unable to enter with the car so Jewel walked in to see if he had his own parking place. Billy and Issa pulled into an adjoining parking lot. Billy put the car in park and looked at Issa and through uncontrollable nervousness he leaned over and kissed her passionately. He got out of the car and walked toward the place where Jewel got out. She had found no special parking place for Dr. Montgomery. Billy decided that he should at least go in and see if he could locate his office and maybe even see him. Thomas had emphasized the doctor's specialty in transplants so Billy knew he could just walk in and at least find the doctor's area. He adjusted his breasts and asked the girls to take the car to the other side of the hospital and wait for him there. Billy tried his best at swinging his butt, and he heard over his shoulder, "don't try swinging it so hard Gloria" he smiled and opened the door to the hospital.

XVIII

Billy did not know where to start. Since he was now a blonde, he figured he could look lost for a minute while gathering his thoughts. As he looked around he noticed the doctor's picture holding an honor of some sort. He read the list of names in order to find which one was he. At that time a lady from the front desk asked if she needed any help. Billy was startled and almost answered in his normal voice, when he saw his reflection in the picture he was looking at.

"Why yes he said" with a slight southern draw. "I was looking for Dr. Vincent, Vincent Montgomery. Is he here today?" he asked with a big smile.

"Well I am not sure. And you are?" the receptionist said with a smirk.

"I'm sorry I am Gloria... uh Benson." He fumbled. "And I was looking for him for my son is in need of a transplant. I don't wish to get into details, but I was hoping to meet him. I have already talked to him on the phone and he suggested I stop by so we could go over some things." He concluded, and was quite proud of his story

"Well it looks as if he will be back around 2:00 shall I make an appointment for you?" she asked.

"No, I have something scheduled at that time, I will call back and schedule an appointment later. Thank you and have a good day." He smiled and walked out trying not to shake his behind too much.

As he walked toward the girls he was grabbing himself and rubbing his breast, causing them to laugh. He was proud of his success in the hospital, but he knew that he had some homework to do, to not draw any suspicious attention to the whole plan. Somehow he needed to talk to the doctor before he got in the hospital and talked with the receptionist. He told the girls all that happened. Jewel thought that he had over acted and put them in an awkward position. Billy agreed. Issa said they would have to wait until the doctor came to the parking lot and for Billy to go and talk with him about Gloria's so called son, who needed a transplant. They all knew that their plan was getting too hopeful. However, they had to keep going in order to get the doctor in the right place and lure him back to the hotel. Jewel then thought of trying the cell phone directory. Dr. Montgomery might not have his number listed, but it was at least worth a try.

Jewel saw a coffee shop down the street and motioned them to go there and try the directory. The only listing in the area was for a Cecilia Montgomery. Jewel got the number anyway. She hoped that it might be his wife and that could go somewhere. She dialed the number and when the woman answered, she asked for Dr. Montgomery.

"Who is this?" she replied in a distressing way.

"This is Gloria...." She looked to Billy,

"Benson" Billy mouthed to Jewel.

"Benson, Mrs. Montgomery, I presume." Jewel said anxiously.

"Well this is Dr. Montgomery's wife...and he is not here. Why are you calling Ms. Benson?" she asked.

"It is for my son, he is in need of a transplant and I, out of desperation, got your number off of the directory and therefore called to see if he was available." Jewel said with nervousness.

"Why not call the hospital Ms. Benson, for he is always there. Or at least he says he is." She said with an uncertain tone.

"I did and they said he was not there so I decided to try this number. Do you know how to get in touch with him?" she was trying to sound more desperate.

"You sound desperate Ms. Benson. I normally would not do this, but I'll give you his cell number. You can tell him I gave it to you so he does not think otherwise. I wish you and your son the best of luck Ms. Benson." she gave her the number and ended with a "Good day" cheerfully.

"My son and I thank you dearly. Time is running out on us, the sooner the better. Thank you again, and good day to you too." Jewel was acting tearful.

"Gee Jewel you really laid it on thick. She must be a nice lady to give you the number, being a stranger and all." Issa commended.

"Yeah well it got us what we needed. Now Billy put on your best Gloria voice and call this guy before he hits the parking lot. Maybe we can have the accident now and skip ahead with our plan." Jewel instructed.

Billy practiced his voice and story to Issa while Jewel was in the bathroom. Issa thought it too sexy but she knew that was the way people from the south talked.

Issa saw Jewel coming out of the bathroom, so she motioned Billy to follow her in the bathroom. Billy looked in the mirror and focused on his mouth. He wanted to use it in a girlish manner. For if he had to talk to the doctor face to face, he needed to look and act properly. Issa was watching him from outside the bathroom door and butted in to help him some.

"If you keep on acting like that, you'll never make it as a girl. Since you can't act natural watch me." Issa said.

She gave a little 'drawl' to her voice and proceeded to act a little naive as if talking to the doctor. Billy watched. After ten minutes there was a rap on the door, it was Jewel.

"What the hell's going on in there? I thought we were about to call the doctor about a transplant?" Jewel was not happy.

"We'll be right out. Issa was just showing me how to... uh... be a... woman." Billy and Issa were laughing, Jewel looked to see if anyone overheard them.

"When this is over, I can't wait to get me some myself." Jewel muttered to herself while waiting for them.

Issa looked at Billy. She stared into his eyes and gave him a long kiss. As she pulled away, she whispered to him...

"You will make this happen. You must become, and be Gloria. She is our only hope. You are smarter than all of them; it has gotten us this far. We will stop this man. This doctor is the only way. I believe in you William Ruoff. Now go out there and reel him in.

Billy was smiling the entire time she spoke. He knew she was right. He thought how he could be so lucky to find a girl who would go through all of this and still have such tenacity at this level of risk. Almost all of the cards were in his hand, he just needed a little more order to them before he had to play them.

As he picked up the phone he immediately changed into Gloria. His voice and stance propelled him into his final role. Not a clone, not a high school misfit, not even little Billy Ruoff, but into a new part of himself. He was in control. The doctor answered the phone and Billy knew that this was the first major step in controlling his life.

"Dr. Montgomery?" Billy spoke as Gloria with a strong accent.

"Yes, who is this?" he responded.

"I am so sorry to call you on your cell phone Dr., but it is my son. He is in desperate need of a transplant. You see..." he was cut off.

"Who gave you this number? You could have called my office." He was acting nervous.

"Well sir, your wife gave it to me and she said to tell you that she did. Any way the utmost urgency is required for my son. Can you meet with me today and tell me if he is too late to hope for a transplant?" Gloria was laying the accent on heavier, in hopes of sounding more desperate..

"I understand uh Ms., I am sorry I did not hear your name?" he asked politely.

"I am sorry my name is Gloria Benson." he responded.

"Well Ms. Benson I do have a busy schedule, and I do understand the nature of a transplant is usually of the utmost urgency. What is your son's condition?" he asked.

"Dr. Montgomery I wish to discuss this in private and not on a telephone. My son is my world, however with this issue of time, I wish to bring him to your office today even in the next hour if at all possible. I am not at all worried about the cost. He needs help desperately. I even have a donor that is very near and able to give their kidney to Daniel. That's his name, Daniel. Yes he needs a kidney transplant. He only has one at the moment and it is failing and the dialysis is becoming to much for him. I might sound like a prude but my son is very important and he must get this operation as soon as possible." He was out of breath. The girls stood there with their mouths wide open.

"Ms. Benson I am aware of the importance of a kidney transplant. However, my schedule is not very flexible and there are other doctors that can perform such a procedure. I suggest that you call my office and my secretary can give you the numbers of doctors that can help you immediately. That is the best I can do at this time, I am sorry I personally cannot help you." He finished.

"Well Dr. I understand your position, but if you are headed to the hospital at this time I would like to ask if I could at least meet you in person. Perhaps in the parking lot or in the lobby, just to let you meet Daniel and me. Time is of the essence but I feel that if you meet us both you might be able to help us faster than the others. Is there any time in your schedule for that Doctor?" His accent was thick and somewhat seductive. Billy could not believe that he was talking like the voices he would hear while surfing the internet as a young curious man.

"Well I see no harm in this. I suppose that we could meet at my car. Now I can only give you a few minutes and we will have to decide if there is indeed something I can do for you... and Daniel." The doctor now sounded more interested in Gloria than Daniel. "I drive a blue Experate and I'll park in the south lot designated for staff. So if you can wait there, I should be there in about twenty minutes." He said.

"Oh Doctor, that would be great. You don't know how much this means to me and Daniel. We'll be there. Thank you so much we'll see you then." He hung up and jumped for joy.

Jewel and Issa looked at Billy with wonder. They only heard his side of the conversation, and in between their giggles, they knew that he got the information on the car and fixed the problem with the doctor knowing that a Gloria Benson did talk to Dr. Montgomery before he returned to the hospital. They were excited to find out that through Billy's accent and conjecture if the doctor could be persuaded by subterfuge, to give them what they needed.

The time was nearing for the meeting in the parking lot. They all felt that Jewel should be the one to play Gloria. She needed to say that Daniel was not up for the meeting in the parking lot. At that point she needed to use some bedroom eyes and the Southern accent to see if the doctor could be ensnared by the powers of a woman. It was all they could come up with on such short notice.

XIX

Five minutes later, a blue Exparate pulled into the parking lot. Jewel looked at them both, finished putting on her lip-gloss, pushing her breasts up, and said, "Wish me luck!" and she was off.

Billy and Issa watched as she walked over the Dr. Montgomery's car. She went to the driver's side and then walked around to the passenger side and got in. She was in there for almost fifteen minutes. Issa remarked that she had never practiced her southern accent and was worried she might foul it up. Then they both got out of the car at the same time and Jewel walked around and shook his hand. He held it for a moment as they finished talking and as Jewel walked away the doctor watched her for a moment. Issa and Billy looked at each other and smiled. They were fairly certain that this doctor was an easy mouse to lure into their trap.

Jewel walked into the coffee shop to avoid their car. Issa and Billy soon followed. To anyone they looked like three women in the corner gabbing away.

"He was as easy as they come, and he is cute. That made it easier to be a tease. At 7:30 he is going to meet me at the Court Yard Bar on 15th street. He seemed very nice, but I could tell that he is sleazy, because he is married and the way he came on to me in the car was flattering but a little pathetic. He hardly even seemed interested in poor Daniel." Jewel acted upset.

"I think that we should all go to the bar and you two act as my girlfriends that came along for a few drinks and then we can all go back to the hotel, with him thinking that he will end up with all three of us. Then Billy can rip off his wig and say to him. 'Do I look familiar?' and just freak him out. He'll go from horny as hell to scared straight in seconds. That's when we'll have him right where we want him. Plus we will be able to use the fact that he is at a hotel with three women and he is married. It seems almost too easy and too fun." Jewel was full of herself at that point.

"Damn sis'. Where in the hell did you dig that plan

up?" Billy asked.

"I am not sure, but I like it and it is almost fool-proof from the likes of the guy I just met." Jewel replied.

"Well it is set. That all sounds good to me. Now we just need to find that bar. I hope they do not card at the door. Jewel is the only one with i.d. that will get her in. We better find the bar and scope out the scene. Billy, go and pay for our coffee, you need some more practice walking as a woman, and we will be waiting in the car." Issa said.

They found the bar and luckily there was no one checking identification at the door. So they went back to the hotel and freshened up. Jewel made herself look very sexy for the doctor. She did not want to screw this up. Issa dressed a little less sexy but still looked good. Billy was still a man dressing as a woman.

After they ordered drinks they were just talking and laughing at the fact they were all dressed up and actually out having a good time. A few men started showing attention and Billy got worried. So, he leaned over and started kissing Issa on the lips. Jewel just laughed as the men who were checking them out turned away in disappointment.

Just then, Billy noticed a man walking towards the bar and looking around. It was their man, Vincent, all dressed up and looking for trouble. Jewel put up her hand so he could see and after paying for his drink. Vincent walked up to the table with a big grin.

"I see that we're not alone. Hello my name is Vincent and you are...?" he said with a large smile.

"This is... Tammy and .... Sheri, my friends were here when I walked in, so they joined me while I waited for you Vincent. Do you mind if they sit while we talk?" Jewel, who was now Gloria, asked.

"Why no, the more the married, I mean merrier. Ha ha." He said with a very dry laugh. "I am sure you all know about her son so there are no secrets here. I was not sure how or when this all might come about, with you and Daniel. My schedule was open until a prestigious client unexpectedly arrived and now I am not sure when I will have an opening. You see," he leaned in and lowered his voice. "This client is very important for my line of work, so I have to give him precedence, for he could make me millions." He leaned back and took a drink.

"Well Vincent that is wonderful for you, but seems to put me in a holding pattern until this client is gone." She pulled her chair closer to him.

"Maybe with all those millions you can cut me a break, and my Daniel can be normal again." Jewel was rubbing her knee against his, and smiling very big at Vincent.

"We'll see about the millions, but the closeness of that time depends on how long I have to wait for you to come through with your new end of the bargain." he said looking at her form breasts to her eyes.

Jewel shot a smile to Issa. Issa grabbed Billy by the arm and mentioned that she needed to go to the lady's room. After they left, Jewel turned to Vincent with big eyes.

"We should go to my.... no I think that we should go to a hotel, just so Daniel does not see me with you before the surgery. Does that sound like something you would like Vincent?" Jewel asked, whispering close to him.

"Yes, yes I think that this could work. I just need to umm....call my ...wife and tell her I'll be late." He said with a small uncomfortable look on his face.

"You look a little uneasy about all this. Look I am not trying to get a discount by being with you. I am somewhat attracted to you, but not to the point of bad feelings, especially if this is going to affect Daniel. He is the most important part of this relationship." Jewel said while stroking his lapel and chest.

Vincent grinned and held her hand. After a moment he said:

"It is just that my wife, she is so nice to me, but just does not satisfy me sexually and women like you come into my life and well, sometimes a man's got to fulfill his wishes and...."

As Issa and Billy had returned to the table, Vincent and Jewel pulled away from each other.

"I think it is time to leave. We were going to stop off at the Palace and have a private cocktail in my room, if you two wish to join us?" Jewel added.

As they arrived at the Palace, Issa and Billy were getting hot and heavy before they even got out of the car. Billy stopped and fixed his wig and as they got out, he saw Vincent peeping at them through the room's window.

At first Billy became angry. Vincent was a doctor that worked for people who were out to use him and eventually kill him. Vincent now had his hands on his sister. Issa came up beside him and clasped his hand. Billy flashed an angry look and then came back to reality with a smile of confidence. He realized that they were trying to make Vincent their ally and not their foe. Issa asked what the problem was and he smiled, just shaking his head. Issa looked at him with a little strangeness.

They went into the room. Vincent was in the bathroom. Jewel actually glowed a little, from Issa's perspective. She was also a little tipsy from the bar, and excited from kissing Vincent. Billy was not amused, overhearing Jewel's whispering to Issa. He was trying to fix his bra, because after kissing Issa, his tits were crooked. Issa then pulled out a micro-cassette recorder, turned in on and hung it behind a picture on the wall. As she turned to the window, she saw the three of them in the reflection. Issa and Billy also turned to look at each other in the window's reflection, as the door to the bathroom was opening. Billy mouthed 'show-time' and threw up his hands.

Jewel turned first and walked over to Vincent. He was wearing a big smile and threw out his hands saying:

"Well it is just the four of us in this nice......room. What shall we do next?" he said slurring.

"The girls and I were thinking that we wanted to know a little more about you and your line of work. After all, it is my boy you are going to be working on and we need to know a little more. So is your work as important as say your marriage, Vincent?" Jewel asked as Issa and Billy turned around.

"What I do on my personal time does not affect anything I do at the office. I feel that at this time, this pleasure of being with you ladies does not at all mean that little Daniel will be compromised. I remind you all that I was invited to come to this room with you. I feel that you all need... to ... uh." He was losing his train of thought.

"Feel! That's it Vincent. Feel that if you think this is about business, then we need to show you that it is about the business you are in and right now it is...." Billy's eyes got big and his voice was changing a little.

Issa grabbed his arm and kissed him. This was all she could do, to not blow the set up. Vincent had a perplexed look on his face. He mumbled rather loudly that 'Tammy' seemed familiar and then stared off.

"Sometimes Tammy gets a little strange when she drinks. Let's let Sheri calm her down and we can talk more about you Vincent, oops! I mean Dr. Vincent." Jewel stumbled into his lap into the chair

Issa was holding Billy rather tightly and then kissing him deeply. She did not care what this looked like to Vincent. She was stalling, thinking what to do next.

"There is nothing I like better than watching two women kiss. And you know that the other day I was....." he was cut off by Billy.

"There is something I'd like to know Dr. Vincent Montgomery. Where does your wife think you are?" he asked.

"The lady that is my wife.." he hesitated, "Has no clue where I am. You see ladies, my wife is let us say a half-wit, an idiot. I cheat on her not because she is so stupid, she is just boring. She does not have fun any more." He finished taking a drink of water.

"So she does not care that you are here with us? Doing what we are doing?" Issa asked.

"Oh she would care about this, but what could she do to me? Divorce me? Ha!" He drank more water.

Jewel looked at Issa, and then Billy. She smiled real big and looking at Vincent, laid a big wet kiss on him. She made the sound of their kissing rather loud and sloppy sounding. Then Billy and Issa started kissing again. When Jewel noticed that they were kissing and Vincent was starting to watch them, while kissing Jewel, Jewel pulled away, letting out a wicked laugh.

"Well whatever turns you on sister." Vincent said with a grin.

"That's right Vincent whatever turns you on." Billy said in his own voice, but by the time that Vincent looked, who he thought was a girl was now a man.

"Whoa... Shit.....Man ... What the F... is .... Holy shit man, you look like .. Ahh... Ahhh ... I think I know what is happening." He made a break for the door. Issa ran into him, her cross block knocked him against the wall and he fell, Billy jumped on top of him.

"Oh shit man. Never, never in my wildest dreams did I think this would happen." He was staring spellbound at Billy.

As he looked at Billy he whispered, "It is true, It is true."

Vincent started talking and instantly started to sober up. He had been told by one of his colleagues that his client the Shapur was into 'Live-Stock'. That was the term given to the people who lived very long through the lives of others. The Shapur, however took it to a new level when he 'acquired' a doctor in the last Terrorist-Territory War in the middle east. This doctor cloned thirteen women with his stem-cell genes and only five survived. Most of them died at birth. Some grew beyond their abilities to handle the rapid growth. He stopped talking for a minute and gazed at Billy.

Jewel and Issa were in shock. Billy registered everything that the doctor was telling them. He wanted to strangle the doctor between every heartbeat.

"Well regardless of the past Dr. Montgomery, we are here to stop the future. And with or without your cooperation we will succeed. We have you on tape and I am sure that we could drum up some witness to all that has happened with you and us tonight. Sorry to drag you into this, but you are the closest link we have to bring this man down. We are wondering if you will help us? I will give you a minute to answer." Billy stood back and started to take the rest of his dress off.

Issa started to shake and clutch at Billy. She had never really thought about how it would feel to hear how Billy was conceived. She kept getting closer to Billy, shallowly crying to herself. Jewel was just looking blankly at the wall.

Billy finished changing clothes when Vincent started to move.

"Whoa, mister. Don't get any funny ideas. I am extremely aggressive right now and I won't have a problem hurting you." Billy was standing there with no shirt on, ready to go.

"I ah.....I ah....need a little longer to weigh this out. I mean these guys are worldwide. My whole life is going to change from this moment on. I am going to lose my wife either way, possibly my Medical license and then my life. So I need to decide which way I can get the most out of this before I die." He again reached for his drink.

"Wow Vince... you surprise me with the way you are handling this. I mean you are a good kisser and all, but considering that you are a lier, a cheat and someone who is working for the other side, I'd say that you're .....gonna make the right choice." Jewel finished with a hopeful smirk on her face.

"Whatever sis. This guy is still untrustworthy and now I need to know how we are going to get this guy to help us. So I don't want to hear any more about kissing and...." Vincent interrupted.

"Hang on.....Mr...... What is your name anyway?" he asked.

"It is William Ruoff, or Billy. Don't forget it." He answered.

"The only way this can work is if we can get our government to protect us from the Shapur's men. I mean what are you going to do? I can give you proof that you are a clone of the Shapur, but then what? Someone will kill you and then they will figure out that I had something to do with it and then I'm dead. So what is your big plan after that William, or may I call you Billy?" Vincent said.

"Honestly Vincent, I do not have a 'big plan'. However this turns out I need proof that I am his clone. From what you just said and from what I've heard in the past, I should not be alive anyway. I am going to find a way to expose this man who has completely screwed up my life and killed my mother. Whether I die or not, I am going to fight! Now are you with us or are things going to get real nasty for you real soon?" Billy asked Vincent, pointing his finger in his face.

"Billy, I think you made your point..... Vincent is for sure going to make the right choice. The ethics regarding cloning are kicking in his head and we are the best solution, right Vincent?" Jewel was leaning in next to Billy, as they both stood over Vincent.

"Because if he does not, he will mysteriously have an accident, and therefore..." Issa was next to all of them.

Vincent started to squirm a little, darting his eyes left and right. The three of them pulled back as they realized they were very close to him.

"Let's get this straight; what are you going to do after I have the proof that you are indeed a clone of the Shapur? How can you alone expose something that,.. is already known, but not brought to a large crowd's attention. After all he was a terrorist that became a leader and now is actually doing some good for his people. What do you have planned for the Shapur?" Vincent leaned back in his chair.

"I am not telling you anything Dr.. I know for a fact, that even if you agree to help us, little will be divulged to you along the way." Billy said as he leaned up against the door.

"Now we are at the great impasse. I have no reason to accept your plan. I can not help you because you don't wish to tell me anything. So the next thing that I would do Mr. Ruoff, is to think how I must be convinced of your plan?" he smirked.

It was eerie for Billy to look at him. The smirk he

made was very similar to the one he himself would make. Billy turned to Issa, who was still trying to deal with the situation. She was thinking on what was happening between Billy and Vincent. Jewel was looking away, for the alcohol left her feeling sorry for Vincent.

Billy went towards the mirror and then to the window and peered out. Then it came to him. Let it go. He had a little bit of evidence for black mail. He wants to get a sample of the Shapurs blood and then the doctor can go.

The more Billy thought, it seemed kind of weak, but time was of the essence and most of his hand was already played. He knew he needed to make something happen tonight; it was all he could think of. Billy told Vincent his idea that he only had to get a blood sample of the Shapur's and not be visible in any way. In return, Billy would give the tape of the evening's events with no copy.

The girls came out of their reveries as they heard Billy. Vincent looked back and forth, between Issa and Jewel and then just watched Billy. Either way, he was going to have to take a chance. Vincent agreed, but Billy still did not fully trust him. He had to figure out how to trail him or somehow see how he reacted, when meeting the Shapur. He had to let him go. He wanted to talk to the girls before he left though.

"Just like that you agree, huh? I am a little surprised at how quickly you agreed to this plan. I need to talk with my family. Give me the keys to your car, your wallet and your cell." He asked.

"Well if we're all about to trust one another, then give them to us and wait outside so I can talk to them in private. If you leave, then we will go directly to your wife and say you left these with us. So what is it going to be?" He started to open the door.

Vincent gave up the keys, wallet and phone. As he went out the door he looked back with a trusting smile and said "I'll be right back".

"Give us fifteen minutes." Jewel said.

Billy shut the door and turned, looking out the window. Issa instantly ran up to him and embraced him.

Jewel came over and hugged the two of them. Time passed slowly, with Billy pulling away first.

"Well? What do you think?" He said whispering as he finished looking out the window.

"How do you feel?... Billy?" Issa was frightened.

"I can not feel right now. I am just trying to keep this flowing. If I think too much about this, my emotions will screw this up. I love you, I love you both. Let's think now... Shall we?" He finished with an English accent.

That lead him to instantly think of Thomas. This would be a great time to consult with him, but there was no time to do so. He thought of what he might say.

"Basically we need to not lose this guy until he delivers us the sample. What do we do with the sample once we get it? How do we know that it is the real one?" Jewel asked.

"When this sampling is going on, we should see if we can keep the doctor within our reach." He paused. "What's up with you Sis? Do you like this guy or something? Is that what I was sensing?.. he paused, "Man, this is just a day in the life, huh?" Billy looked dumbfounded.

"I am not sure what you mean by 'like' this guy? I am fond of his lips at this moment, but I don't trust him either. What do you mean keep him within our reach? How are we going to do that?" Jewel snapped back.

"We'll that's just why I asked about all this 'liking' stuff. I think if you can pull it off, you act as the go-between sister, and find out what side he is really on or at least some way to verify that the sample is in fact the Shapur's." He was smiling.

"Are you insisting that Jewel acts as the double crossing sister?" Issa asked.

"Well that sounds interesting, I was not really thinking that, but he doesn't know any different. What do you say sis', wanna give it a shot?" Billy said.

"Why not, it is at least something for now. You were right though, we cannot let him out of our sight until we get the sample. By the way, what are we going to do with the sample after we get it?" Jewel questioned.

"I will give a call to Thomas first and see if he can help us out on that one. It is rather late. I am sure that he will want to go home and so we will have to follow him to have a better watch on him. I think we should just be up front and tell him that we are going to stay around him until this is taken care of. Jewel will hopefully be the main person in charge. And we must get the next part set up to go to the Kennedy Center. I'll need a new dress and new shoes...." Billy tried to be funny, for he had been too serious for too long. The girls laughed and for a moment....they all calmed down.

Soon after: "I think that....:" Jewel was cut off by the knock at the door.

It was Vincent, "Hey, it's been more than fifteen minutes. What's going on?" He said.

"Well, Jewel?" Billy asked.

"Hang on Vincent I'll be right out." Jewel said while staring intensely towards Billy.

Jewel went outside and then peeped her head in after a few minutes and said that she and Vincent would be back and that she was taking the car. Issa said to be careful driving that tipsy. Jewel blew a kiss and yelled a 'I'm comin' damn it' to Vincent.

Issa turned to Billy and made the comment that she was acting like he was her boyfriend already. Billy said it was just the liquor. At that point Issa's back was to Billy and he snuck up behind her and then slowly pulled her to his body. He whispered into her ear, 'just let me hold you for a while, I really need to hold you' and she fell into his arms. After about half an hour, they were both sound asleep.

XX

Billy awoke and noticed that Jewel was not back. He panicked for a moment. He prayed, and as Issa awoke to a grim look upon Billy's, there was a noise at the door and it opened with Jewel standing there with coffee, Danishes and a very bad hairdo. Billy laughed at her hair but then after she put down the bags, he gave her a big hug. Issa was awake just smiling.

"What happened? Did you stay with him all night? You look like hell, but you seem all right. What's in the bag?" Billy asked with a perplexed look on his face.

"He showed me his house, I think. I mean it could have been any ones house. I wrote down the address, but he had no mail to prove that it was indeed his house, so...Then we went to an office which in fact was his and we talked and I lead him on to think that after we get a positive match on the blood that you two were going on to deal with some stuff and I would not be needed. He isn't stupid and he is nice, he said that he jumped on the needs of the Shapur in order to get some experience and some money. I felt sincerity from him at that point, but there was something that he was not telling. I could not get him to be totally comfortable with me, unless we were kissing." She started to drink some coffee.

"Here we go with the kissing thing again." Billy retorted.

"Whatever, anyway in two days is his preliminary visit with the Shapur and then to schedule the actual surgery there after. This is before the Kennedy Center dinner, so after the preliminary visit he will have a sample. He said if we like, that we could draw your blood at that time and show you the proof then. I said that I doubt it. Did you talk to Thomas?" Jewel finished.

"No, we uh... fell... asleep and woke up just before you arrived." Issa said.

"I came back around two thirty and you all did not move." She ate some of her Danish. We just talked. He never once asked a question about you. I mean being a doctor and all, he did not really talk much about his profession. It was kind of strange, the way he was acting and all. I have only been around you all for the past month and it was like I did not know how to act or feel around a stranger. Especially since he was not acting at all like how I expected a doctor would act. Then of course all of the drinks I had. I was impressed though with my performance. We got what we needed, and I feel good about what is going on. I'm also going to meet him tomorrow night at a bar across town, so I'll need the car Buck-oh. You two can watch movies or whatever." She was acting sassy.

"God, you go out and get a little and you start acting all full of yourself and stuff." Issa said with a little Ebonics.

"It feels good, but it will only last a while, I am sure he is acting or hiding something." Jewel responded.

"He is acting sis, he is married. He acts one way to her he acts another towards you. Some guys are just that way." Billy said with a consoling manner.

They finished the coffee and Danishes and Billy got dressed and called Thomas. After twenty-minutes of calling friends and relatives houses, Billy tracked Thomas down in of all places, Baltimore, Maryland.

"Thomas I am finally able talk to you. I feel like I have just talked to half of your friends and relatives to reach you. How are you ol'boy?" Billy said with an accent.

"William, what a surprise this is. I must say you are a persistent chap to have found me here. How is your lovely wife, Issa?" Thomas asked cheerily.

"She's wonderful, although there is a mad person after her husband." Billy snickered back.

"That reminds me. I have good news and bad news. First, the Shapur is to arrive in the U.S. day after tomorrow and is to meet with his doctor. However, he will be guarded heavily and is to go to an undisclosed hospital for a check-up. Now the bad news, he got a new pancreas. We do not know if it was from a clone or a donor pancreas.
This is very strange. For the likely hood of his need verses the ability to get one is rather slim. My colleges do not think it was a donor. We have a strong feeling that there are more clones. One of my colleges has speculated that they are younger boys that are out there and not being able to understand due to youth. It is sad what he is doing to the young lads and they are just too weak to stand up to him." Thomas stopped as if someone else was talking to him.

"Thomas, are you there?" Billy asked

"Sorry I was interrupted. You were about to say?"

Thomas replied.

"We are not far from you right now and we have just met with and hopefully lured into helping us, the doctor that is to check on the Shapur. But we do not trust him, for sure, and we need to also know if we have a way into the Kennedy Center, because if our plan goes remotely close to schedule then we will have a blood sample. Then we were hoping that you could help us find the right place to have it tested against mine for the complete proof that we need. We'll also maybe need a in with some news people so they will be glad to air the proof to the world that this is for real and it is happening in this country, that was Issa's idea." Billy paused.

"Good show old chap, however, there is one thing that you left out. What are you going to do after you expose the Shapur? Don't you think that he will want to talk to you?" Thomas asked with a fatherly tone.

"I am glad you brought that up Sir Thomas." Billy said respectfully.

At that moment, Billy wondered. He wondered what the heck he was thinking when he heard the news of the Shapur's coming to America. As he was drifting off, he heard Thomas' voice off in the background. He was not listening to it. He was thinking of a way to draw attention. Then he thought of the news people and what their reaction might be, could Thomas help with a connection. And with all of the security there for the important people, and he technically being a U.S. citizen, he would demand protection and with the way the media covers everything to exploit their views and twists in their words of opinion. At that moment he came back and heard breathing on the other line...

"Thomas, I am sorry are you still there?" Billy asked.

"Yes, are you?" Thomas replied.

"Sorry, my mind was wondering and I just had to tune you out and let my mind go as it does sometimes. I was on the thoughts of using the news media people to help in my shelter from the Shapur? Do you know anybody to leak this two but not before we are all actually there, at the Kennedy Center? I am going on the pretense that they will treat me as a U.S. citizen and protect me as one. I hoped..." Billy was cut off.

"Slow down old boy. You mind works well when under pressure. Just as I remember your, I guess father acting. I know that is a harsh reality for you William, but it is the truth. Without him you would still just be an angel of some sort." There was silence.

"Yes I do know someone who could be vital in aiding us in your safety. I will get on that, but as far as you being a U.S. citizen that will only last for a short time. You were not born into America. You were born in...." Thomas stopped.

"Where was I born? Do you know?" Billy asked.

"I do not. I just know it was not in America. The chances could fall in you favor if they look at you as and adopted child that legally became a citizen, however, you are now an issue of world relations between America and the territories of the Middle East, which right now are in good standings. America cannot and will not hold the Shapur. He will likely be outcast, but that could be as far as the U.S. will go. You will need to figure out during that time where and how to go. You and your sister will need to separate. Issa I am sure will be with you, but she will also be at risk. You need to think of others as you enter into this level of exposure, William." Thomas stopped to take a drink.

"I know. I do need to be reminded of these things. I do sometimes think of him as my father, even though he was to use me then let me die. Issa and Jewel are behind me and I will remind them of his dangers once I am exposed, but I forgot to mention what Dr. Montgomery said about the Shapur and all of this doing." Billy said.

He told us of what happened and how I was more or less created. Only five of the clones lived and they were considered 'live-stock' by the people who knew of such atrocities. Thomas did not reply. Billy assumed that he already knew this.

"I would have told you some more after this was

over. Now that you have begun to hear about this insane quest toward immortality, I will only tell what I know when I am asked. When you are ready William we will talk." Thomas said this as consolingly as possible.

"I will Thomas, but for now I must get the most out of our Dr. Montgomery. My sister is working on him, in more ways than one. I just hope she stays focused. She has been lonely for to long." Billy finished.

They talked a while longer on the ways to cover all bases that would enable Billy and the girls to be safe. Thomas said that Billy should get a new costume as a girl with different hair color and such. He should stay in the outfit until he is able to expose the Shapur in front of the biggest crowd of press people and public. Billy was hoping that the connection Thomas had would take care of this, but Billy was starting to think of his own ways just in case. They had realized that they had been on the phone for over a half hour and left it as they were going to talk just after the Dr.'s meeting with the Shapur. After saying good bye to Thomas, Billy sat and felt the feeling of an almost true father, helping him.

Issa came over to him as he got off the phone. Jewel was lying on the bed.

"Who is watching the Dr.? Jewel, how do we even know what this guy could be doing right now? What the hell is happening?" Billy felt slightly panicked.

"He is sleeping right now and after his 1:30 appointment he is meeting me at the coffee shop where we were the other day and then we are going out for diner. So if he stands me up then I or we will wait for him at his office or something, but I know that he will be there, I just know. Now let me sleep, you two go out for a walk and get some new clothes for Gloria. I thought I heard Thomas mention something to that effect. Please just be quiet." Jewel rolled back over with a pillow on her head.

"I guess that will do for now, we'll be back." Billy answered.

Billy dressed up as Gloria and they went out looking for a new look for him. When they returned to the hotel,

Jewel was gone and had left a note giving the address of the Dr.'s office. For some reason, that made Billy want to change rooms, he thought of the Dr. giving that information to the Shapur's men.

Issa took a shower after they moved and Billy was watching television almost asleep. She got into bed and they snuggled and instantly fell asleep with the television on.

The next morning Issa went over to the old room and found Jewel there, alone and still in her clothes from the night before, very tired and grumpy. She said she did not even notice that they were not there. She told Jewel the room number and said to come over before 11 am for they had checked out of that room. Jewel seemed confused but agreed.

This would be the last day they all had to relax. The whole day Issa watched television and Billy laid with her staring but not really watching. After dinner Jewel went out with Vincent for a drink, but came back rather early.

Billy got into the shower and while alone Issa finally asked Jewel what was up with her and Vincent. Jewel hesitated. Then she broke into a small history of her love-life that was all of short relationships that were mostly sex, and too few that really stood out. She went on a little then dipped into a philosophical disclaimer about how acts of the past made it easier to do this with Vincent. Issa seemed lost and the look she gave to Jewel said 'I am lost'. Jewel recognizing this sat up in her chair and said;

"But if you think for a moment that I would ever sell my brother out, you're fucking crazy! I don't know what may ever come of this but Vincent and I *are* having a good time. If that's all I might get, I better get it while I can." She said this rather calmly, having heard the water in the shower go off.

"Who would ever say you would do anything of the sort, but I was curious and I felt, considering the circumstances we are about to go through, we had a right to know." She stopped as Billy walked out of the bathroom. "Want to know what? Oh, yeah sis what's up with the Dr., huh?" Billy asked while drying his hair.

"Ask your wife" she replied, as she grabbed her bag and went into the bathroom.

Issa told Billy some of his sister's love life, but made note of unhappiness and no respect. "With Vincent she is getting both...... of it, and with no ties to you. There could be other reasons why she is feeling this way. You have me and she only has us, so just remember she is on our side." Issa finished with whispering that he should go and talk to her, alone.

Jewel came out of the bathroom and then Issa went in to the bathroom. Billy stood up.

"This is all so hard on us. We must keep talking. You are all I have left of our family. So if you could just stick with us until this is over and then...." He was cut off

"I ain't going anywhere Buck oh! He just feels so... right. I know that he is a cheat and such and who is to say that he won't do it to me, but, I don't know Billy I guess I just wanted some love. Just like Mom playing that Bob Marley reggae all the time, and such, I just needed some love." By this time they were sitting next to each other and smiling. They both started singing the melody but only remembered the chorus of 'Three little birds' and 'every little thing is gonna be all right' over and over they sang.

"So I am just going to play it easy and by tomorrow we should have the blood sample. How are we going to know if it's his blood?" Jewel asked.

"I need to call Thomas and see what he has found out. He did say by tomorrow he could know more on that stuff. He was also going to find a way to leak this into the news media and so the exposure is large." Billy went on to tell her more of the conversation with Thomas. Issa came out of the bathroom and the conversation turned into going to a thrift store so Gloria could become a brunette, get some different clothes and more comfortable shoes.

Issa and Jewel got dressed quickly. This excited them greatly but Billy was indifferent. They returned from their shopping spree in which they managed to only spend twenty dollars. They traded some clothes for clothes and haggled more for the clothes.

There was a message at the front from Vincent to Jewel. Billy and Issa started laughing. Jewel read the message then joined in. The clerk looked wide eyed at three women laughing, and then started to laugh himself, for no reason. They stopped when Billy, being taller than the clerk, lunged at him who then immediately stopped laughing, as they all did. The clerk smiled uncomfortably then left. She was to meet him later at Cindy's, an Italian restaurant nearby in about two hours.

Billy put the new outfit on to get use to it and asked Issa to fix it up a bit. As Jewel was about to leave Issa attacked Billy, still all dressed up, and then Billy said 'you two better not try this stuff in the restaurant. We don't have much time to fool around. Ya hear?!' he said with a hick accent.

Knowing that Billy and Issa were fooling around during the time she would be gone, Jewel started to just sing, 'every little thing's gonna be alright.' Vincent was late but came in and happy to see her.   He seemed so genuine to Jewel. She found it hard to just get the initial business underway. Jewel resorted to being flirtatious and having fun at that. After diner she asked how the meeting with the Shapur was and if he did in fact have the blood sample that he promised. Vincent went into the conversation that he had with the Shapur and at that moment it really came to Jewel to whom Vincent was talking to. Her brother's father. He shared that the Shapur momentarily alluded to the fact that he was going to use her brother to keep on living. She could only imagine the feeling of even talking to her father, not ever having one herself. Over hearing Vincent talking brought her back to the restaurant, he paused in his remake of the conversation with the Shapur and his colleges. Vincent finally went on to say that at his office was a sample of his blood. He covered his tracks by putting the blood with a different Doctor's name on the label. He thought of no other way to make is safe. As he spoke to Jewel he mentioned that if this whole thing turned out to be bad then he would hope that they could somehow go hide out together. Jewel could not believe this guy.

Jewel thought to herself: He is at least fifteen years older than me. She was talking to herself under her breath when she noticed that he was trying to listen.

"It's alright to talk to you self about it. I do. Also remember that I can prove that he is in fact a clone. I want to be trusted." Vincent finished.

"I want to believe you but right now, I can't. Lets go and get the sample and let me prove to myself and to Billy that it is in fact the Shapurs then we will talk more about us." Jewel felt self-assured and stuck to business.

They went to his office and after he gave her the blood sample and an ice pack. She grabbed his arm and said; "Our relationship seems rather odd, I know that I used myself to lure you into this, but you see the situation I am in. These people caused my mother to die and my brother to grow up very uncomfortable." She paused, then turned her body to his. "I feel something towards you. You are much older and you have a wife, however, I am always thinking of the future, so maybe you could keep me in mind after all of this is over, huh?" She leaned in a kissed him as passionately as she could to convey to him that she meant it. At first he smiled, looked at her for a moment and said for her to call him soon. They kissed again then said good-byes.

On the way home she was very proud of herself and knew that if he were true then time would let her know.

Upon arriving at the hotel she thought she saw a mysterious car parked across from the hotel. She would be sure to mention it to Billy. Trying to be quiet she opened the door to find them sleeping. Just upon closing the door she looked out and saw the same car drive by and then sped up. She got a small sick feeling in her and she just reacted.

Jewel immediately started packing their stuff and simultaneously waking them up. Issa saw what Jewel was doing and began to help. Billy asked what was going on and then subconsciously started to help. Jewel told them about the car, at which point Billy started slowing down on his packing. Issa did not. She asked how it went with Vincent. Jewel went on to explain everything and that she had the sample. At that point Issa expressed they needed to go soon. It was the first car that gave anyone of them the creeps. She also made the point that they had the sample now they should go and find Thomas and see if what they got is real. Jewel agreed and thought to herself that it could prove that Vincent was somewhat trustworthy.

Silence came over the room. They all keep getting their stuff together. They were just looking at each other waiting for one of them to say something, Billy broke first.

"Let's see if this car is in fact a 'goonie'. I think that I will try out my new outfit. Do you think my butt looks better in this skirt that the last?" Billy was squirming into his new outfit.

"And just what do you suppose is going to happen when you go outside, the car is gone?" Jewel stammered.

"If it is in fact a 'goonie' car, then they will be in the vicinity of this hotel. I just wanted to walk in my new shoes and see how I fare as a brunette." Billy was adjusting his wig. "How do I look?" He started for the door.

"You look great. Now wait a minute there missy. I want a little bit of the new Gloria, plus you need to fix that wig and don't forget the glasses." Issa came strutting up to Billy and fixed his hair then gave him a kiss.

"Good god you too." Jewel replied.

"Sorry Sis." Issa answered.

Billy went out and stumbled as he got use to the new shoes. He paraded down the street in front of the motel. A car honked a horn, but Billy thought nothing of it. Then when someone whistled, Billy turned and saw that someone was actually paying attention to him. At first he glared then looking down at his fake breasts he put on a smile and turned to swing his hips and strut away. He was walking with a prideful look on his face when he came out of his happiness he realized that he was walking right towards a car that looked all to familiar. Billy could not believe it. He had seen the car before, but it was not like the others that followed him. As he came closer to the car the window came down as to talk to him. A cigarette slid out of the crack and paused not to fall, but it was held back. Then the window went further down and much to Billy's surprise he recognized the face, it was Jarin, the delivery guy back at the food court in the mall. Billy worked his face so hard to go from disbelief to a sassy girl smile for Jarin was starring right at him.

Billy then thought of his sunglasses. They hid his face well. He smiled and started in.

"My, what a beautiful day isn't it?" Billy said in a thick southern accent.

Jarin just smiled slightly and replied "Yes it is Mama."

Billy kept on walking. He tried not to walk faster than usual but he knew that they had to move fast. He walked down the road until out of sight of the car, and he took off his shoes and started to run back towards the hotel. Billy found an ally that went right behind where Jarin was parked, Billy got lucky. A van was going the same way and he was able to run along with it. He regained his composure as a woman about a block before the hotel. He briskly walked up to the room. Just before he went in he heard and felt a car coming with a low tuned exhaust. He went on passed the door and headed for the stairs. The car stopped but Billy continued walking up the steps. He heard some voices talking. It did not sound like English. He was able to see them through the railing of the stairs. It was Jarin and one other man.

They started pointing in the direction of their room. Billy knew he had to make a diversion. He could tell that they were unaware of him and the coincidence that this same woman is at the hotel they are staking out.

Billy crossed the upper walked way and back over towards the office. He walked in and told the clerk that there were some suspicious looking men who seem to be trying to break into a car. The clerk looks suspiciously at Billy.

At first Billy did not know. He knew that he used his girly accent, but was unaware of his breasts being slightly out of balance. As Billy noticed he went to sneeze and came up all fixed with a smile. The clerk chuckeled to himself and called the police.

Billy started to wonder if he did the right thing. He saw himself in a mirror in the lobby, he looked scared and so he straightened himself up and walked over to behind the desk and called their room Jewel answered.

"Hello?" Jewel said very nervously.

"It's me. Listen, there are two guys outside, hopefully by now the hotel guy is over they're seeing what they are up to. I think that we should combine our bags and get on a bus or a train, get to Baltimore and find Thomas. There is more but I need to get you guys out of that room first. Tell Issa the same and I'll call back or something so stay put." Billy hung up and walked out from behind the counter just in time for the clerk returned and said that he saw the two gentlemen, but the were just standing there smoking a cigarette, and that he was going to go and meet the police when they arrive.

Billy did not think that the cops would do much to scare Jarin and his friend. They might go away but would stick around the area, he had to act fast.

Billy walked briskly around the back of the hotel. As he started to round the corner he tripped and caught himself on side of the building. With the momentum that persisted, his head just went around the corner; there was Jarin and his companion in the car, waiting around the back. Billy paused and then slowly pulled his shoes off and started running back the other direction. He ducked into the stairwell as he heard the car door slam shut. He had no idea of what to do next.

He heard a door opening around the corner, he put his shoes back on and checked his outfit. Just then a man came out of his room. He smiled nicely at Billy. For a moment Billy just stared at him, then realizing he was a woman, he turned to the man and touched his arm.

"Sir, would you mind doing me a favor, A man is

coming this way and I need to uh...lose him, I was wondering if I could duck into your room for about five minutes, do you have five minutes to spare?" he said as he twirled his hair and distracted the gentleman from looking at his feet.

"I don't really like to get involved with strangers, but you seem to be a mess from something so... I guess that I could help you for five minutes, what's in it for me?" he replied with a grin.

"Well I have no money and I am in the mood for nothing else so, nothing." Billy said his girlish voice.

The man looked very perplexed. "Here's the key, you do what you want." He responded rather irritated.

Billy smiled and took the key and went for the door, the man followed. Billy went for the television and turned it on rather loud. The man looked at him even more strangely followed by a sigh. Billy saw the shadows of Jarin and his partner go by. Billy turned to see the man standing there. Billy's eyes were darting around the room. He was not sure what he had gotten into. The man looked at his watch and then at Billy.

"Look lady, or whatever. I am starting to feel uncomfortable and I am not a man of confrontations, so if this is....." he stopped as he saw Billy's arm go up.

"There is nothing to worry about; I am a detective observing some suspicious people. I am sorry that I used you in this way, but you saved me from doing something that I do not like to do." He was talking normal and slightly cocky.

"Like what?" the man asked.

"I am not ...uh at liberty to say sir. We'll only be here for another few minutes or so then we can go. I need to use the bathroom, excuse me." Billy went into the bathroom. He could not believe that what he just did, worked.

After using the bathroom, he fixed his hair and boobs. When he walked out of the bathroom, he noticed that the man had gone, with the door left open. Billy walked up slowly to the door and closed it; peaked out behind curtain and looked at the clock by the bed, the phone...he called the girls.

Jewel answered, "Hello?"

"Hey I am in room 134 and we need to leave right now. If we do not meet up, take the bus to the train and then to Baltimore. You can call Thomas once you are on your way, but we should all make it together. We need to get to the bus stop that is down the block in about ten minutes. I saw a bus schedule in the office and the bus will be stopping down on the corner so leave in seven minutes, I will be there, I hope." Billy stopped talking.

"We will be there, where are our friends?" she asked.

"I do not know for sure but they are still around here. I need to go now. I will see you at the bus. Good luck, I love you sis." He said.

"Love you too, buck-oh." She hung up.

Billy went back into the bathroom to fix himself and noticed that the man had left his toiletries. Billy found some rather large toenail clippers. He thought of the brakes on Jarin's car. Billy looked at the clock, ten minutes to the bus.

He walked out of the room and around the hotel, down past their room and back toward Jarin's car. He didn't see anyone. He executed his new routine, fake twist an ankle, fall landing right next to Jarin's car. He rolled under and got out the clippers and started knawing at the rubber part of the front brake. Once he broke through the brake fluid started dripping out. Billy rolled out, got to his knees and looked at himself in the side mirror. Fixed his wig again, got up and walked back towards their room. Just then the door opened and the girls walked out. Jewel and Issa had again dyed their hair to platinum blonde and now Billy was the brunette. Up the block the bus came into view, Jewel noticed their reflection in the big hotel window. They arrive at the corner as the bus stopped.

As they boarded the bus Billy saw two people walking back towards Jarin's car. He smiled and Issa asked what was so funny. Once they sat down and was moving he told Issa and then to Jewel. Jewel said, "Only my brother." Billy just grinned.

XXI

The bus took them twenty minutes to the train station. They instantly notice that there were a lot of suspicious men there with almost identical suits and hats. Issa said something out loud first.

"It feels like a conspiracy. Or is it just me?"

"It's just us. We must keep telling ourselves that." Billy replied.

"Where is the train to Baltimore?" Jewel asked.

"I have never been to a place this big with so many people.

"There is information let's go over there." Issa said.

The found out that the next train to Baltimore did not leave for forty-five minutes. They went and got their ticket and then Billy noticed some private phone booths and called Thomas.

After telling Billy where he would be picked up, Thomas mentioned of some rather large people interested in his story and such. Billy became excited, but he knew that he needed to take care of exposing him before this was to be exploited. They were brief with the rest of the conversation. Thomas said he will be in a black BMW to pick them up.

When Billy came out of the area of the private phone booths, he saw two men with those suits talking to the girls. He became very nervous. He held his composure well as he walked over to them. He smiled as they smiled and chose not to say anything.

"Thank you very much" Issa and Jewel said.

"What the heck was that?" Billy asked.

"They are Amish and they are here for a gathering. The accepted the use of the trains for their only other means of transportation. They gathered at the capitol this year. That's why there are so many of them." Jewel explained.

"No shit I have never seen an Amish person, nice

hair." Billy mumbled.

"Billy... what did you say?" Issa asked.

They all laughed a little and started toward the train platform. After a short wait they were aloud to board. As the train left they all had safe feelings on their minds and on their faces. The smiles turned to yawns and they were asleep. The train ride was only twenty-five minutes to reach the station that Thomas told him to take. Billy woke up only to see that they were coming into the station. No body talked. Not even the people around them. It was as if they entered a different place. In the train station things came back to the usual sound of the station, however the three of them were feeling a little uncomfortable with the place.

"Where are we going Billy?" Jewel asked.

"We must take the right street and Thomas will be there in a black car. I am sure he looks the same although it has been a while since we have seen him." Billy stated.

"Is that it, over there?" Jewel asked.

Just then the window went down and Thomas greeted them with a smile.

"Welcome William, ladies. I assure you that things will be a little quieter while you are with me. We will be going to a friend of mine's laboratory to see if what you have, does in fact match William here's blood. I'll be extremely curious if it does. We do however have a back-up plan. You all just sit back and relax, you'll need it." Thomas proclaimed.

They did just that. It was another hour until they stopped driving. The traffic did not allow them to travel very fast. Jewel gave Thomas the sample as Billy started to change into some other clothes they had brought. They parked in an underground parking lot and entered into a dark bricked building, after Thomas flashed the guards the proper identification. A lady with a white coat came into the room they were in and prepared to draw a blood sample from Billy.

Thomas showed them to a room with some cots and said for them to get comfortable and he would be back.

Later, Thomas peeked into the room where they were all sleeping, knew they were safe and decided to let them sleep as long as they could.

After almost four hours Thomas came into the room. Issa and Billy were starting to stretch and look around.

"I saw that you were tired. With all of things that you have accomplished William, you should be tired. I come with good news." Thomas was smiling.

"Is it a match?" Billy asked.

"Exact. It looks like Dr. Montgomery did what he said after all. That poor chap must realize that there is a remote chance that he could be linked to our cause and be in much danger." Thomas noted.

"He does. That is why he feels that his efforts might be needed in the future for us. Vincent knows that one of his colleagues will rat him out. Therefore he is finishing up what he can right now in order to join us later." Jewel said this as she stepped into the room.

"I see you have become more than just acquainted with Dr. Montgomery. What are his plans? How is he to find us?" Thomas asked.

"After examining the Shapur, Vincent told me that his health was stable. Vincent knows once we've exposed the real Shapur, then they will look for him to help them. Vincent also feels that they will be very persuasive.

Jewel went on to tell them that Vincent was tired of his marriage and was over trying to gain something out of being tied to the Shapur. At that point Billy cleared his throat rather loudly and butted in.

"So we know most of the rest of the story. However, Thomas had some other news about Dr. Vincent Montgomery. Thomas?" Billy snorted.

"It seems that the Dr. had a bit of trouble at his internship and it was fixed by a friend of the Shapur's. The favor was passed back to the Shapur and that is why the Dr. is doing this, not only for you. He hopes to tag along, hopefully getting himself out of his own mess." Thomas stopped and motioned them to follow him.

They went through a door and it was like they were

in someone's house. The smell of flowers and lavender filled the air. Thomas smiled as the looks on their faces became large smiles and total relaxation came over their bodies.

"I like your friends Thomas. They can sure make a girl feel very comfortable in this house." Jewel remarked.

"They have quite the knack for comfort-ability. I myself have used their ways of pleasing the eye as well as the nose, in achieving this feeling." Thomas added.

Thomas told them to relax until a few more bits of information came in. It would only be another hour and then they would know exactly what to do. He was not completely sold on the doctor tagging along with them after they exposed the Shapur. He went on to say he could create more attention and even be a weak link in assuring their safety. Thomas digressed into a scenario where the doctor could tell the wrong person of their whereabouts or even be tracked on his cell phone. He was not sure how powerful or long the Shapur's reach was in this country. Thomas knew that he could take care of them for the time being. Having the doctor around might not be too good. He never spoke about it again.

The look on Jewel's face, as Thomas was talking, went from angry to sad. She understood what Thomas had said and agreed with him. She was now worried that Vincent might forget that she existed or worse turn on them, upon figuring out that he might be left alone and unprotected. Issa saw these emotions appear on Jewel's face. Issa walked over and sat beside her, as Thomas excused himself.

"I can see what you are feeling. He came into your life to help your brother. We need to focus on getting your brother safe. Vincent is a big boy and if he got himself in this trouble then you should be glad that you are not in the middle of it. He could even be the type that could drag you into it." Issa stopped as anger returned to Jewel's face.

"He was trying to tell me something, maybe this is it. That he is in trouble and did not want me in the middle. I don't know." Jewel was tearing up.

"Let's put our attention to Billy until we are sure that we are safe. We are the one's that need protection and Vincent even joked about the potential loss of his career. Thomas knows what we need to do. We need him now and to put pressure on what he is doing for us is not good. Dr. Vincent's strikes against him are building up. You should think some more before you put any further energy towards him." Issa was holding her hand and being very serious.

"Sis, I am behind you and Vincent might be good for you or us, but for the time being we need to help ourselves before we can help others. Vincent got himself into this trouble and our plate is full. I understand your feelings for this guy but they are rather new and came to you under unusual circumstances. If his intentions are real then they will come to fruition soon enough after we are more secure with our ability to live a life without looking over our backs all the time." He stopped as his hand was stroking her arm.

"I know, I know. To think that this doctor was actually interested in me and not just trying to use me is far fetched. All the guys I have dated have used me in some way, why should Vincent be no different." She was still sobbing.

"I wouldn't say that. You said that he was trying to tell you something and this was probably it. We are behind you and if this is to work then it will. Vincent is going to have to have his own plan and not skate on the tails of ours. I would welcome him if that becomes a possibility, but for now let's just get through hopefully our last move to break the Shapur. We need you as much as ever. Then we will try and get you a guy and a life." Billy was smirking after the last sentence. Jewel looked up and laughed a little.

Issa had left the room during all of this and upon noticing this Jewel started talking about their mom. They had not talked about her since they left the house over three weeks ago. Billy said that he has just been trying not to think about her while in the car and with all the stuff happening. It had not surfaced until he saw her so upset with the latest news that Thomas had told them about

Vincent.

They talked about how crazy it had been since he graduated and then they thought about Aunt Nell and Grandma. Grandma probably thought that they too were dead. They talked about how the funeral might have been. What music was played and how mom looked in the casket. They know that she hit her head so they wondered if it was an open casket. Thinking of them and Mom was very hard for the both of them. Issa overheard them as she walked by the room. She entered and as they all looked at each other, they all started to cry. After a few minutes, Billy started to try to speak.

"I... know ... that they need to know that we are all right. I am sure by now they have received a visit from our friend. I... just...hope that they did not harm either one of them. They are so old and have no idea just what is happening. Right after the dinner I am going to call them to let them know that we are all o.k. and to find out what happened at the funeral. I wish I could do it right now, but I could not handle it at this... time." Billy was having a hard time talking through the tears.

"We gotta make this work, Billy. The more I think about it I go crazy. I am so thankful that Thomas is on our side and I believe in him, but we must make sure that this exposure does work and scare the Shapur out of America and hopefully shake down this live-stock ring that the Shapur had created for himself. Where is Thomas? We need to know more and get this thing locked down before tomorrow." Jewel was teetering on anger and rage.

"I know sis. We are going to. Let's just clear our head and then go down to the kitchen, I think that is where he is." Billy said.

As they went towards the kitchen they heard a loud voice coming from a room down the hall. He was shouting something in a foreign language. Billy started to stay and listen to the man, but was pulled forward by Issa.   They found Thomas in the kitchen talking to a woman and they went in. The woman smiled and left the room. Thomas sat up and smiled.

"Well are you well rested? I hope so, because we are in for a bit of work. In order to get you in, we are making you a fake press pass, stating you're working with a friend of mine's news crew. You're going to be going in with a camera crew, but you will have to lay low until after the dinner. We are working on a way for you to do an interview with him after the dinner. Then you can expose him right in front of the camera. He is never too worried about young women interviewing him so you can start a normal interview then with a cue to the camera man you can pull your wig off and immediately accusing the Shapur of cloning you for your body and on and on. We will make sure that you then are swarmed by the same news crew and hopefully others. With security as tight as it will be, the scene should turn into a small paparazzi with you at the center. There has been a lot of talk of this kind of behavior in the undergrounds of the Middle East. A lot of journalists have been waiting for some real proof that these things are true. During this time our people in the crowd will try and move the action towards the door. Depending on what the security men do, we hope to either get you in a car outside or have you detained by security. Although you must not trust all of the security, if you loose contact with me we will know your whereabouts by the small device in this broach you must wear. That will only be important if we do not get you in the car. Now I know this is a lot William, but I am giving it to you all now so you can come back later with questions and I will help you." Thomas looked directly into his eyes.

"We are all here to help you. All these people here have come on their own accord. They have gathered information to help people. And for me to know them and then to meet you is beyond all possible thought. Somehow, by the day after tomorrow, the world will know what has happened. The name William Ruoff will be known as a survivor and a hero." Thomas smiled with a small gleam in his eye.

Issa came up behind Billy and hugged him from the back. Jewel placed her arm around him also.

"You make sound so like a movie. It's like I am actually going to be able to walk in and do all those things just like you said. I sure do hope so. I think that we need to drive down there and scope this place out. I mean I would like to know a few things before I go down there and risk.............." He was stopped by Thomas shushing Billy, with his finger to his lips.

"Relax William, I know that. You will have plenty of time to do that tomorrow. I thought you might want to do that. I arranged permission for us to walk behind some of the doors at the Kennedy Center. We also need to get you some sexy glasses to help hide your face a little more. We have to cover as many angles as possible. Getting you next to the Shapur is very important, it is all about..."

"Timing" Billy cut in.

"Your absolutely right William, our timing has been blessed by the spirits. I just hope that this one time we can do it. Our back-up plan is for you to be standing in front of the media cameras and as he walks by you can get his attention and having the cameras on you as you make your speech. Have you thought out what you are going to say?" Thomas asked.

"I have tried but the arrangement of the things I want people to realize is hard to control. These are so emotionally charged facts and part of my struggle. I feel that when that times comes the words will come out as they are suppose to and I want the Shapur to feel these words and see the look on my face as he hears them. It will probably be the first time he has ever met one of his offspring." Billy started to ponder that thought.

"I believe you are on the right path of how to tell your story, but you are only going to get a minute at most before something happens. The cameras will be still rolling but the surprise effect will switch to panic from the Shapur's men and security. Whichever reacts first, this will get you the camera's attention. We will be pushing the crowd toward the door, but security will want to keep you in the building for protection and questioning. Of course Shapur's men will try and surround you and bully their way out and get you in a car and out." Thomas was using his hands while talking. He let them down and sat back in his chair.

"We have worked on this scenario and we think that it will go relative to what we have said. The big variant is the placement of you with the Shapur and the news people." Thomas concluded.

"I think that I can put on some flirtatious looks and gestures that will allow me to move in to him. I just hope that I can handle the awkwardness that will come once I am that close to him. The pressure of keeping my composure will be hard until I reach the media, but then I can let it all come out." Billy was pondering the moment to come.

"Now don't over do it old boy, remember that the focus on you will be brief but we will have wide exposure. I again suggest that you go over what will say in order to keep their attention as long as possible. Now I am going to get some other things in order, you and the ladies go and rest and have Issa work with you on your little speech. I'll come for you all when dinner is ready." Thomas gave a quick smile and went out the back door.

Issa put her hand in Billy's and winked. Jewel mentioned something about a book she found and was going off to read. The two of them were in the kitchen alone and both laughed and went towards the refrigerator.

` After some small snacks, they gathered up the food and went back to their room. Issa shut the door and said:

"We can work on the speech a little later; I have some other things to work on." She said as she was spreading a hummus spread on some pita bread.

"I would like one of those too." Billy said.

"One of what?" Issa responded.

"Actually I want all of it." Billy said, as he slid over on his knees and wrapped his arms around her waist, squeezing her tightly.

He pulled her gently to the floor. After finishing the pita bread, Issa rolled on top off Billy. They kissed. As it became more passionate, Billy opened up his eyes briefly only to see the wig and bra he used for his Gloria outfit and without thinking he grabbed Issa by the shoulders with slightly aggressive speed. Issa pulled off.

"What...? Are you O.K.?" Issa asked shockingly.

"I am sorry....." He paused. "I saw my wig and... started to think of him and all I wanted to do was enjoy you and...I think that you should just hold me right now. I need to digest what Thomas has told me and...I just can't blow this... I need to just think... while I am with you. You're the only one I can bounce things off of. As much as I would love to bounce off of you right now, I need space for the other. And right now there is none. I am sorry, but...." Billy was hushed by her lips.

"I understand, of course I understand. Lay here. I am getting some water. I'll be right back." She got up and looked back at him with a smile and mouthed 'I'll be right back'.

Billy started to tear up. He thought of his mother. He was not even nineteen years old and about to face the man who made him, who was him, but not entirely. As he rolled to look out the window he heard several car doors close outside. With his curiosity he looked out. It was Thomas with a few men. He watched for a moment and just as he was about to look away, he saw a man grab Thomas' arm from behind and pull him to a different door of the house. Billy's eyes were filled with tears. He let out a whisper-cry of 'No'.

He turned and grabbed as much of their stuff he could. He was trying not to whimper. On his knees with the bag in one hand he went out the door. There was no one around and no sound. He got to his feet and walked towards the stairs. He whispered 'Issa', and then heard a creak from the stairs. He looked and saw her eyes were also big and tearful.

He motioned her to stop. He came down and whisper to where Jewel was. Issa pointed to a room just down the hall. Billy showed her the bag and nodded towards that room. They walked in and Jewel looked up and said in normal tone...

"Gee I thought you all would still be humping'..." At that point Billy covered her mouth.

Then Jewel noticed both of their eyes. Her face looked scared. He whispered to her "We need our shoes. We gotta go now, without Thomas.' Then somewhere in the house, they heard a door slam.

They heard someone mumbling at the bottom of the stairs and started to draw nearer. Their shoes were also at the bottom of the stairs, there was no way to get them now. Billy turned to the window and moved towards it. The girls looked out the other window to see if the route was possible. Billy was opening the window. The roof was four feet down which ended up on the garage roof. Billy started out the window.

Issa heard more voices and started pushing Jewel towards Billy. Billy suddenly left the window and Jewel's head poked out to see. Then Billy grabbed his sister and pulled her out. Issa went out feet first. Her last sight was a shadow of someone coming towards the door.

They went toward the front of the garage and Billy saw a van that was parked close enough to jump onto. He went first and turned to grab Jewel then Issa was there next to him before Billy could turn. He smiled and pecked her on the lips.

Jewel was down and started to run down the street. The first car Billy checked had it's keys in the ignition, he whisled lowly, the girls saw him. After they all got in they heard loud voices coming from the house. The car was slightly blocked in. Billy started the car and bumped the cars around it and went out through the yard and Issa silently yelled that she saw someone come out the front door. She thought it was Thomas, but she was not sure. Billy took the first turn and kept driving. There was silence in the car.

"We're getting kind of good at this" Billy noted.

"I don't wish to get better at any of this, Buck-oh. Jesus, just get us far away from them." Jewel was almost in tears.

Issa told Billy to go toward the sign up ahead and

see if they could see through the trees, she knew that it was a shopping center. Again, it became eerily quiet. As they pulled into the parking lot, Billy spoke.

"We must ditch this car and get on a bus, how much money do we have?" Billy asked.

"In the rush I didn't grab all of the money, I only have forty bucks." Jewel responded.

"I have twenty." Issa added.

"We need to go back to the house. My outfit is there and so is our money. We could get a room tonight and then one of us could go back and try to get in. We don't have enough money to replace my clothes and eat and such. I hope Thomas is all right. They seemed very adamant towards him so who knows what they might do." Billy stopped to think.

"He is not alone and he has a lot of friends. The goonies came when no one else was at the house. They must have been tipped off, since they came after we had only been there for less than a day." Billy said.

"Well at least we are safe for now. Look there is the bus stop. Let's park as far away as possible. Whose car is this anyway?" Issa asked.

Jewel, sitting up front, looked in the glove box. Sure enough it was one of the goonies cars. After Jewel said as much, Billy saw one of those concrete barriers and gave a quick look around to see if any other cars or pedestrians were near. Then he smiled and Issa and Jewel instantly they braced themselves. Billy crashed the car along the side of the concrete barrier. He stopped quickly and backed into it; turned down a parking aisle and parked the car.

As they got out an old lady was staring at them with a concerned look on her face. Issa watched her, saw her shake her head and go on her way. They ran through the shopping complex to reach the bus just in time. The bus pulled out and Jewel pointed out the window to three cars quickly pulling into the parking lot on the opposite side. Billy and Issa looked at each other, smiled and sat back. Jewel still looked somewhat worried.

Billy then thought back to Thomas, and wondered

what he would suggest they do. He had no idea what was around them, where to stay or whether to go back to the house. Issa noticed his mind drifting and grabbed his hand and kissed it. Billy turned to acknowledge her, but still had a somewhat blank look on his face. Jewel saw them turn to one another, and as she noticed the look on his face, she said:

"Looks like you aren't getting better at other things as easy, huh Buck-oh?" Jewel said with a sour tone.

"Just lay off alright. We all know this is hard and he is dealing with it, we are all dealing with it as it comes, Jewel. None of us need to start with attitude at this stage, alright?" Issa said insistently.

Jewel's eye got big. She had never heard Issa speak to anyone like that, let alone her. Billy looked around towards Jewel saw her eyes, and thought to change the subject and come out of his stupor, time was short.

"So do you think that someone tipped off the goonies? Did Vincent know where..." he was cut off.

"No he didn't." Jewel jumped.

"I was not sure. Besides we did know where we were going... or are." Billy said.

"Let's get off the bus and get some food then look for a motel, a cheap one and then think of how to go back to that house and get our stuff." Issa suggested.

Just then the bus stopped they all looked at each other and Billy stood first and as they exited the bus, Issa notice a man intensely looking at them and then suddenly reaching for his cell phone. Jewel spoke which turned her attention away.

"Sounds good to me, but I already know who is going back to the house, me. Because you and Issa must stay together for if they catch me I am spendable, and ..."Issa cut in.

"No one is expendable, but I must be feeling paranoid, it seems that everyone is looking at us or for us. I just saw a guy staring at us and then jumping on his cell phone. He acted nervously and he was in a suit like the other 'goonies'. I don't know what to think. Are you guys.........?" Issa stopped to stare at a group of people and see if any of them looked back.

"Get it together Issa. No one is trailing us. We lost them when we got on the bus." Jewel snapped back, she had been daydreaming too.

"Let's not start another confrontation. Here is a coffee shop. I would like to sit outside and have a coffee and Danish. Is that acceptable to everyone?" Billy asked as he turned into the shop. The girls followed without acknowledging each other.

Billy ordered for all. The girls were still stand-offish towards one another. After getting the order, Billy just walked past them and to a table outside. The girls followed and after a few minutes, Issa finally spoke.

"I am sorry that I snapped on the bus. You know as well as I that Billy uses humor at the worst times, but that is just the way he is and ..." Jewel tried to speak.

"Let me finish before you say anything. This is hard as can be. We have not had a break since your Mom died and we are so close to see if all of our efforts are worth anything to anybody. I think that the reason that I said what I did was because... I ... don't know. I guess that I had had enough too but, he is all we have and I guess I took it out on you first. I am sorry. You are my sister too and I love you very much. We are going to get out of this it's just a matter of time... What the heck?" Issa was distracted by the noise of car tires squealing. Billy stood up.

"Short lunch, gotta go." Billy said as he grabbed his sandwich and then Issa. Jewel was already standing.

"That can't be them coming after us. How could they know?" Issa stated.

"It must be something on our clothes. We need to get rid of our clothes and that backpack. Let's go into this clothes store." Billy said.

"He we go back to stealing. I know I know it's our only chance" Jewel replied.

They ducked into a clothing store down from the coffee shop as the cars pulled in front. Issa saw the group of suits go into the coffee shop in a hurry. She felt that they were tipped off instead of following a signal from their clothes.

They rushed in and the store attendant noticed their frantic actions and asked if she could help. Billy thought to distract her as the girls grabbed some new clothes. Jewel saw a backpack on the floor grabbed it and walked towards the back of the store to switch the stuff from theirs to that one.

Issa was already changing clothes and then stuck her head out of the dressing room door and as she looked the other way she notice that there was a delivery entrance just past the dressing room door. Jewel was finishing the backpack and saw Issa. She looked up to Issa and grabbed a shirt and skirt she saw in front of her, looked to where Billy was. She saw the back of the attendant and walked quickly to Issa.

As Billy was talking to the attendant, the phone rang and she excused herself. He then saw some pants, fumbled through them for his size. He looked over towards her and saw that she was looking the other way. He crouched down a little, trying to hide and ran towards the back. As that happened, Issa and Jewel came out of the dressing room and went for the back door. Billy pulled off his shirt and put on the new one as they went through it. Just as the door was about to close, Billy grabbed it shutting it slowly and quietly. He peeked out the door just to see the goonies outside the door looking around; one of them was holding some small device. Next to the door was a chair and he put it under the knob of the door. As he turned to run he hoped that the clothes did the trick. They went through one more door and found that they were right by a four lane road. Billy looked for the stop light and started to run for it, the girls followed.

Back in the store, as the attendant was hanging up the phone, four men entered the store and moved rather quickly to the back. She asked them if she could help and then thought of the man she was helping. She walked behind the men and found them in the girl's dressing rooms, holding the backpack and talking in a foreign language. She asked again if she could help, but in a more insistent tone. One of the men smiled at her and said 'No thank you' and they went toward the back door. The attendant asked them to stop, they did not and she watched as they tried to open the door. One of the men then started aggressively pushing on the door. Staring in disbelief, the attendant turned and hurried to the phone and dialed the police. She said that there was a robbery happening in her store and while she was talking one of the men came towards her, she screamed and dropped the phone. Then there was a loud slamming sound from the rear of the store, the man coming at her stopped and looked back, he then looked at her with disgust and ran to the back again. The attendant was whimpering with fright.

She heard nothing. Walking to the back seemed to take forever to her and as she saw the back door open she heard the sound of a police siren. She turned and ran to the front and out the doors just as the police pulled up. She threw her hands up and pointed to the store.

XXII

Billy was at the stop light first and saw a bus coming their way. Looking to see the bus stop down from the intersection and then to the girls, he pointed out the bus stop and they stopped, looked and crossed. They all met as the bus came to a stop, got on and the door closed. Before the bus was out of sight the back door of the store flew open and men were running out, looking around.

They rode the bus for a while. They were mentally drained, but Billy knew that they had to get back to Thomas' house, it was there only hope. The bus then turned in the direction of the house. Billy saw the street sign, Nelly Ave, and recognized it and then the bus came to a stop. Billy stood and pulled on Issa's hand and she then grabbed Jewel's. They were getting off as Jewel said:

"Didn't we just leave this neighborhood? Why in the hell are we back?"

"Yes and we need to get the stuff now while they think that we are as far away as we can be. At least I hope that they're all gone." Billy hoped.

"O.K. that's far enough, I want the both of you to stop and tell me where to meet you guys. Like I said earlier I am going for the stuff and you two are staying put. Now it is just down two streets and then right, Right?" Jewel said.

"Really sis, now that's mighty brave of ya." Billy was looking around. "Yeah, yeah it is a right, then the second house. That backs up to that building. I'm sure that you'll recognize it. We will walk down this parallel street and wait for you to come through the back yard of the house. We are going to hide somewhere between the houses until you give us a 'hootie-hoot' and we'll come out. Try to grab a different bag other than ours and just the money and my new Gloria wig and such. Good luck and just act like you live there and walk right in or something. I'm sure you'll do fine, Love you." Billy gave her a hug and Issa joined in, clasping his hand around her back. Jewel smiled, "I love you guys, wish me luck." She started jogging down towards the house.

Billy and Issa started walking down the same street for a block and then cut over one street to see if there was a way from behind Thomas' house to that street. As they walked Billy could see the house beyond the trees. When Issa saw it, she grabbed Billy, who was still walking towards the yard behind it.

"Come on Billy, if someone sees you we're done. Pull that hood up and hunch over or something. We'll walk to see if there is any place good to hide. Issa kept looking over through the trees to see if there was any movement around the house. Billy then spotted a small box trailer that was backed up to a fence. He pointed to it and they both went over to stand behind it. Billy then heard the sound of a car approaching. As it came closer, Billy whispered 'I recognize that sound' and after it passed he peeked out to see it was Jarin's car, he again whispered 'Jewel'.

They waited for almost an hour. They heard no sounds at all. Then across the street a lady came out from behind one of the houses. She walked down the street carrying a bag but her hair was not Jewel's color. The woman started looking in her purse for something then stopped. Wind blowing, her face was covered by her streaming hair. The wind picked up a little and the hair blew back from her face, it was Jewel.

"Pssssssst. Hey!!" Billy was trying to get her attention.

Jewel looked over at him and smiled. She pulled her glasses out of her purse and put them on. Just then a car started coming back up the street. It was Jarin's car, and Billy knew it. He waved at her to keep walking as the car came in the opposite direction. It slowed as it passed Jewel, but she just kept walking and the car drove past.

Issa pulled Billy back as the car passed. They slid out on the other side and waited for the sound of the car to be gone then they ran to Jewel.

"What happened?" Issa asked to Jewel.

"We need to find cover near the bus stop and hope that it comes soon." Billy said as he pulled them onward.

"I walked up to the back door and I heard talking in the kitchen so hid by the window until they stopped then I peeped through the window and saw Thomas eating alone. After he saw me he waited then came to the door and let me in. He had to hide me in a closet there in the kitchen for most of the time. He talked to me through the door. He was able to go up and get our stuff, he thoroughly checked for bugs. There are two of them there, but they haven't harmed him yet. We need to call a number he gave me as soon as possible. It's someone that can help us and him out. That's about all that was said, you can tell that it was difficult. Let's see if we can get to use someone's phone around here, it will also get us off this street." Jewel still looked rather scared.

They all started walking quickly back toward the bus stop that they had got off at and saw no cars or people on the street. When they got to the bus stop the schedule read that the next bus was due in fifteen minutes. Across the road was a man in his yard, Jewel pulled off her wig and threw it to Billy, ruffed up her hair, told them to wait and then ran over to him.

Issa watched for cars and Billy put on the wig. It was almost too messed up for him to look decent enough, but it hid his face. Jewel went into the man's garage and then he came out alone. They were hoping that she could have some privacy for the phone call. Billy wondered since the clothing store how much of that escapade was known to the public by now.

"Once this person finds out what is happening at Thomas', there are going to be a lot of people involved in this. I hope it does not blow my chance of exposing him at the Kennedy Center, I really want to do that." He looked up as he spoke. Issa did not say anything, just kept looking out for cars.

Jewel soon came out of the garage and shook the man's hand. He waved as she walked away. They saw the bus turn the corner as she came over to them. As they boarded the bus, Issa saw a black car turn and go the opposite direction, she looked upward and whispered 'Thanks'.

"Did you talk to anyone?" Billy asked.

"Yeah, it was a woman who seemed rather shocked when I told her the situation. The man's name I was given was not there so I hope that the woman I talked to can be trusted. She said she knew Thomas well, and was going to call anther mutual friend to get help and for me to call her back in an hour. Thomas also gave me one hundred dollars for us to use, so we now have almost two hundred. I am wearing your outfit under my clothes. He didn't find any bugs, but you should check that wig once again." Jewel started taking off clothes, Issa quickly stood in front of her.

Billy felt a few small hard balls in the top of the wig. Issa then found one in the bottom of the pants that Jewel had on under her long skirt. Billy was just prying the last one out when bus came to a stop, he dropped one as the bus started moving again. Issa was looking around for it and stopped as she looked out the back window, three cars back was the black car. Issa could feel that it was one of them for sure. She tapped Billy's shoulder and pointed out the window.

"Let's get these balls together, Are there any more? Give them to me. When it looks like quite a few people are getting off, I'll slip them on someone. Then let's go get a room, I need to get out of here." Billy voice was starting to wear thin.

"Amen brother, let's hope these are all of the balls." Jewel replied.

Four stops later the bus pulled up to a small crowd waiting for the bus. Issa saw that the car was still back there. Billy got up first and a man in front of him got up to let out the person beside him out. Billy saw the pocket on his blazer and dropped the balls in. The man sat down and looked up at Billy and his hair; he just shook his head and pulled up his newspaper. Billy mumbled 'Thanks Mr.' and walked on out.

They dispersed through the crowd and hid in the remaining people waiting for another bus and the black car went by. After it was gone, Issa jumped and yelled 'Whoopee!' and then ran to Billy and kissed him. Jewel saw a near by cafe with a 'Free Internet' sign and went in and soon came out with a small list of hotels. He turned and put up his hand to hail a cab. A half hour later they were at a hotel near the train station. They only had one full day before the dinner at the Kennedy Center.

Billy plopped down on the bed exhausted.

"I need to talk to Thomas. When you talked to him, did he still seem to think that we should go through with this? What did the men do to him? Does he know who tipped them off?" Billy was slightly panicked.

"I am not sure of any of that. He was mostly concerned about getting me out of there and getting someone there to help, fast. You gotta go to a pay phone from another hotel or something and call Thomas. I really think that Issa should go and ask Thomas questions. After all of this it seems that the goonies are thick around here and they might even know what we are up to. After talking to the lady for Thomas, I now know we are not the only people being abused. These guys are going to be all over the place. Now that we have a little extra money maybe we should look for some different..." Issa stood and placed her hand gently on Jewel's shoulder.

"Wow, uh you need to slow down sister. Let's just ease up and relax for a moment. Think about all that has happened and all that might happen. I really feel safe here and we should turn on the television and see what the rest of the world is doing." Billy sat back and grabbed the remote for the television and started switching channels.

He stopped on what looked to be a Baltimore news station. The news had just started. The segment was showing the back of a shopping center, which Billy instantly recognized. The reporter was describing what an attendant said in describing the events that occurred. By this time Billy was out of his seat pointing at the television.

"That's the one we came out of!" Billy shouted.

The camera followed the reporter in the back door as he described what happened. He went on to briefly show a small segment of the security camera tape, but then the camera panned back from the video, to the reporter who said:

"The suspects you see aren't the only ones that the authorities are looking for." The reporter said with an inquisitive look on his face and eyebrows raised.

They went back to the video, which played long enough to show the three men attempting to break open a door, but then the segment stopped and there was a long pause until the news returned to the studio. The news anchorman apologized for the cut off, but as he started to return to the news segment, he hesitated as if his attention was drawn else ware. The look on his face was disturbing as he started with other news.

"What in the hell was that?" Jewel yelled.

"This is all too much; we need to talk to Thomas now!" Issa said as she jumped up.

"We need to double check the clothes that you got for any bugs and then I am going to dress as Gloria and go the hotel lobby down the street and call Thomas on his cell. Give me that number of the lady you talked to earlier and

I'll call her also." Billy was pacing.

"I am going with you." Issa said.

"Well hell we should all go. Six eyes are better than four. Here you check this pile and I'll double check the bags." Jewel stated.

They all worked the clothes over and Issa did find one more. She immediately flushed it down the toilet. After that Billy started combing the wig and Issa was straightening up his outfit as well as her own.

Jewel was ready so she got all of their money together and divided it up evenly, in case they got separated. Issa was standing in front of the mirror, combing her hair when Jewel walked up and pulled gently at her hair. They looked at each other and smiled. Jewel pulled out a pair of scissors, snipped a little bit of her hair and then gave Issa an inquizative look. Issa smiled and nodded so Jewel started cutting Issa's hair into a very short style. Issa returned the favor by puting a bob in her hair. Billy came over in his new outfit and after he put on his wig, Issa grabbed one of his hats. Just then there was a knock on the door and they all jumped.

"I'll get it." Issa whispered as Billy went into the bathroom.

She looked through the peephole at the maid holding extra towels. Issa said 'No thank you, we're fine' and the maid went on her way. Billy came out of the bathroom shaking.

"Wow that really scared the crap out of me. Let's get out of here and call Thomas; I need to know what is going on." Billy grabbed their small bag and stuffed in a change of clothes and their toothbrushes.

"I am not taking any chances. We might not come back here, so grab what you think is important." Billy said in a sad voice.

He started for the door but Issa grabbed his arm and kissed him. As she pulled away Jewel was laughing in the back ground.

"You two look hysterical, I feel like it's Halloween or something. This is getting to be too much, already.... I don't know...." Jewel was mumbling as she walked pass them and out the door. They did not realize that it had gotten dark since they checked into the hotel. As they realized the lack of light, Issa spoke.

"We are under cover of the night, sweet."

Two blocks down was a hotel. Billy went in the lobby while Jewel went around the left side and Issa follow Billy from far behind.

Billy called the cell number. It rang a long time but there was no answering service picking up. Billy knew this was not right. He called the house and still no answer or machine pick up. Then he tried the number that Jewel had. A woman answered.

"Hello?" She said.

"Hello," Billy's voice broke from man to woman. "I am a friend of Thomas Mallory and you talked to my girlfriend earlier, you mentioned to call in an hour and it has been several since ..." he was cut off.

"Madam, I have no use for that product and do wish you would stop calling!" And she hung up the phone.

Billy did not know what to think. Maybe it was a code, the wrong number or he dialed it wrong. Jewel wrote it down wrong. No, he knew it was right. The lady was trying to tell him something. Billy noticed himself in the mirror across from the phones, and then the phone he was using rang. He saw himself jump and then looked around to see if anyone was watching. Looked at his reflection in the mirror and then the phone and picked it up.

"Hello, Hello. Who is there?" The voice had an English accent.

"Hello?" Billy kept the woman's voice.

"I am sorry did you just call here?" he asked.

"No, but there was a gentleman who was" Billy responded.

"I might be able to help him is he still there?" he asked.

"Your name sir?" Billy asked.

"Thomas Mall..."

"Thomas, it's me!" Billy shouted quietly.

"William, Oh god I am so thankful that I can talk to you. They told me that they had you, but I did not believe them. They were asking me questions that lead me to know that you were o.k. Now I can only talk for a minute or two, so listen. All is still happening like we said, except that I won't be there. I'll be outside in a van waiting to help if needed. With what happened at that clothing store today, we are helped and hindered at the same time. They are looking for you as well as Issa and Jewel. But once you reveal yourself you should have fair enough protection, however, you need to wear a bullet proof vest. I know this is shocking but you are now a problem to the Shapur. You must still go as planned. This is your best bet for protection and to save countless people from this misuse of life. William, like I said, I think of you as one of my son's, I love you and only send you to do this because it is your destiny, to save yourself as well as countless others. I am honored to help and assist." Thomas stopped.

"I too am honored. Thank you. I" Billy paused, Thomas cut back in.

"Time is still short William. Channel Nine News van is where you need to send Issa or Jewel at around 3:30 tomorrow afternoon. They will have the vest and your passes to get in the place. Act and dress professional and wait until after the dinner that is when the Leaders will be walking in front of the press. The Shapur's security is going to be tight so we now think that you should come up to him and try to interview him. A man from the crew is going to approach the security and say that you, as Gloria are going to inter..." Thomas stopped.

"William do you have a pen?" he asked quickly.

"Yes" Billy replied.

"Write this down- 555-232-5674, now call back in twenty minutes and ask for Alan." Thomas hung up the phone.

Billy slowly turned, scared to see himself in the mirror, tomorrow was really happening, he thought. He paused and straightened himself up then walked out to find Jewel and Issa. It was an upper class hotel and Billy was noticing more as he walked out. He found the girls with the valet, standing there in the parking lot. The valet looked to be their age and was telling them of a nightclub to go to that was within walking distance.

Billy just stopped and said nothing. The girls said good-bye to the valet and the three walked away. Billy started telling them what he found out on the phone and that he needed to call back.

They were walking towards a convenience store while Issa told Billy about the nightclub and that maybe they could chance getting in. Jewel said she was tired but did not care. Billy was not listening.

Billy went to the pay phone it did not work. There was one for cars he walked over and picked it up. It worked, he dialed, and a lady picked it up.

"Is Thomas there?" He asked.

"There is no one here by that name." She replied.

"Huh, uh then is Al... Alan there?" He remembered.

"Yes he is. May I say who is calling?" She asked.

"Um, a ...friend, please." He did not know what else to say.

"William?" Thomas asked.

"Yes. Please tell me something good." Billy begged.

"I believe I left off where you are to interview the Shapur, now I know that you only have tonight to think on this and what you are to say but your hair must cover some of your face and you must have some eyeglasses that will shade your eyes. Once he recognizes you, you'll have to act quickly, so you must get the jump on him in order to get his reaction for the cameras. This will probably be our only hope to get the most coverage and protection all at the same time. You all must leave Baltimore first thing in the morning and go and get familiar with the area around the Kennedy Center. Then hide out until 3:30 tomorrow afternoon. I will be there but you won't see me. Tell Jewel to only go to the grey bearded man named Arnold. We know that there is a leak somewhere within the people who are helping. Thank god we made it through that one. Now be careful when you approach the Kennedy Center. Walk with some attitude and without the girls,the Shapur's men will hopefully not notice you, because they will be everywhere." Thomas stopped to take a drink.

"This is really happening isn't it Thomas? Tomorrow I am going to meet the man who made my life possible and also whishes to take it from me. I am feeling nauseous and there is a car wanting to use this phone I am on. Is there any way I can talk to you tomorrow?" Billy asked.

"Yes just go to a pay phone and call the three places that you previously called when I called you back earlier and I shall hopefully be able to call you as I did before. If I don't, try half an hour later and so forth. God's speed my boy and I give you all the luck of the Irish. It runs in my veins so I am sending you some luck, I......love ya laddy, good luck." Thomas' breathing was a little heavy.

"O.k. Thomas I am going to be alright. Good-bye and...Thanks." Billy hung up the phone and a car pulled up towards him, pushing him away. Billy staggered in his girl's shoes.

The girls came out of the convenience store and saw Billy staggering in the distance towards them.

"What happened? You definitely did not look so bad before. Is it bad? What did Thomas say?" Jewel was excited but Issa cut her off by giving Billy a squeeze.

"It's these damn heels! I guess as I walked over here I am more realizing of what I am going to and have to do tomorrow. As far as what Thomas said, that since they have not found me, there is going to be a whole lot of goonies around the Kennedy Center. Anyway, I am now going to try to interview the Shapur on camera. I need some dark glasses so I can shade my eyes, then I will pull off the wig and glasses and get his reaction on camera." Billy was now taking his shoes off.

"Really, I was hoping that we did not have to go or something." Jewel was now acting depressed.

"What has gotten into you sis? I mean one minute you're going leaps and bounds and now you don't even want to go? What gives man?" Billy was staring at her in disbelief.

"Easy honey, I think she's got some woman issues to deal with." Issa replied.

Jewel was walking away as Issa caught up with her, Billy followed behind slowly. They walked along a busy street towards the hotel. Billy tried to put his shoes back on as his feet were cold, but he was unable to walk correctly or comfortably in them. This caused him to become rather far behind them and he could just see them ahead. He missed crossing due to a light change and could no longer see them. Then a group of men in a car started harassing Billy. One of them said by the size of his feet that he was a transvestite and then one of them started to get out of the car. Billy panicked and at the corner a cab stopped and someone got out. Billy immediately hopped in begging the cabby to drive off. The cabby laughed, but did so and Billy was safe for the moment.

Suddenly Issa turned to look for Billy and could not see him. She let go of Jewel and ran back only to see Billy running to a cab and a man getting out of a car and running towards him. Issa screamed 'NO'. Jewel ran back to her and Issa told her what she saw. They both thought that they had been found again. Issa looked back to see the man who went after Billy look up the street to her. He waved both his hands in disgust towards her and got in the car. The car then came towards them. Jewel grabbed Issa's hand and pulled her over in a doorway. As the men passed, Jewel felt a doorknob and turned it. They both somewhat fell in the door as the car passed. Issa shut the door from behind her.

"What the hell was that? Either those were just guys harassing Billy or they found us again. Why didn't they come after us?" Issa was listening to what was happening outside.

"I don't think that they were after anything. They would have followed Billy if they knew it was him. We should just go to the hotel. He will be there waiting since he is in a cab." Jewel reached around Issa and opened the door.

The girls walked out and saw Billy's head sticking

out of the cab window.

"You girls want a lift anywhere?" He asked.

"Anywhere with you girlfriend" Issa said with a southern accent.

The cabby looked at the girls strangely and raised his passenger rate on the meter. He drove them to the hotel. Issa and Billy just stared at each other while Jewel looked out of the window. None of them spoke until they walked into the room.

"Why did that man run after you?" Issa asked.

"Because he saw my feet and thought I was a transvestite and so he wanted to beat me up or something. The cab showed up and I just reacted. Did you see this happen or something? You guys turned the corner just before this happened." Billy said this while taking off his wig.

Issa told their story while he undressed. Jewel walked straight to the bathroom and did not come out for at least an hour. When she did, Issa and Billy were asleep and the television was on. She tried to find the remote in their bed. After noticing they were naked under the sheets, she stopped and thought of Vincent and manually turned off the television and got into bed.

XXIII

Issa woke at nine-thirty and went to shower. In the middle of her shower Billy joined her and when they came out Jewel had found the remote and was sitting there switching channels.

"I don't know why I said what I did yesterday, Billy, but I am sorry. I guess that this time my period just really hit me and I wasn't in the mood to bleed." She said as she laughed at the picture on the television.

"No sweat sis. Just next time leave out the details.

"No problem. So what are we doing now, today?" Jewel asked.

"We are going to get rolling and go and check out the area around the Center and then wait around 'till 3:30

and you are going to the Channel Nine News van and find Arnold only. He is a older man with a grey beard. He is going to give you our press passes and a bullet proof vest. Now don't you two freak out. Thomas said that I am now a problem to the Shapur and all precautions must be taken, so I am going to do as I am told. With the passes we will go into the building and scope out the area that I am going to do the interview at. Then after the dinner, Arnold's men are going to try and arrange an interview with the Shapur and me, as Gloria of course. Now the security will be tight around him so you guys are going to have to be out of sight. We don't want any of their men spotting you. When we go there we will be able to see what the place is like. We're going to have to buy me a different wig and a more professional outfit. I don't want to go in there looking the same twice, so we need to get moving, NOW!" Billy realized that they had a lot to do before 3:30.

Issa was already packing their stuff. Billy started applying makeup, and then pinned his hair back. Jewel was thinking of all they had been through and started to cry. Issa came over to her and could tell that her period was really putting pressure on her emotions. Billy tried not to pay attention, while he pulled his tights up and stuffed his bra.

Jewel calmed down and was getting herself ready. They were on the bus by fifteen after ten and on their way to the train station. When they arrived at the station, Jewel went to a phone booth and found a costume shop that was near the station in that part of the District. All was fine as they left Baltimore and it did not seem as if anyone was following them, although they still felt paranoid.

On the train they realized that the hundred and twenty dollars they had was it. Issa got all the money together and mentioned that they could still sell or trade their clothes for different ones. She was trying to get Billy and Jewel's attention. Their minds were not really there on the train, it was fairly obvious.

When the train stopped, none of them moved, Issa jumped and pulled Billy and Jewel toward the door. The two of them were like zombies, but Issa kept strong. She asked Jewel for the page that Jewel had torn from the phone book. Then she went to a security man and asked for the best way to the Kennedy Center and to the vicinity that the shop was. He was very helpful and even complimented her hair style. Issa had not received a compliment from a stranger in so long that she did not immediately react to his compliment. The man stared at her strangely as she walked away. She came back to find Billy and Jewel holding each other and staring at the ground.

"The security man said that we need to take a bus towards George Washington University and he said there might be a costume shop there, though he was not sure. Are you two alright?" Issa asked

"Yeah we'll be alright; Jewel is starting to get really worried." Billy said.

"I am just trying to get my head together before we go in there, that's all. I just don't want to lose anyone else, I am just trying to deal." Jewel said as she turned and walked a few steps away. Issa followed her as Billy looked skyward and mumbled some words to his mother.

Issa found the bus stop and read the schedule, they had to wait for twenty minutes. So they walked around near the bus stop and just looked out over the Potomac River. Billy's wig was being loosed by the wind and a few other people around were looking at him strangely. Issa noticed them and went up to Billy, kissing him passionately. The people stopped looking and walked away shaking their heads.

"I would think that in our nation's capital people would be a little more open to two girls kissing. There is the bus, let's get out of here." Issa grabbed Jewel and Billy's hands again.

They got on the bus and they were all looking out the window at all the buildings. None of them had seen Washington D.C. and they were too busy looking to notice that they had passed their stop. Issa realized it first. She immediately went up to the driver and asked him their options. Upon returning to Billy and Jewel, they were laughing at a pedestrian they saw and for a moment they were all smiling and laughing at what they saw. The driver said that they should just stay on the bus and in about a half-hour they would loop back around. Billy liked the idea of riding; he mentioned that he felt safe and that this was a good distraction for the time being.

As the bus came back around, they got off and just marveled at the old buildings and the outskirts of the campus.

"It does not even look like a campus. Are you sure we are in the right place? And where are all these shops that the man told you about?" Jewel was asking.

Issa stopped a passer by and he pointed down Smith St. and Billy saw more people walking and a coffee shop just past the people, he started to walk and then his heels got caught in bricks in the road. As he pulled the shoe out he studied the road. He had never seen a street paved in bricks. He proceeded to take off his shoes as the girls came to his side. Issa saw the coffee shop and pointed, Jewel shook her head as her head was turning from side to side in awe of the old houses.

"There is so much history here, what a great place. Maybe when it is all over we can start a new life here and stay. I really want to stay here, I like old stuff." Jewel said.

"What about Vincent, have you forgotten about him so soon?" Billy interjected.

"No, but I really like it here." Jewel replied.

"Well from the likes of our situation, we are going to be in the Washington area for a while, at least I think so. I just hope the right people get to us first and protect us.

As they entered the coffee shop, Issa saw that they had internet access computers against the wall. She inquired at the register and paid for the coffee along with a half-hour of internet time. Billy was asking Issa what she was doing only to watch her look for a shop in the area first and then punch up the address of the house where they last saw Thomas. She was also able to get an internet address of the house, so she e-mailed the house a small note. Just before she hit send, Billy stopped her.

"What if the wrong person gets this message, they

might know where we are and then it will be the same all over?" Billy was very concerned.

"What, we are sending it from this coffee shop in the University. They have no way of tracking us and soon we will look totally different. There is no way for them to see us. I just wanted to thank the people for doing what they were doing for us. Plus Thomas has not heard from us. Hopefully he will get this message. Were you going to try to call him again or were we to just go and rely on this Arnold guy who we do not even know. He could be the leak that set us up. I just don't trust anyone but Thomas." Issa was looking hard at Billy.

"Look I am going to Arnold, you guys won't even be seen so they won't be able to get you if they get me. Since we will have access to enter the press area, there will be too many people around for the goonies to really come and take us without making a scene. They are only going to see me until after the dinner, by then I will know where you are going to be and Issa and I will be able to find... out..." Jewel was cut off.

"O.K., O.K. we get the picture. You're the only one they are going to see and such. Let's get out of here and get some new clothes and I need to go and think. I need to prepare or something. It is 11:30 and we need to get going." Billy grabbed his coffee and started towards the door.

Issa looked at Jewel and then followed Billy. He was putting his shoes back on and realizing that he should at least keep pretending that he was a girl in order to get into the right mindset. He knew that time would go by quickly and before he knew it, he would be staring right at the Shapur. His ankle gave out again just after putting on the shoes, so he stopped and looked up again.

Issa came up to him and put her arm inside of his. She made a comment on his breasts, which made him smile. He used his Gloria voice to talk to her.

"I do declare that you are most beautiful to say so, may I now see yours?" he replied.

She was slightly surprised, with such a response from a female voice she hardly knew how to respond. So she smiled and as Jewel passed by walking, Billy picked up the pace so they all walked together. At that point, Issa mentioned that she talked to the cashier who said there is a shop called the 'Fashion Point' just two blocks over and they should have what they needed. She then mentioned that they were going the wrong direction. Billy stopped first and turned, the girls followed.

They walked on with a few stumbles by Billy and a few whistles from men checking them out. Billy would shake his butt a little aggressively after each acknowledgement.

The Fashion Point was somewhat crowded with young college students, which also ran the store. Issa and Jewel instantly went to the back where they saw the wigs. Billy stared at all the people, who in turn stared at him. Most of them smiled at him but some sneered. Issa yelled for him, luckily calling for Gloria. At first Billy did not realize that the call was for him. He was too busy looking at himself in a mirror that was down the aisle from him.

The outfit she picked up was the right size for him. As he was sizing it up to himself, a man who worked there came up to them.

"Were you planning on purchasing an outfit, our fitting room is over there but...," he paused to look around. "If you guys are planning on doing something stupid and rip us off, you should..." he stopped as Billy walked up to him and looked down on him and cleared his throat.

"Hey I don't want any trouble, but your faces look familiar, our boss faxed us a picture of the three of you from that other store that you all ran through. I noticed that you all are not in a hurry, but there is not anyone chasing you, so I figured that there was more to the story as to why you made the news last night. The cops are looking for you and I just don't want any trouble in the store, the boss has already had trouble before, so he is pretty paranoid." He stopped again as Billy put his hand on the worker's shoulder.

"That's awfully nice of you, and no we are going to buy these clothes, but I am wondering what you're going to tell your friends or what your coworkers are going to say. We are being chased by some bad people, and do not want to involve anyone else, so if you could just let us buy some clothes, we will be out of your store and nothing else will happen. Also there aren't any bad guys following us today, you can be sure of that." Speaking in his Gloria voice, he went back to sizing up the outfit.

"Will you need shoes with that outfit?" the worker asked.

"As a matter of fact I do. Do you have something that will work better than these?" Billy pointed to his shoes.

The man motioned over to another store worker and she looked at Billy and Issa, then back at her coworker. He acknowledged that it was all right to help them and she went on to help all three of them find new outfits. For the girls she found them each a woman's suit that was slightly outdated but went well with their hairstyles. As for Billy, it took some time to find clothes that fit him well. Eventually they found a pair of black slacks with a matching jacket and a white blouse that came up to the neck. Billy went into the wig area where Issa had already picked out one that was a dark auburn; she thought that since she and Jewel were going as a blonde and brunette respectfully then he should round it out by being a redhead. Plus she thought it looked good on his darker skin and with his new suit. However, Jewel came up to him at that time with some facial powder. She thought that they needed to tone down his dark skin. While putting it on him, Jewel was becoming a little leery of the workers; she did not hear the conversation with the one who spotted them first. They all kept looking at them and whispering. She was trying to get Billy and Issa's attention but they ignored her to avoid any discussion that might be overheard, as the store was still very crowded.

They were gathering their old clothes after they changed into the new and put them in the bag that Jewel had brought. As they went over to pay, the first young man who saw them came over to the register and excused the girl working the register in order to ring them up personally.   "Did you find everything that you needed?" he asked.

"Yes I was pleased with your selection. Now what happens? Are you going to call the cops or anything after we leave?" Billy asked with a sultry voice.

"No sir, I mean, no madam. We here at Ol'Fashion Point know all too well the works of the outside world. Some of us hide in these clothes in order to not become one of them. College keeps us out of their world and we could tell from the news and as well as your demeanors that you three need help. We don't really want to know more, unless you wish to tell us." He said this with an inquisitive smile.

"I wish I had the time to tell you all of it. You have shown us more consideration in the last twenty minutes than we have had in months and if we had more time I would.

Jewel came up to the counter and started negociating the bill. She did a double take at Billy to get used to the fact that he look very convicing. They were able to get their new outfits for have price due to the fact that they were leaving the old ones. They thanked the employees that were around the counter. One of them said 'Good luck' as they walked pass them. Billy gave a sultry 'Thank you' and was out the door.

As they walked back the way they came Billy was very quiet. Jewel was back to staring at the buildings and Issa was looking at their reflections in the windows as they walked by. Just then they all heard the sound of a car that they all knew. Issa turned to see the car in another window reflection. It was not the car they thought. Billy had stopped walking and was anticipating anything. Issa grabbed his hand and pulled him along.

"They have no idea where we are or what we look like. Let's just get back on the bus and we can go walk along the river. You can be alone or we can talk and just collect our thoughts on what is going to happen today. It's 1:05, which gives us enough time to go back there and get ready." Issa said this carefully.

I just want it to go our way and let this truth be known in the largest possible manner. There are others like me out there in the world. They will be put at a greater risk when this story gets out. From the Shapur's men coming at Thomas' people and also having so many men looking for me, I just can't help but think of them. The others like me, but they don't yet know that they are a clone. In just a short while I am going to possibly be standing by the man I was spawned from. I don't look at him as a dad or anything, but he is the reason I am alive." Billy just looked up again and smiled as he drew back the tears and breathed in hard to stop the fluid from running through his sinuses.

Jewel walked up just as Billy finished speaking:

"Those pants really make your butt big Buck-oh!" She yelled this swatting him on the ass.

"Really, I hadn't noticed yours yet. You should get some pants to give you an ass, Sissy-oh!" He said this as well as he could, but some of the other emotions still remained.

Jewel looked at him funny, until she realized that he was confused, scared and still trying to walk as tall as possible. She came up besides him and wrapped his arm around her waist, tilted her head into his arm and started humming a song. They all joined in, no one really singing the same song, but it had reggae beat to it.

They got back to the bus stop that was just down from the Kennedy Center, got out and started walking slowly in that direction. Jewel spotted a news van coming around one of the sides and then away from them to the other end of a building.

"Did you see that news van? I think that I will take a short walk over there and see where they are parking. You two stay around here and I'll be right back." Jewel said rather authoritatively.

"Be careful, we'll be down over there, we'll be looking for ya." Issa answered humbly.

"Just in the last few hours, Jewel has changed. I like it but it's weird." Issa said.

"I know. Let's go over here and sit for a while. I just want to think and stare at the sky. Thank god it is a beautiful day." He grabbed her hand and started to walk.

It was a while before Billy spoke. Issa knew not to say anything. After they had watched birds soaring over the Potomac river, Billy started in.

"I know that in a few hours our lives are gonna change again. I pray for the best, but expect the worst. Since Mom died, I have not really had time for closure on that one. I feel that I need to do that before I see my actual father, but I can't do that unless I am standing over her grave. So..." he was sniffling. "So I must somehow do it now: Mother, Katherine, I'm so glad that they gave me to you. They sure did not know who they were dealing with. They probably thought that you were a dumb white American mother of one that needed help, so they gave her, me. I think that being good, clean and honest can get you a long way. You taught us that along with a strong belief in oneself and the power one gets from having it. Today, however it may turn out, will be done in your honor to give dignity to you and other mothers who have suffered the same consequences. I feel like this is a speech, but I am trying to sum up all the days I can remember doing something with you. From the beginning of my trying to play any sport to just being a loner, you always said that it was not me that was to blame, you said to believe in myself and my destiny would come. And here we are today, right here and just down the way, we will find out the future." He paused, looking over the Potomac. "Good bye Katherine. Jewel and Issa and I will be fine." He looked skyward and then to Issa, and then noticed a man looking directly at them and walking towards them.

Billy's hand squeezed Issa's arm and then he pulled her to directly walk towards the man and not run but confront him, with a few pedestrians very close made him more comfortable doing so. Issa looked at him and then to where Billy was looking. Billy did his best to walk well and act feminine.

The man did look at them again as he got close, but he walked right by. Billy looked back just as the man stopped. Billy turned and guided Issa over to where Jewel went.

"Let's hope that Jewel turns up soon, I don't want to go over there just yet and I don't want to leave this area and have her looking all around for us either." Billy was looking around as he spoke.

"Why don't we walk towards the river and stay in this area and wait for Jewel. Now I want you to finish your homage to Katherine." Issa said with a proud look.

"I don't know how to start again. I wish that Jewel were here too. She probably has not had closure either. It's just that she was there with us in the water and then, then she was gone, just like that. I feel that since I have graduated this whole thing has escalated too fast and we have not had time to feel or mourn or anything relating to her death. She was my mother. She might not have bore me, but she gave me life, and showed me how to respect life. Not like the one we are living now. Even when this all started to catch up with our family, she held on to us and did not let us down. I know that I keep saying that, but it is one of the things that I learned that kept us going. How many times have we almost come to a dead end, and if we gave up I would have been butchered up and dead. Because of the life she gave me, she showed me to never say die, we are the Ruoff's and not a Shapur spin off." He started to tear up. "Today we make a mark for the Ruoff family. Aunt Nell and Grandma had to burry Mom, I did not even get to see that, but today I will be there to burry my dad, in some form or way, and that might be my only recourse, but at least it will be in your name, Mom." Billy pulled away from Issa and stepped up on a bench, raised his arms up and tilted his head back. He remained like that until the wind almost blew off his wig.

When he came down, he wiped his eyes and sniffed. Issa was looking the other way for Jewel. She had been gone a long time. Issa mentioned that to Billy, but he was still thinking of his Mother. Issa walked away from him to look further down the river looking for television vans. She had seen a few coming in as Billy was talking. She saw a black one that had just turned the corner. She put her arm around his shoulder and guided him towards that area, his head was down.

The wind picked up again and Billy did not react to it very fast. His wig pulled up again as they were entering a place where the people present were not just pedestrians, but quests going into the Kennedy Center. Billy looked up after catching his wig just in time.

"That was not good; do you have any more of those bobby pins? I just lost two of them to the wind." Billy leaned into her ear while pulling his wig straight.

Issa nodded yes and pointed at the end of the parked vans and they went in between them to fix his hair.

"You better be careful, these are the only ones I have left, we don't want that wig coming off before you take it off in front of the cameras. I don't know what you are going to say to him but you are just a man and he is a world leader with a lot of power. The anger that you have inside of you is not what you need to show him because you will just be like him. Be Billy Ruoff, a man who is thoughtful and good, if you anger him more then he might make it worse for us after. He has already exposed himself; you are just making it real for all of those who wished to ignore it. You just need to make it real for you and the others that are out there. This could very well be bigger than we think. Who is to say that other men or women have not made clones for the same purpose? We have come this far for a reason, we need to just put the word out, and we don't need to cut our own heads off. I love you and am right here for you. I am leaving this building with you today and we are going to succeed today, I just know it. Now let's walk out from these vans, find your sister and get inside. It will be safer inside with all of the people around. Hey, look at me; everything is going to be alright, right? Just like the song says, "every-little-thing." Issa pulled him close, after a few seconds his arms surrounded her and he almost pulled her off her feet.

As the came out from between the vans, Issa caught a glimpse of the back of Jewels head, she knew it was her, as no one had that color and style of hair.

"Hey, you with the hair." Issa yelled slightly.

Jewel turned slowly and then ran up to them. She

had the passes and the vest in a channel 9 news bag for Billy,and had learned from Arnold that Thomas was all right and that the people he works with was able to have some of Shapur's men arrested, so there were fewer of them to be here. Issa could see a little relief in Billy's face as he heard this. Jewel went on to say that most of the television crews were informed that something big was happening after the diner, and that they will be waiting for the event near the south entrance, Thomas will be there outside to also see the event take place. She said that Arnold told her to tell you specifically that Thomas will be here to see the big moment. He will be able to hear it all through a sound feed that Arnold has set up for him. She thought that this would bring Billy a little more confidence. "Did you get some time to think? I did not expect you guys over here, did anything happen?" Jewel asked.

"No not really, we thought there was a man coming towards us but he did not seem to be after us, so we just kept walking this way and then we found all of these news vans, we were hoping that you would be here, we did not feel like looking for very long out here for you." Issa replied.

"Well let's go in and get familiar with the set up, it looks like a lot of the other crews are heading in, it will be a good time to enter. I can go to the ladies room and put this vest on under my jacket. Hey Sis where are those passes?" Billy asked.

Jewel pulled out the passes, which hung around there necks. They got through the security with no problem, except that one of the security women looked very strangely at Billy, he said a loud 'Thank you' in his partial southern accent and kept going. With all of the news people coming in the security lady did not wish to pursue him any further.

Issa and Billy went to the bathroom to put on his vest. It was rather akward to make his breast look right even thought the vest was for a woman. Issa helped him with his outfit until it looked good enough.

They walked around and looked at all of the

exhibits. They did not know that it used to be a place specifically for the performing arts. Now it was also used for conferences and big dinners. All of the works of art from sculptures and paintings were still displayed. The three of them did not say much as they walked, Billy was lost in the artwork and nearly forgot he was a girl. Issa caught him scratching him self at which point he started to talk like himself while there where other people around. He voice drew a few eyes, but they were minimal glances.

They came back around to the entrance of the hall with the dinner. Billy became extremely nervous as they approached the door.

He stopped just as Issa grabbed the handle. He grabbed her other arm and looked at her with a very long face and eyes filling with tears.

"You must do this now Billy, face the music, he is in there and you have to get comfortable being in the same room with him. Soon you are going to be standing next to him and talking to him face to face." Issa pulled her arm up and let her hand go into his; she opened the door they all went in.

Billy saw a lady look at him strange as they walked in and then realized that he needed to be a woman entering a large hall. With people everywhere, he became Gloria to his finest he tried to adjust his breast with his arms as he walked. Issa grabbed his hand and pulled him back slowly, for he started to walk ahead of them. None of them knew where to go.

There was a person speaking at the head table, Issa's eyes glanced along the head table and she instantly saw the Shapur. He was looking rather pale. Billy was still just looking forward to not make eye contact with anyone until he had his composure. Jewel was also looking to the head table, and notice the Shapur and almost simultaneously with Issa they each put an arm into each of Billy's arms and turned passed the next table steered Billy down the back of the room and out another door. Billy was just coming into his character when he realized that he was walking out.

"Hey girls what is going on? Where are we going? I

thought that we......were... going into." Billy stopped talking since neither of them where responding.

Just down the corridor it went into another display of the theatres and stages of the performing arts. There was an area that was away from the people in the hall. Jewel saw it and pulled everyone in.

"What are we doing? I thought we were going to scope out the hall and see him. Did either of you see him?" Billy's voice broke back to his own.

"It was to much for me I did not know what to do or how to act as we walked through, but I did see him." Jewel said first.

"I saw him to and that is when I became uncomfortable. It was coincidence that Jewel and I grabbed you at the same time. I also felt that we had no place in there. Plus that dinner is not over for two more hours. We need to walk through this side of the place and find the area that the news people are setting up and then you need to get things straight in your head. Those two hours are going to either feel like an eternity or a matter of minutes." Issa was speaking directly to Billy.

"I know I know. I just wanted to see him. Get a feel of his presence. I am being chased by a man that I came directly from and still have not seen. I think that we should go and find the news people and then I want to go back in that hall and see him for myself. I know it will help me get focused and ready to stand be side him and try to not be me until it is time. There is only once chance for this to happen. I really don't think that he could imagine me being here, although,... to him since I am a part of him and could actually in some way think like him then; he could feel just like me and would do the same thing that I am doing. That is what I have to prepare for. The after wave of whatever is to come. Security and news people and his people and on and on and on will be taking me and you two should not and will not be seen. Who ever takes me; it is your job to find Thomas and then me. He is our only outside person whom we can trust. If it does come down to that then you two should work apart, not be together. Who ever tipped off the goonies from inside Thomas' people then could still be around and they might be able to identify you if they see you. Always be looking, put on your sunglasses even if you're inside, after of course my main show down with Shapur. Because once the word is out then they will be looking for you two, and if the goonies gets you then they might use you for leverage or something, who knows. What else have I been thinking?" Billy stopped to look up again.

"That all sounds good, but let's look at it as if we are going to walk out of this building together. Let's go walk over to where this is all going to take place. Arnold told me that it was just down the hall here where there the camera crews are going to be setting up. There goes a man with a news jacket on, let's follow him." Jewel pointed over to a man walking by.

They slowly came out of the enclave and they saw a man with a Channel 9 jacket. As they walked behind him, they came into a large entrance way into the Center, there was an area over to the left where the camera crews were setting up and then Jewel saw some men from Arnold's crew setting up towards the middle of the cameras. Jewel grabbed Billy's arm and pointed over to his crew, he acknowledged it and then pointed it out to Issa.

They walked slowly around the area. They noticed that there were only two doors that did not have any emblem on them. Billy saw that one of them had a heavy duty door handle and lock on it, which made Billy nervous. He pointed it out to Issa as they walked passed it. As they were about to exit the room, Jewel saw Arnold and he looked up to her and just stared. She flared a smile and then quickly turned to follow.

Billy expressed the urgency to use the bathroom. He walked away and was walking towards the men's room and at the last second he felt a hand slip into his and then pull him around to head towards the lady's. Once he realized why, he swung his butt a little bit. His felt himself not being able to concentrate very well and he thought that after this they definitely needed to eat. Issa pulled tightly on his hand and guided him to the lady's room.

"What's going through your mind? Are you trying to think other things or what? You need to concentrate on this." She stopped as he turned to face her.

"I need to eat first and then start thinking. We have an hour and twenty minutes until the dinner is over. I will talk after we eat, O.K." his voice went in and out from Gloria's to his.

Issa pushed him into a stall and then went into the one next to it. As they came out of the stalls they walked up to the mirror together and Billy looked awful. Issa noticed it more in the mirror than before. She somewhat ignored him until the two women who were still in the room left. She immediately went for his hair first with a small hair pick that she had and made his hair a little bit more presentable and covering his eyes slightly. While she was doing it he was smiling and adjusting his breasts, he did it almost sub-consciously.

Jewel was talking to a news guy that noticed her press pass and was making small talk as Issa and Billy walked out. He straightened up a little more as the two of them walked up to Jewel. Issa smiled at him and Billy just looked down and away. Jewel finished up their conversation and he smiled again at Issa and glanced over Billy and said; 'See you later.".

"Who was that?" Issa asked.

"Just some cute guy wanting to know what I was doing after this?" Jewel replied.

"Not now Jewel we need to get......" Jewel cut him off with her hand coming up to his mouth.

"I am just playing the role to act just like everybody else lay off, I still gotta be me." Jewel whispered with a smile.

They walked back passed the hall and Billy looked in as a door opened while they walked by, he did not stop but he slowed greatly and as he turned to walk straight a man came out of the hall with most of his head turned away from Billy, just before the man went into the men's room, he looked back towards Billy, Billy saw him through his hair, it was the Shapur, but the Shapur did not see him.

Billy sped up his step as he walked past the bathroom door, and he started to grin.

Jewel and Issa did not see him. Billy did not mention that he saw him and felt that if he kept it inside it would give him his own strength and not alarm the girls. They ended up at a food court area that had some coffee booths that offered sandwiches. After getting food they went to a corner table and ate in silence. Jewel broke it first.

"I wonder if he has a clue as to what is to happen to his world in about an hour? I am starting to feel a bit comfortable with what is about to happen with all that is behind us, I can now say, just before the moment of truth is about to happen, that this has been some shit to go through man, I mean come on! I really believe that if Mom were here things would just be a little...more...comfortable. I am hoping that I don't lose it here just before the show, but has anyone really said anything to Mom or for her?" Jewel paused.

"I...really... miss...her. There are things that we are bound to go through. And the mother usually dies before her children, but...not...in front of them, 'pause' in the water...helpless. I know you know what to say Bill, but we need to make him hurt for her." She was just about to fully cry. "His men killed her!" her voice got loud, Issa quickly moved over to her side to calm her, she was crying. Issa look frighten to Billy.

"I am alright, I am alright. We need to go back outside. It would be really nice to go to the river and look at it and think about her."

From her, we still think the same." Billy said as he helped her out of her seat and looking at Issa smiling.

As more people were entering the Center they received a few more looks from the more conservative audience that were there for an evening show that was going on in another theatre. As they somewhat fought there way through the crowd Billy got lost from the girls and then ended up outside before them. He waited near a bench to look for them. He looked down at himself and then as he looked up he saw a police officer coming right at him, not looking happy. Billy immediately put on his sunglasses.

"Good day officer." he said with his best voice while praying to see Jewel or Issa.

"Look here fella, I don't have time to deal with this kinda shit but I ain't about to let it go unnoticed. Now you just take that 'trying to be sweet' ass of yours and beat it." The officer was totally in his face talking with a soft voice.

Billy just looked him straight in the eye and smiled and pulled back and walked away from the Center. He noticed his press pass had blown around to his back, so he pulled it around as he turned and kept looking over his shoulder and trying to find Jewel and Issa. The officer was watching him the whole time.

The officer started talking on his radio and then walked briskly over to another area. Billy ducked behind a group of people who were gathered outside and he saw the officer going away from him. He had not seen the girls at all. He had no idea of what to do. He had to get back in and now was the time. He started moving. While he was going back to the doors he had just come out, he realized that he needed to go through a different entrance, specifically for the press. Billy realized that it was in the opposite direction the officer had gone.

He looked one last time for the girls. He could not believe that he did not see them. He realized this was going to be his only time alone, to really figure out what he was going to say to him. It's like a small part of him wants to embrace him, but then he remembers all that has happened and what his sister is now going through. The remorse and pain that he has suffered all because of this man was clogging up his brain.

He came around to entrance that he needed and just as he started through the door he saw the officer just inside. He had not seen Billy yet, so Billy turned slowly and walked towards the police vans. Looking at his pass he realized which news station he was with and then looked for their van. He thought he could find a little solitude over there and not be questioned.

Issa started to panic a little when she did not see Billy. Jewel was just looking at the ground as they walked. When Issa stopped and turned them around and as Jewel looked up, she asked where was Gloria? Issa stared at Jewel with a look and feeling that Jewel was either joking or losing it. Jewel broke through the foggy look on her face and said:

"I think if he is caught there would have been a larger scene, so either something or someone made him leave without us. I need to get out of this crowd for at least fifteen minutes, so I...am...going...over there, so...I...am...going." Jewel mumbled the last part not facing Issa.

Issa turned as she saw the back of Jewel's head fade into the crowd. She heard most of what she had said. Issa stood dumbfounded and walked over to a bench, proceeding to stand on it to look where Jewel was headed. The crowd faded fast and she looked the other way for Billy.

Billy was leaning up against the Channel 9 news van. He caught his reflection in the side mirror of the van. He walked up to it to get a closer look at himself. He imagined himself older and put it with the glimpse that he just saw, inside. He became frightened, he knew that in a little more than half an hour he would be looking into the exact same eyes and standing right next to someone who is physically exactly the same.

"I know who I am and I am just his clone not anything else and I will tell him how it feels to lose a home, a life, a mother... He paused; I just don't know what to tell him. Except that the game is up and now everyone is going to know it." He stared at himself a moment or two longer.

He knew that he was his own being and that the Shapur had no right to take it, even though he created it. It was not his fault, and the Shapur was not going to be in charge any more. He felt his confidence building. He looked once more and pulled his hair back so he could see only his face behind the wig. He stared hard and looked pissed, then cracked a smile. He knew that the words would just come to him while he was standing next to the Shapur. He felt the nervousness fade.

Billy straightened up checked himself and walked to the corner of the van, he looked around before he came out. The officer was within eyesight again, Billy saw him first went back behind the van. Just then a man approached Billy. He looked side to side then to the man.

"So you're the new interview lady? You should come back over here so I can help you do the best you can. Don't worry, Hi I am Jamie." The man easily pulled Billy back over to where he had originated.

"Look pal I don't know what you can do for me......." Billy said in his voice.

"I know about the plan, don't worry I am the camera man. What I see, the world sees. Just listen to me, O.K.? Good." He spoke very politely.

Issa knew she had fifteen minutes to find Billy and get back to Jewel. She thought of him and what he might do. She knew that he had already been to the river so he might be walking around.

She just started going toward the entrance they just came out then realized that she had to enter through their special entrance. She started walking that way and glanced over to see all of the news vans. She picked up her pace and went towards the van that they were supposedly a part of, she felt drawn towards it. As she walked up to the van she could hear talking from the other side, so she looked around it carefully.

As she saw the back of Billy's skirt, Issa pulled back to listen, the man he was talking to was very serious and began talking about the interview with the Shapur and the way he should conduct the interview. He continued saying that he should just ask some questions about his visit and how long he is staying in the U.S. and if he had any other plans while here. To have him talk about himself and have him looking at the camera the most. Jamie stopped talking. Issa walked around the van, he immediately acknowledged her.

"Can we help you?" he asked

"Issa what happened to you and Jewel?" Billy asked.

"The crowd was thick and we lost you. Jewel is over where you were earlier and I need to get back to her soon, but what is the cue for you to pull off the wig?" Issa asked.

"Oh right you're with this crew, I am Jamie and you are?" he asked

"This is Issa, my wife. Jewel is my sister that she mentioned. So what is the cue I am to give you?" Billy asked as he put his arm around Issa.

"It's nice to meet you Issa. Well the cue is for you to say after all of the other small talk is: What is the biggest surprise that you have found on this trip to the U.S.? Then after he answers or if he does not, you can say something like: How about this for a surprise or something like that and then pull off the wig and go into your story or whatever you are going to say. Don't use any curse words or slander. You just need to let the camera know the truth about what the man is doing and that you are the proof. Now you do have the blood proof or something, right? Good, so then there will be a frenzy because a few of the other camera crews know the cue so they will pulling their cameras to you and then I am sure that security will swarm to you and hopefully get you into a secure room fast. It is unsure as to what the Shapur's men will do. Do you have the vest on?" Billy nodded. "Good. They will have there own procedure I am sure for this type of situation. So be alert and watch them as you take off the wig, they might shoot, who knows. I am not trying to scare ya kid but a lot is going to happen after this believe me. My advice for Issa and your sister is to not be in the area, so leave and go some place and sit tight. Billy you can have someone go there and get them after things settle down. Now we have about a half hour until the Delegates will parade by the cameras and you will have your moment. Are there any questions?" Jamie asked.

"I guess not. Hey do you have the keys to the van?" Billy said

"Yes, why?" Jamie asked.

"Well there is an officer that thinks that I am here to scam as a transvestite or something and I would just rather stay put for the next fifteen minutes or so with Issa, because I don't know how long it will be until we can talk again so..." Billy was saying as Jamie pulled out a set of keys and opened up the back of the van.

"Be sure it is locked when you leave. I need to go and set up and tell the other cameramen the cue and all. Good luck Bill and you too Issa, I hope that I have helped." Jaime gave a little head tilt towards Issa, grabbed his camera and stuff and walked away.

They looked at each other and climbed in the back. After Billy closed the doors, Issa pulled him onto her and kissed him very passionately.

"I love you William Ruoff, I am sure that all is going to be fine and even though we won't be able walk out together, I will be with you all the time. I must say that you look very well and confident, but now your hair and suit are messed up, we need to start over." Issa slowly started to put her hand up his skirt.

"Hey, now I know that you aren't going to believe this but I need to keep focused on the next hour then we can mess around later. I just need to look into your eyes and feel you near me. I need all of the energy from you that I can get. My head is right, right now and soon I will be face to face with him. If we can just be here together feel all that we have been through. I just want to hold you and think of nothing else for a moment." He said this as he pulled her close.

A few minutes passed and then Issa pulled back.

"Jewel, I need to go get her, she might be worried." Issa said excitedly.

"Just a minute longer, she will be fine. What she needs is some time alone. It is weird how she and I both like to think by a river. I know that she is my sister through and through. I feel her right now and she can feel me too. I will let you go in a minute." He said this very softly.

Issa went back into his arms and closed her eyes. Billy closed his too. After what seemed an eternity to Issa, Billy sat her up and kissed her. The kiss was long and deep. Then Issa got up and said that she loved him and will be there with him in spirit. She looked one last time at him, got up opened the door and just before she closed it she sang 'every little thing, is gonna be alright'. She kept singing it as she walked away from the van. Billy mouthed the words as he heard her voice fade away.

Billy moved towards the front of the van to look out the window, looking for the officer or any other officer that might be around. He figured that they all knew about him so he needed to make a break for it if none were around. He caught his reflection in the rear view mirror, fixed his hair, looked at his dress and breasts, straightened himself and got ready.

"Its show time" he said in his Gloria voice, opened the door locked it, turning he walked towards the entrance.

He saw an officer stop to talk, so he walked on and kept his eye on him. The officer laughed at the person he was talking to and walked on. Billy quickened his pace and pulled his pass out for the security guard, held his head up and walked in.

Once he was in he headed towards the area where the cameras were set up. As he caught some people looking at him with smiles, he just kept his eyes forward walking tall.

Chapter XXIV

He walked past the doors that went into the hall where the dinner was. He felt the nervousness come over him again. He was just passed them and they started to open, people starting to come out filling the foyer. He quickened his pace to get to the camerea area comfortably ahead of the croud. He rounded the corner, saw Jamie and walked towards him. He was talking to some other men.

"Jamie, where are we going to do this so I know my area and when to approach him?" Billy asked with a shaky Gloria voice.

"Bi..Gloria, we are doing it over by that mural. He knows that we are doing this interview, so his assistant said, so we hope that he does so without any delay. You got about five minutes until he is to show." Jamie started walking towards his camera.

Billy turned and caught his reflection in a window; he also saw a goonie coming over to the area. As he waited to turn, he saw two more come into view. He became more nervous and searched his feelings for Issa. He closed his eyes and after a moment, opened them and heard Jamie calling his name.

"Gloria, he is coming, over there, get ready." Jamie went back behind his camera.

Billy turned and saw him coming down the hall. He looked over at the goonies who where not paying attention to the Shapur. As he came closer, Billy put on the glasses that would hide his eyes. A man from the crew went up to the Shapur and signaled Billy to come over. He put his head slightly down and walked over.

"Sir, this is Gloria, she will be conducting the brief interview that you agreed to do and we will be done. On behalf of Channel 23, we would like to thank you for doing this, Gloria he is all yours." the man smiled at the Shapur and then turned to Billy and winked with a smile, and walked off.

"Well it is nice that they gave me to you, I don't like these thinks but from the looks of you I won't have to much trouble talking. Is this going to be brief because I have an appointment to make that is a little bit a ways from here." the Shapur asked with a slight English accent.

Billy froze for what seemed forever. The Shapur asked if everything was all right, Billy snapped out of his stupor, cleared his voice and spoke.

"Why yes your Excellency I just...uh... needed a minute to clear my mind, I have a lot on it." Billy replied in a perfect Gloria voice.

"Good, now shall we get this over with, dear?" the Shapur asked.

"We need to step over here and when... Bill, the cameraman cues us I am just going to ask a few normal questions and we shall be done, O.K.? Good." Billy replied.

He turned away from the Shapur and looked

towards Jamie, he looked back and then into the camera. The Shapur stood beside him but was distracted by one of his security men. Billy looked at the Shapur and watched his eyes as they were looking intently over at one of his men. He turned back to the camera and Jamie asked if he was ready. Billy nudged the Shapur and first he did not respond and then looked right at Billy with an inquisitive stare.

"Are you ready Sir?" Billy asked.

"Yes..., I hope so." the Shapur replied rather sheepishly.

They both looked at the camera and Jamie said: "Whenever you are ready."

Billy straightened up and gave a nod to Jamie. A red light appeared on the top of the camera.

"I am here today with the Shapur of the now Tennise region who was a guest of the United Nations dinner here this afternoon at the Kennedy Center. He is here for this dinner and for a short visit in the eastern U.S. It looked like a good dinner sir; did you find it worth the visit?" Billy asked and turned to the camera.

"Yes Gloria it was rather nice and I am very happy to be invited I love coming to America." he said.

"Your stay in America is for several weeks. Is this just for business or is there any pleasure involved with this visit?" Billy asked.

"I am going to visit a few places in the Virginias I believe, but seeing how it is such a short trip, it will be mostly business." he replied.

Billy paused and did not know whether to go into the cue or try to go further with the small talk. He thought of one more question before the cue.

"Will you be meeting with any other leaders or even our President while you're here to discuss any world problems that are in your reach?" Billy peered deep into his eyes and just as the expression on his face started to change, he turned to the camera.

"We, my constituents and I, are working on a few meetings with Senators and I wish to visit a small town in I believe a West Virginia, and a few governors will be there also. It would be rather nice to talk to them and bend their ear as you say. I am always looking for new ways to help govern my people. Other wise I have planned for no other special visits. As far as your President, I feel that if he were to call I would be glad to meet him but I have nothing to discuss with him at this time." His attention went back to the same security man.

Billy looked at Jamie and noticed that other cameramen were done filming their interviews with the guest. He turned to the Shapur.

"Sir..., Sir......." he saw that the Shapur was turning to acknowledge him, "One last question. What is the biggest surprise that you have had on this trip?" Billy's hand was starting to shake.

"I am sorry, could you please repeat the...question?" he asked but noticed that a few cameras were being turned on and pointing at him.

"What is the biggest surprise that you have had on this trip?" Billy's voice was cracking.

"Well Gloria, I have had a few minor surprises but nothing to be alarmed about. Now it has been nice chatting, but my officers are asking me to turn my attention elsewhere. I thank you for talking to me." The Shapur turned to walk away and Billy did not know what to do.

"Sir I do have a surprise for you." Billy said in his normal voice and as the Shapur started to walk away he stopped and turned, he saw a lot of cameras pointing at Billy. His eyes got mean as he turned to see his interviewer pulling off her glasses and wig.

"Shapur is it wrong to say that I look a lot like you? Even to say that I am your clone?!" Billy grabed his arm to hold him. "Ladies and Gentlemen let the truth be told today that this man has not a clone, but many clones of himself in order to extend his life. I stand here today, a victim of harassment as a boy to the murder of my mother, in order that I mature only to be given life that he can take and use for his own. I have blood proof that my blood is exactly like his. He is not a good man but a murderer and manipulator of life for his own immortality. That man is not my father or my creator, but a breeder of life as a farmer that comes to harvest here in our own country. I have the...Proof." Billy stopped.

While he was talking, the Shapur lingered briefly to stare with an awestruck look at Billy. As he was staring, one of his security men raced between him and the cameras trying to block his face. Another man pulled the Shapur away. The Shapur looked back, listening to what Billy was saying as his men tried to take him out the door. The security guards started to stop them at the door, but then let them go.

As Billy was telling of his proof, reporters from the other news crews started swarming around him, asking many questions. Billy had a small smirk, but was trying to see the Shapur through the crowd. They caught each others eyes just as the two crowds converged. Microphones were being pushed in his face and just then a hand clamped down on Billy's shoulder. Billy thought that this was the moment that he would be hauled away, but as he turned he was relieved to see it was Thomas with two large men behind him with listening devices in their ears. Billy thought that he was going to cry.

"Now you did not think I would miss the grand finale did you? You were great, and your outfit is most becoming of you William. Now let's get you over to a private room, there are some people who wish to talk with you." Thomas was all smiles.

"Oh my god! It is you. You are here for me. Where are Issa and Jewel? Where are we going? What is going to happen to me?" Billy was frantic.

"I will answer all those questions if you will answer some of mine." A voice said from his other side.

The man introduced himself as Robert Sinclair of the U.S. Special Services. He went on to tell Billy that he and his wife and sister were being held by them for protection from the Shapur. They walked through the news people towards one of the doors with a lock on it that Billy had spotted earlier.

As they went through the crowd he saw Jamie, who gave him the thumbs up and then pointed to his camera followed by the O.K. sign. Billy smiled and knew that the end was near. He could only think of holding Issa and Jewel beside him to feel complete.

After they closed the door behind them Billy proceeded to pull his fake breasts out and rub the make-up off his eyes. Robert pulled out a small recorder and a pad and pen. Thomas finished talking to the men that were with him and then sat down next to Billy.

"Well William, you did it. I was very impressed and surprised that we made it this far. After you were nearly caught at my friend's house, I was expecting the worst. Thank god that they did not think that you would dress up as a woman and get right next to him with a T.V. camera. I must say that the whole thing turned out rather nicely. Wouldn't you agree Robert?" Thomas was still all smiles.

"The Shapur is a delegate and we have no right to hold him. Our constituents have tried to remind him of his actions and how they will be handled from a world court perspective. As for you, your wife and sister, we can only protect you until this matter is brought to court. He will be linked to the death of your mother, which will probably keep him out of this country. However, we are not aware of his contacts in this country and how loyal his men are. We don't know if they would actually abduct you and try to get you out of this country. Therefore we will set up a place for you to stay until we can get further information on the Shapur and his whereabouts. This is a serious matter that you have finally come forth with. We knew that there were people like you in America and other countries, but no one had come forth to state the proof. Speaking of which, where is this proof that you have?" Robert asked.

"It is with my wife. My sister has somewhat befriended the doctor that helped us and I feel that he could assist us further with the proof that I am in fact the Shapur's clone. We are not sure where he is. I am afraid that the Shapur's men might have him, for he was the one that was going to perform some surgery on the Shapur. Thomas knows that he needed a new pancreas and I was going to be the donor." Billy stopped and thought.

"So this has obviously been going on for a while?" Robert asked.

"He has been after me since I graduated high school back in June, but even in high school he had his finger in my life. Even during graduation, one of his men posed as an Army recruiter and tried to lure me to them. It was then I suspected something was wrong with my life. Then I thankfully met Thomas who went to school with him and recognized me or him and we began talking and so on. I am just so thankful that people like you are now aware of my struggle and can help me." Billy started feeling more relaxed.

"We hope that we can ease this life that you have been living, but we cannot protect you forever. The Shapur will more than likely pursue another clone. We will though be able to somewhat track his movements and I am sure after what just happened that he will not be allowed to come to America for any more help. This story will be all over the world by tomorrow and that might flush out the rest of his clones. But they could also be instantly kidnapped as you were about to be. Sorry to put it that way, but you needed to look out for you, not them." Robert looked at Billy consolingly as one of his men leaned in to tell him something.

"I just got word that your wife and sister are on their way. They were found on the other side of the building in a women's bathroom. Now William, or Billy once they get here we need to get this proof and analyze it for ourselves. We will also need the information on that Doctor, Vincent Montgomery. He is the other key for your case of protection. I will not be able to authorize much until that time, but we are not going to let anything happen to you either. Thomas has given me a lot of proof for you, but the blood is the most concrete evidence." Robert was interrupted again.

"I have just received word that the Shapurs plane

has just taken off. A large entourage of men went with him. I am sure he has satellite men here in this country, so all is not totally safe. Knowing their tactics from the past they could still try to do something to you or your family. Are there any other people in your family?" Robert asked.

"I have a grandmother and her sister in Gainesville Texas. It is Margaret Ruoff and Nellie Ruoff. They are old but still have their wits about them. Do you think they could use them to get to me?" Billy asked.

"You never know about the Shapur. He could become a desperate man, if he has no other clone for his pancreas, then he could come back after you if he thinks that a clone is his only solution. We have records of his past attempts at organ transplants which have failed. He has nearly died twice when using other people's organs. He feel that his clones are his only salvation. Thomas has given me quite a bit of information on the Shapur and it seems he has been doing his homework while you have been running. My men and I need to go through it and find out any more useful information. You just sit tight and relax once your wife and sister get here. One of my men wil be delivering the blood sample for testing, once it is confirmed we will take you to a safe house until further plans are made, sound good?" Robert smiled.

"Sounds good, I am starting to feel relaxed. Can I get something to drink?" Billy asked.

"Anything you want, Mr. Stanton here will be with you and he can order you anything you like." Robert replied and then left the room.

"Oh my god Thomas, can you believe it. It actually happened; the Shapur has left the country, and I am still intact! Issa and Jewel are still here and all is going somewhat back to normal. Or at least we won't be running and constantly looking over our shoulders. I won't have to dress like a woman any longer, oh what a relief, if only Mom could be here it would be grand." Billy started to cry.

"You should let it all out my boy. This has been quite the time for all of us, but mostly you and your family. Our humanity is supposed to catch up with us through troubled times. I will see if we can leave you alone once the girls get here. I am proud of you, if I may be, and proud to have met you and helped you through this. We have made history in the world of creation and hopefully put another brick in the wall to stop inhumanity from infesting this world. You are a part of something now William. Be proud, your mum would be proud also." Thomas stopped as the door was opening behind him. Issa and Jewel appeared.

"It's over, it's over. I love you, oh Billy this is the happiest moment and we are all here. Oh and it's Thomas! I can't believe it!" Issa was hanging off of Billy's neck and Jewel was holding them both from the side. Billy started crying even more.

As Thomas was standing, admiring them so happy, the man who brought them there motioned Thomas to step outside the room. Thomas reached to Billy and placed his hand behind Billy's head and gently squeezed. Billy looked up with a smile and tears streaming down his cheeks. Thomas moved his hand down to his shoulder, patted it and squeezed it looked into his eyes and whispered 'congratulations' and then walked out.

"My God Billy, we, you did it. Everyone knows the Shapur knows everything is going to slow down. Oh my god Jewel we are free!!" Issa was jumping around Billy.

"Way to go little brother. I just hope that Thomas will still help us. I was so glad to see him coming into the place like he owned it. He looked a little worn down since the last she saw him, but he did not let down. So now what? Are they going to help us or what? I feel like I need a cigarette or something to calm me down. It is hard to feel, not nervous or something." Jewel was pacing next to Issa and Billy. They were not totally paying attention to her.

Jewel stopped pacing and sat down and chuckled to herself. Billy and Issa broke their embrace and sat down too. Not much was said. They all kind of stared off for a while and then just as Billy was about closing his eyes as to sleep, Jewel kicked his foot and broke the silence.

"What are we doing now Buck-oh?" Jewel asked.

"Well I am not sure. I will ask Thomas as soon as he

comes back. How did it go for you over by the river? Issa said you were going over there to be alone." He asked compassionately.

"I am not sure. I just kind of let go of the feeling that I had never mourned the death of Mom and after looking around at the city and the river, I just stopped thinking about it and started thinking of you, where Issa was and where to start looking for you guys. I don't know, but it was kind of nice to be alone for those fifteen minutes. It was what I needed just before I went to watch you let it all out. So that was my closure for Mom. The only thing that I want to do now is to go stand by her grave with Aunt Nell and Grandma. That will be the final closure for Mom." Jewel gave a teary smile to Billy.

"That will be the best closure for all of us. Now that this part of our ordeal is over we need to see if we can call them. I can't believe that we have not written them at all, but they will understand." Billy said.

"We almost need to start writing this stuff down. We got all of these questions and we will forget them for sure if we don't write them down. Let's just stop there and go over this before we get ahead of ourselves." Issa found a pad of paper and pen on one of the tables.

"Now there are certain things that we need to do and we do need to go back to Bakersville and see Mother's grave and then go far away from there. We'll only return to the area to visit Aunt Nell and Grandma. There is nothing there that I want. If the house is not trashed and there are still things left I would like them, but I never want to live there again. We need to go west. I want to go and see the west. I am not sure what money we will have but something's got to give." Jewel was trying not to cry.

"That sounds good. Maybe we can sell our story to a movie company or even a television network. I think that this is big and we can use our story to our advantage. It is getting to the point that we need Thomas back in here to bounce ideas off of because I can't write this down and keep my head open to these ideas at the same time." Issa was slightly frazzled.

"O.k. but is there anything we need to talk about before someone comes back in? After that, I feel that it will be a while before we have any alone time. Anything?" Billy asked.

"I do. Little Buck-oh I am so proud of you. I cannot believe, looking back over the last three months, that we are here, safe for the moment, and all of us are here, including Thomas. And that if it weren't... for the fact that Mom died... she stopped talking and was now crying. We would have never had the courage and the strength to keep going until our story was heard. Love and luck were on our side... and few side tricks. And you Issa are a true Ruoff, or something." She blew her nose. "I am envious of the love you two have but I am glad that it surrounds me. It makes us, me, have hope for myself in the future." She paused and took a big breath. "I just wanted to say that. Since I got a little time before you went to confront the Shapur, it dawned on me that we actually did it. We have been through so much and it was not until then that I realized that everything IS going to be alright!" Jewel stopped as there was a knock at the door.

Billy looked at Issa with a small tear in his eye and she had big tears in her eyes. They all looked at each other and fell on their knees and hugged together. The knock came again. Billy let go of Issa and really hugged Jewel and then kissed her cheek, she returned by kissing him, in a sisterly way, on the lips. They both smiled big.

Billy stood, placed his hand in Issa's and walked to the door. He opened it and Thomas' voice came through before he did.

"Is everything alright in there?" he asked.

"Oh yes my dear Sir Thomas everything is splendid." Jewel answered back in a British accent.

"Good. We have much to do before the evening is over. There are some real important people here to talk to you, so you better put on your, what do you call it, game face. Thomas was smiling with a firm brow.

What seemed like an eternity was actually only two weeks, but in those days they told their story to the government at least a dozen times and to the press two dozen times and it was not until they got seriously asked to sell their story to the press and mostly exploit it to the maximum that Issa found out that she had become pregnant during all the excitement. They put off selling the movie rights and just told their story to an autobiographer that Thomas recommended. Thomas tried to talk them into moving to another country and, as far as the press knew, they did just that. However, they remembered a place they saw on their travels through the Virginia's, that is where Issa wished to go. Thomas worked it out with both sides. The government was still willing to help keep their whereabouts a secret and agreed as long as Billy, Issa, and Jewel all stayed in touch with them. The news media was still hounding Thomas for more info, so he struck a deal with one writer in order to keep the others at bay.

 Xavier Ruoff was born in a remote little cabin on the West Virginia, Virginia border. He was 7lbs. 7oz. born on Kathryn's birthday, June 13. Jewel did meet back up with Dr. Montgomery, and though it seemed too good to be true, it was not. Jewel moved in with Billy and family and got used to being just an Aunt, for a while.

Final

     The Shapur only lived another two years, mostly in exile. He never found a working donor pancreas, he lived a short while without one and suffered long until his body finally gave out. After his people ousted him from his post, his followers, only a few, helped him in his exile. Just before he died a world law was passed that no country would tolerate any cloning of humans. Even so, after many scientists and doctors were taken to trial, it did not stop the practice.

     Throughout the world a few others were discovered as having clones made in order to live longer. Most were from rich people and since Billy exposed the truth, and gave the clones some fortitude, the clones came to their governments for protection. Some, however, were not as lucky as others. Reports came back to America that a few were being imprisioned by their makers, with little hope for them. Thomas was unable to keep this information from Billy. Billy express the notion of going out directly and persuing them. Thomas thwarted his notion with the mention of Xavier and Issa. Billy did however start a web page to try and reach out for those who he felt he could help.

Billy lived only to be 60. Being a clone caused his body to age to that of a 85 year old man. Without much hassle from the outside world he and his family lived on the state line. He pursued a lawyer degree to help and understand the twisted world that perpetuated the likes of the Shapur. He help put away many doctors and scientists for participation the practice which allowed them to travel a lot. As Xavier became older, Billy would take him only on special hommages back to the area that the Shapur came from to identify with the people there. Before he died a movie was made and many past public interviews and speaches were played and brought a lot of attention to Billy. However, even with him still telling the world, their web page got visited, mostly hoaks but some genuine, a clone would appear and would need a lot of help. Xavier and Issa still tries to help any who come to the web page. Througout the years they have made a lot of contacts, and this method of immortality still happens.

www.ingramcontent.com/pod-product-compliance
Lightning Source LLC
Chambersburg PA
CBHW070842120626
46556CB00002B/840